THE QUEEN OF HEAVEN'S DAUGHTER

MARY TREPANIER

TALES OF THE END TIMES

THE QUEEN OF HEAVEN'S DAUGHTER

MARY TREPANIER

Published by Cwtch Press, Redmond, WA

Cover design by Mariah Sinclair

Second edition.

E-book ISBN: 978-1-947234-30-7

Print ISBN: 978-1-947234-33-8

Trigger Warning: Graphically violent scenes in this book might be disturbing to some. The material is not appropriate for people under age 18.

This new edition reflects updated language and corrects errors made in the first edition.

Prologue

$\mathcal{A}$ strip of red sunset flared over a lava flow, black and rusty brown. Beside lay the ocean, a froth of foam at the waves' edge.

"It has begun," the Star Mother said. Tiny motes of life formed in the sea. Last rays scintillated on the water, dotted with points of light.

"Shall we do this dance?" someone asked.

"Some will lead, some protect, some challenge."

Standing outside time, the spirits saw futures in the bubbles of new life: beings of one cell, jellies and anemones, trilobites, dinosaurs, humans.

"All full of suffering."

"But beautiful!"

The Star Mother said, "It has begun."

One spirit stepped out, watching as life split and formed.

"My daughter," the Star Mother said, "they shall call you Hekate Soteira. Hekate Savior."

The goddess returned the Star Mother's smile.

Chapter 1

*A*s they drifted to consciousness out of dream, images flickered: a mountain frosted white against a lavender sky, a hill of sand snaked with furrows driven by the wind, the edge of a murky ocean under rain.

It had been a while.

They tried sitting up.

Ow.

They fell back supine, fumbling for language.

Hung over. That was the term.

The body Puabi-Ekur had entered, as it happened, was a male one. S/he—they—had entered by consent—they were careful about that. Though the person asking had perhaps not known what he was asking for or that he could receive it. Did this lack of knowledge count in the greater pattern— karma, as some called it?

Such questions were best left to the philosophers.

Puabi-Ekur let the body go back to sleep. Floating up

and away from it, they surveyed the room: small, with a scratched wooden floor and a metal bed frame over a desk topped with some sort of composite. A drumbeat filtered through the wooden door. The room smelled of marijuana and strawberry incense.

Puabi-Ekur inspected the borrowed body: stubbled face, muscled shoulders, the penis and balls well-formed, even impressive.

What was this boy, Clayton, so concerned about?

"I wish someone would take over my body and run my life," he'd said. "I'm so tired. I wish I was dead," he'd said. "I don't even have the energy for suicide." These, with variations, over and over, went out into the ether. Puabi-Ekur had heard.

Approaching cautiously, Puabi-Ekur had given the boy a few dreams, even a night with a favorite incarnation.

Maghavatii. That was long ago—there were so many calendars—yet no time at all. The white stone dais faced out into lavender twilight; at its edge, she touched her lover's shoulder. A handmaiden, she could fade into the shadows. Soft makes soft softer—so the Tantric priest said of women with women.

No one had pierced their heart as her rani, her princess, had then.

A breath in: lips like dark garnets. Downy skin that smelled like clove. A kiss: thin lips, thoughtful. And the long black hair, released from its veil, brushing and brushing it. The skirts fell aside, and she kissed the dark and pungent blossom below.

When retribution came, the worst was waiting for the

knife, hands tied behind her back, before the dark eyes of the bored and seething crowd. She knew somewhere Maghavatii, the new widow, waited too. She could hardly bear to think of Maghavatii's pain. It would be greater; she would burn.

Remembering it stung Puabi-Ekur. But the dream had made the boy happier, at least for a night.

The boy's consciousness was stirring, and Puabi-Ekur hid. There was much to reconnoiter before fully taking over, if that ever happened. But Puabi-Ekur had all the time in the world.

"...so often what they need is human touch and reassurance, not even sex. Though they like the sex."

Joanie nodded. She sat with Hayley in their favorite hideout, a coffee shop a few blocks off campus. Someone had painted mushrooms and ladybugs on the chocolate brown walls, a hippie reference. It bothered Joanie.

That style had been over in the '70s. Here and now, it was cynical.

But whoever had chosen the mural was elsewhere, and the baristas left the students alone.

That late morning, she sat nursing a cappuccino, Hayley a latte. They'd split one of the shop's starchy scones. Joanie pushed crumbs around the small plate with her fingernail.

She'd met Hayley one midnight on her boss Tammy's grey-leather sectional office couch, waiting for Tammy to get off the phone. Pretty soon she and Hayley were best friends. Both were sophomores in their third quarter, Joanie in economics, Hayley in social work.

Hayley, a big, blonde girl, usually wore jeans and Indian print shirts, but for work she dressed in slinky knits and a fall of faux gold jewelry. Joanie was slender and dark, with eyeliner-drawn eyes and a mop of brunette hair. At work, she went braless to emphasize her shallow breasts, wearing tiny slip-dresses in black or dark purple. Otherwise, she dressed in jeans, black t-shirts, and a leather thong necklace with a leaf-twined pentacle. She dabbled in witchcraft, occasionally meditating on a candle or reading Tarot for a friend.

"I saw Phil again last night," she said now, splitting the last chunk of scone in two and eating half.

"Phil, your regular guy? Is he becoming a problem?"

"Sort of. I think he likes me too much."

"What are you going to do?"

"I don't know. I might ask Tammy." Tammy ran the escort service where they both worked. "But he's nice, he's good-looking, I don't have to fake anything, and he's been tipping one hundred percent. So I hate to drive him off."

"You could make him your sugar daddy."

"I don't think so." She raised her ink-spot eyes to meet Hayley's. "It's not like he's awful. He's fine. But I just don't see it."

It was hard to put into words why. And there were other things.

"Something more ongoing, I'd be afraid my family'd find out. I'd never live it down."

She frowned into her coffee. It was okay if Uncle Jeff

pawed her in a closet, but her mother would go ballistic if Joanie said was having sex for money.

"Besides, this is just for now, to have money to live on. It's not my life work."

Hayley shrugged one shoulder. "You could argue it relates to either of our majors. Social work is obvious. And it's a study of pure capitalism."

"More of the grey market."

"I suppose. But also, I enjoy it." Hayley shook back her long hair, then tied it into a ponytail; she had a yoga class next. "I like people. I like helping them; I like making them happy." She scratched her lower lip with a pale-blue fingernail. "I feel for some of these guys, you know? I'm like the therapist they'd never hire otherwise."

"I've had that. Like that guy a week ago. I felt like I was helping him heal some old trauma. But with Phil, it's pretty transactional, if pleasant enough."

"Not a sugar daddy thing?"

Joanie shrugged. "Time will tell. Speaking of time..." she checked her phone. "I should go. I have a bunch of reading to finish."

Or she could find a tree to sit under in the park, pull out her journal, catch up with herself.

Sex work had been remarkably okay so far—a few weirdos, but worth it for the money. She set aside the scat-play outing where she ran out of the apartment and had to pay Tammy's commission herself.

But now Phil was falling in love, maybe. She didn't want that to go south.

Maybe she should talk to Tammy.

"Do you want the last bite?" she asked Hayley, nodding at the scone. Hayley shook her head. Joanie ate it.

Maybe she should talk to Tammy without letting her know how much Phil was tipping.

They were in Clayton's tiny single dorm room. Clayton burned his usual strawberry incense. The resident assistants didn't care if students smoked weed discreetly, but Clayton had long ago made incense part of his smoking ritual. Now no insult from his friends could stop him from lighting it.

"We'll just call some girls and—you know," James said, taking a hit off the bong he'd brought. He sat back, smiling beatifically.

"What are you talking about?"

"What, are you stupid? I mean prostitutes. I've done this before."

"That's kind of gross, isn't it? You want to hook up with some crack whore?" James acted like he was some man of the world, but half the time he didn't know what he was talking about.

James sat back, shaking his head. "It's nothing like that. I've worked with this agency before. The girls are young and hot. Half of them are college students themselves."

"Really?" Clayton tried, and failed, to imagine the girls from his classes whoring themselves. Those sorority girls, those hippie chicks? That hot Korean girl in Data Analysis? No way.

He felt himself getting hard and adjusted his jeans.

"If it's what Rahul wants," Clayton said. At the end of spring quarter, Rahul planned to fly home to India to marry a girl his parents had found. Rahul had no complaints; the girl was pretty and well-educated. But he wanted to have some experience when he took his bride to bed. "I suppose he'll pick the cutest one."

James released a mouthful of smoke. "He should. It's his bachelor party."

"And your girlfriend doesn't mind if you—?"

"She'll never know."

Clayton frowned.

If he had a girlfriend, he'd treat her like a queen. He wouldn't look at other women. Let alone go to a hooker.

Curled up in a corner of Clayton's consciousness, Puabi-Ekur smiled.

They met at an economy hotel on the outskirts of town in an early June twilight. A strip of red sunset flared below a cobalt sky. The evening star flamed as big as a headlight.

They converged on James's Chevy. First Danny, then James, stepped out. James dangled a pair of room keys from two fingers. "Suites 201 and 202," he said, waggling his eyebrows.

Rahul giggled. James and Paresh exchanged looks. Clayton, wreathed in strawberry incense and Axe Body Spray, tried to pretend he wasn't there.

If he'd been asked (no one had asked), Clayton wouldn't

have been able to articulate his issues with the party. He wasn't quite a virgin. Two years ago, as a freshman, he'd walked a girl home from a party and gone in with her. He'd spent himself in three minutes, and he'd never seen her again.

He didn't want the guys to know he was hair-trigger. He'd hear about it for the rest of his life.

But that wasn't the reason, or not all of it. The other reason was also something he would never tell his friends.

He wanted a girl who loved him.

As a compromise, he'd gotten stoned as close to insensibility as he could and still stand up.

They climbed the stairs to the second floor, James last, with a bag that held several bottles of cheap champagne to oil the party. "Come on in!" James swung the suite door open to a room in tones of tan and olive. He'd shaken the other four down and gotten two suites across the hall from each other, both with a living room separate from the bedroom. Rahul had insisted, and Clayton was thankful.

One girl, a busty blonde, sat near the door on the living-room couch. She flashed a smile as they entered and stood.

"Hi, boys! I'm Hollie!"

He guessed that was a fake name.

The other girl, dark and slim, wore an aubergine slip-dress that showed a slender body. She sat further away on a recliner, her face closed, as blank as possible. The blonde shot her a look. Putting on half a smile, the dark-haired girl said, "I'm Jenny."

A moment of silence. The five guys stared at the girls.

Even James hesitated. Danny's mouth hung half-open. Clayton shut his own.

The girls were both so pretty, and normal.

A pentacle tattoo showed on Jenny's ankle, but that was her only marking.

He could have sex with either of these girls. Both of them. Both of them together. Watch them have sex with each other. He was paying for it.

"Who's the lucky bachelor?" Hollie asked. James gestured to Rahul. Stepping forward, Hollie stroked Rahul's hair gently, grin turned up to dazzling. "Is it me you'd like, or my friend?" Jenny stepped forward, still wearing only a half-smile, nothing like the wattage of Hollie's. But now she looked pleasant.

"I'd like you," Rahul said to Hollie, shyly. He looked around at the other guys. "Mind if I get the keys to the other suite? I'd like some space to myself."

Something clicked into place for Clayton.

It was Rahul's first time.

James handed over the keys. Hollie took Rahul by the arm, and they sauntered out. Jenny turned to the four who remained.

"Who's next?" A moment of pause. "No hurry. You guys have got us all night, if you want."

James cleared his throat and straightened his shoulders. Clayton eyed him.

James was as scared as he was.

"How 'bout me?" James glanced at the other three. "Why don't you guys go out and get stoned?"

After some time, James emerged. Jenny stayed in the bedroom with one of the bottles of champagne. Leading Clayton and Danny, James crossed and knocked on the other suite's door. "Doin' okay in there?"

Rahul opened up, towel wrapped around his waist, smug as a cat. Behind him, Hollie sat on the couch, back in her slinky olive knit dress, feet tucked under her, sipping champagne from a plastic hotel cup. "Just fine," said Rahul. Hollie switched on her shiny smile again.

Paresh stared at Hollie. James nudged him. "Go on, it's clear you like her!"

The door to 201 closed, and Danny and Clayton looked at each other. "Rock, paper, scissors," Danny said. Clayton lost.

"Come outside and get stoned," James said to him.

Full night had fallen. City light made the edge of the sky fuzzy mauve; at the zenith, a handful of stars winked. James took a big hit off the glass pipe that Clayton produced, but when he handed it back Clayton shook his head. "I don't want to be too stoned."

James smirked. "I doubt it's an issue. These are great girls. Jenny's amazing." He offered the pipe again, but Clayton passed.

Please let it work out okay.

"Come inside. I brought some music."

Not much later, Rahul knocked. "I've gotta go hit the books. I've got two finals coming up." Like Clayton, he was an engineering student. Clayton saw in his mind the pile of books on his own desk, and set the image aside.

This was going to be worth it.

"I'm going to go out and get stoned," he said. James gave him a wry look as he passed.

It was something to do.

After midnight, Paresh still hadn't reappeared. Danny had passed out on the couch in Suite 201's living room. James was watching television.

In the suite's bedroom, Jenny sat propped against a snowy pillow, wearing her aubergine slip-dress, sipping champagne.

Clayton sat at the end of the bed, staring at her. At the edge of his range of vision, the walls were bubbling and moving in waves.

Too much weed.

Jenny set aside her plastic cup, slid out of bed, and pulled her dress over her head.

Clayton swallowed hard.

This wasn't going to work.

Puabi-Ekur, watching in growing impatience, did something then that they rarely did. They pushed Clayton out of the way.

They could set it up so the boy thought it was his memory. But they weren't going to fail here. They had a job to do.

"Are you sure we have to use the condom?" Puabi-Ekur asked, as Clayton. "They make me lose my erection."

Jenny purred, "Honey, keeping you erect is my job." She slipped across the comforter into the boy's personal space, stroking his hair. She kissed him, first lightly, brushing his lips with hers, then softly mouthing his mouth, licking and probing. Puabi-Ekur responded.

His fingers went to stroke her rosy brown nipples, squeezed one. She moved against his hand, encouraging him, and he put both hands on her breasts, kneading. She let out a happy sigh.

Puabi-Ekur pushed her down on the bed and ran his hands over her pretty body. Such smooth skin. He mouthed, squeezed, and bit her breasts. He stroked her pussy and inserted one then two fingers. She let out a squeal. She was very wet.

"You like this, don't you?"

"I want you inside me."

They guessed she said this a lot, but this time it might be true.

"Are you sure we need a condom?"

"I can put on the condom with my mouth. Let's see how you like that!"

Grabbing at the nightstand, she found and tore open the package, positioning the rubber over the tip of his cock. She slid the condom on, mouthful by mouthful, finishing with her hand.

Then she mounted him and rode, positioning him so he hit her G-spot.

Clayton woke up, wanting to be on top. Puabi-Ekur let

him, flipping the girl so Clayton could thrust into her. With soft grunts and moans, she thrust upward, meeting each motion as Clayton pounded into her.

Puabi-Ekur smiled. They hadn't lost it.

Letting Clayton stay present, Puabi-Ekur held the girl's thighs, managing the energy, guiding, guiding... there.

She cried out in orgasm as Clayton came.

An explosion, a whiteness in space.

They collapsed together on the bed.

Puabi-Ekur floated away.

Let the two of them think it was the marijuana that made it intense. At least Puabi-Ekur had done part of their job, despite the condom.

After a few moments, Clayton awoke, the dark-haired girl curled in his arms.

Wow. Was that real?

The girl sat up, wriggling her shoulders.

"I know this is going to sound fake, but that was amazing. I don't think I've ever come like that." She shrugged and smiled. "You're a pretty special guy."

Clayton shook his head. "Just lucky." Something about her confession made him feel loose. "I've only ever had sex once before."

"Really? You're a natural."

He doubted that, but he wasn't going to argue.

"It's your weed I've been smoking all night, isn't it? Wanna go outside and smoke some more?"

"Sure." They emerged, a little bleary, into the tan living room. From the couch, Danny snored lightly. James stood and flicked the television off.

"Let's go smoke a bowl," said Clayton.

In the middle of the night, through the warm city haze, summer stars shone from far away. A breeze wrapped the three of them. Jenny shivered a little, and Clayton put his arm around her. James eyed this but said nothing. The coal flared in the bowl as he drew, then the red light died away.

"I should go wake up Paresh." He handed Clayton the second key to Suite 202 and went inside.

Clayton and Jenny stood in the parking lot, leaning on James's car, by a small concrete island with a juniper tree. The warm air carried the scent of its berries, mixed with marijuana smoke and some elusive scent of the girl's.

Puabi-Ekur watched them both.

There was much that could be done here—many life threads weaving. This boy and girl could fall in love. Such sex was binding.

They also sensed this girl was one of their people.

"I've never hired anyone before," Clayton said, "but James wanted to give Rahul a gift. He's getting married in India. He wanted to learn a few things, he said."

The girl beside him smiled. "I'm sure Hollie showed him, if he asked."

Clayton snorted. "I'm sure he had a good time. I'm guessing he didn't ask her a thing."

"Maybe not."

He swallowed hard.

He had to speak.

"I'd like to see you again."

She tilted her head to one side.

He didn't want to fuck this up. "For money. I know it's your livelihood."

"Sure. You can book through the agency."

He'd been hoping for a real date. But maybe she didn't want to get in trouble with her agency.

"Okay."

Clayton's first reaction, waking up the next morning, was pure fear.

Last night, he'd had sex with a whore.

Part of him said it could never happen again.

But why not? It had been amazing.

He crawled out of bed, yawning and scratching his head. Watery light filtered by clouds floated into his dorm room. A lazy Sunday. He had two finals left: Geotechnical Engineering and Structural Design.

He'd spend the day studying. But coffee first.

Putting on jeans and a t-shirt, he wandered down to the cafeteria, where he saw James hunched over a plate of scrambled eggs. Grabbing a cup of coffee and some oatmeal, he sat down across from his friend.

James looked up smirking. "Great night, wasn't it?"

"Yes, it was."

"You impressed that girl Jenny. It's hard to impress a whore."

James didn't have to be like that about it.

Was it so bad she was a whore?

But he didn't want to debate it.

"So are you staying in the dorm for summer session?" James asked. Clayton nodded. He'd gotten a good internship the previous summer and wanted to finish early if he could. "I'll be around too."

Clayton looked up from methodically shoveling oatmeal into his mouth—like paste laced with brown sugar, but it was food.

"Yeah," James said. "I think I flunked Structural Analysis."

"That sucks, James. I'm sorry."

"Not as sorry as me! But I'll be here. We should hire that girl of yours again."

"Of mine?"

"You liked her. But I liked her too." James was watching his face closely. Clayton retreated into blankness, hiding his reaction.

He didn't want James near Jenny.

Chapter 2

etal surfaces, muted earth tones and neutrals, cherrywood cabinetry: nothing declared a personal taste. The condo's surfaces lay glassine, smooth, except for one long-piled wool rug in front of the gas fireplace, beside a faux-bronze urn with a handful of alder sticks. The narrow kitchen was painted blood-orange, the strongest visual statement in the space. Clearly a designer had chosen the accents; they all said money, and that Phil was rarely there.

It looked like a room in an upscale hotel. One of the few personal touches was a pair of framed photos on the mantle, one of Phil's daughter. Joanie had studied this a while once, waiting for Phil: a blonde child sitting among daisies, beaming, adorable, maybe three years old.

When you loved your parents unconditionally. Before you knew who they were.

The other picture showed a lawn covered with fall leaves, with Phil's well-brushed parents, a younger brother with a goofy smile, and an earlier, unguarded Phil with floppy hair and a golden Lab in his arms.

She'd studied this image too. High school, college? The face showed a sweet nature, now mostly invisible.

She'd seen it in him once or twice, like when he'd gotten enthusiastic about artificial intelligence one time at dinner.

Now Joanie lay curled carefully on the bed, in a black silk negligée edged in lace, waiting. She didn't mind waiting; he always paid for her time. She'd poured herself two fingers of Laphroaig, as Phil had made it clear she was welcome to. The scotch and the clean-surfaced anonymity sent Joanie into a pleasant numbness.

She was sort of like the Egyptian cotton towels for Phil.

Maybe that wasn't fair. It was hard to tell, since there was money involved, and it was a job to her.

A well-paid job. And he'd never wanted anything remotely weird.

She sipped the Laphroaig. Warmth trickled into her belly.

The sex wasn't wild, or hot, like with that college guy the other night. Clayton. She hadn't figured him for hotness. But hotness had occurred.

Phil was more bread-and-butter sex. But fine, especially for money.

She finished the scotch. Still no Phil. She stretched and sat up, poking at her phone to bring up a historical novel on her reading app.

After a few moments, she let it drop. It just wasn't that good.

She wondered if Phil had anything worth reading.

Passing the kitchen nook, she padded into his office, her bare feet appreciating the glassy-finish hardwood and the pile of the Persian rug. On a desk with clean lines and a mahogany finish lay a silent desktop computer. Facing that rose a wall of books. Some were on programming—he'd come to Seattle to work in software and was now a high-level technical evangelist—a few on math or science. At bottom right, she found a couple shelves of worn paperbacks, classic spy and detective fiction: John le Carré, Graham Greene, Raymond Chandler. No women writers.

That figured. She couldn't picture Phil as a feminist.

She slipped out a Chandler novel she hadn't read and turned to go when her careful eye, always on the hunt—the therapist had called it hypervigilance—caught that the desk's lines were not, in fact, even. A drawer sat a bit crooked, as if it had been shut in a hurry.

She stepped up to the desk slowly, as if it would pounce.

She didn't want to pry. Almost always it was a bad idea. But maybe she should know more about him.

The drawer was a locked one, or was intended to be, but closed so crookedly the lock hadn't caught. She tugged gently at the drawer, and it opened.

It showed a neat set of compartments, each with its own secret.

In one narrow wooden box, she saw a tall stack of twenty dollar bills.

To the other side, in another wooden box, sat a set of

police handcuffs. Under them (she counted with her fingertips) lay two, three, four, six—she pulled out a short stack of hardcore BDSM videos. Well-packaged, high-production ones, by sellers she knew, but not mass-market. These were the real thing, real people doing BDSM.

Kinky Teen Sluts, Lesbian Bondage, Ball Torture by Mistress Z. There was no unifying theme.

She set them back in their box.

He'd never talked about BDSM. He was almost too self-controlled. It was a little scary.

As soundlessly as possible, she returned the drawer to exactly the same position as before. With infinite gentleness, she wiped the whole area with her negligée.

Resisting the desire to back out of the office, she replaced the novel and retraced her steps to the bedroom, snagging some scotch on the way. She curled up exactly as she had before.

Her heart pounded. It took several minutes of deep breathing to release her fear.

When the condo door opened, she smoothed the silk on her thigh, as she did smoothing on the persona of Jenny Sex-Kitten. Phil stepped into the bedroom doorway and smiled, showing good teeth. Mid-forties, dishwater blond hair greying at the temples, tan and fit, he'd grown up on the East Coast, with a tennis court in his backyard. He still played even when he traveled. His vintage-finish jeans had cost more than her negligée.

He sat down by her on the bed, a discreet smirk winking on and off his face. "Jenny." He stroked the silk on her thigh the same way she had, slid his fingers up to her pussy. She'd primed the pump and was wet for him.

"What do you want to do?" he asked her.

"Fuck," she said, smiling, because she knew that was what he wanted to hear. He grinned back, pulling his polo shirt over his head and displaying his muscled torso. He was vain about his body.

Slightly numb, with scotch in her belly, she switched her brain off. She'd done all this before. If she thought of anything, she thought of dinner to come, or money going into her bank account. Her body drove, on cruise control, with an occasional addition from her mind.

She kissed him, slipping him her tongue. She let him roll on top of her, kissing a while longer, then leapt up and tugged off his jeans. With a wriggle, she let her negligée drop. Climbing on top of him, she rolled a condom on him, nudged his cock inside her, and rode him, maneuvering so he hit her G-spot. She generally tried to come with her clients, if she could; it was part of her craft. She let herself ride the orgasm out, still on top, eyes closed, thinking of—hmm, Clayton.

She hadn't expected that.

Putting the thought away, she snuggled into Phil's armpit, body thrumming with retreating waves of sex.

"I have something for you," he said.

She came up with a throaty chuckle. "Yeah, you gave me that already."

He sat up. "No, I mean... here." He handed her a small

white box with a red bow. "It's nothing big, but it made me think of you." She saw nothing in particular in his eyes— perhaps a hint of nervousness.

Opening the box, she saw a bracelet, tiny nubs of shining black stones. "It's hematite. The saleswoman said it was protective."

Her gaze flickered to his face.

He looked proud of himself. This was something he thought he was supposed to do.

"Well, thank you." She leaned forward, gave him a softly open kiss. He responded, not deeply; he rarely wanted sex again immediately.

"Where do you want to go for dinner?" he asked.

"I feel like steak," she said.

After steak and a couple of Manhattans, they returned and she fucked him again. She guessed he'd popped a Viagra, but she didn't care.

Let him get what he needs from this.

She didn't claim to understand him.

And now there was that drawer full of secrets, those BDSM videos. She locked it away in her mind, awaiting further information.

It was a short ride home, in steady rain. At an ATM, she put her money in her bank account and Tammy's cut into Tammy's. By one a.m. she was back in her apartment, which smelled of curry and cat pee.

In her chilly bed, she wrapped herself in her quilt, her tabby cat kneading himself a space by her feet. She fell asleep and dreamed of nothing.

The next Saturday night, James and Rahul went out to the bars, but Clayton told them he was too tired. He'd taken his last final that morning, after studying all night the night before. In his dorm room, he sat in growing darkness, the desk lamp the only light. For a while, he sought solace in internet porn, but at last he worked up his courage and found the website: Desiree Elite Escorts.

The pink-and-black background took its time to paint on-screen. A marquee showed pictures of girls; a paragraph plugged "the Elite girlfriend experience." Then some hokey tourist-oriented text described Seattle.

They had to get a lot of visitors from out-of-town.

Most of the girls' pictures were greyed out, tagged "For Members Only." A few showed photos, obscuring the face. There she was: "Jenny. Age: 21 yrs. Measurements: 32" C natural, 24", 34" (81-61-86). Height: 5' 6' (168 cm). Weight: 50kg (110lb)."

It bugged him that the measurement units weren't parallel. Why put metric first on the final one? Clearly it was a cheap website.

"If you are new to our agency, please fill out the booking form here to arrange an appointment. Or email us directly for a personal introduction."

Maybe that's what he needed to do: "Hi, I'm Clayton. I met Jenny two weekends ago and had mind-blowing sex. I want to see her again."

Something like that.

He typed for a few minutes, pretending that it wasn't

important, that it was like any email. His finger paused before clicking the Send button.

Did he really want to do this? He couldn't afford much of her time, at the rate James quoted.

But she'd liked me. Or at least, she'd said the sex was good. But maybe that wasn't true.

He saw in front of him the slippery slope to not doing it. Catching himself, he hit Send.

Puabi-Ekur's first memory was of a mud-brick building, rays of light falling through an open window to a mud-red floor covered with reed matting. The visual winked in, then winked out. They were Puabi then, a young human girl in their first life.

Later, when she was older, she walked up the broad mud-red steps to the temple, holding her mother's hand. She had always been destined for the temple.

As they paused in the doorway, a young woman dressed in the robes of a priestess met them. She took Puabi's mother's arm and drew them both inside. Ahead at the central point of the temple sat the broad altar, now empty except for a shining copper dish where incense burned. To the right down the long aisle stood the shrine, where only priests and priestesses could go. Its door stood open; within rose the statue of Inanna, made of white gypsum with huge lapis-blue eyes.

Beside the altar, the young priestess leaned and looked into Puabi's face. "Hello, child of honey! After the sanga-priest signs you in, we'll perform the ablutions. Then we'll get you to your dormitory."

Beside Puabi, on the floor, her mother's shadow fell. She couldn't remember her mother's face, only the feeling of standing next to her, knowing she would go. Puabi knew she had to be a big girl; she couldn't cry or hold onto her mother's body as she left. But Puabi didn't break down or wail.

The next thing she recalled, fleetingly, was the ablutions themselves, immersion in the sacred cistern meant to symbolize the original sea. Dried, dressed in linen, given a plate of barley cakes, she sat at a low table in the empty dormitory and tried not to cry.

Later she learned to dance to the harp and perform the sexual rites. For a while she entertained the youngest prince, Ditanu. He liked her to dance first, as one of the harpists played; he was liberal with his silver, so no one minded.

Of an evening, in the shadows of an oil-lamp, the curtain open to the lying-down room beyond, he would watch her. His gaze stroked her brown body, picked out her nipples showing under the thin linen. In the night, he clutched her to him and called her child of honey, though she knew he would soon marry.

For him, she danced like no other. She wore blue; her beads were lapis; she danced a river in the land of two rivers. Then she knelt in front of him and put her mouth to him, licking and sucking his slender cock, till it became so natural she could wake with his cock in her mouth, the two of them moving together in their sleep.

Then he married, and he was gone. The matron-priestess, seeing her tear-streaked face, let her take a week to herself before resuming her duties.

But that was a long time ago. Why did Puabi-Ekur recall it now?

The boy lay asleep in his dormitory room, lit cold blue by the lamp he'd left on. He thought he'd nap between chapters of reading, but the nap had become a night's sleep. Puabi-Ekur sat wakeful in a corner of the ceiling.

They set their mind again to the deep past.

Puabi was thirty, at the height of her beauty, long crimped brunette hair falling over small breasts still high on a frame slender but wide-hipped. For her full, rounded ass, she was justly famous. Her beauty had catapulted her nearly to the highest rank, but she hadn't taken on the airs of some of her sisters. She still brought figs home from the market for the little girls, still danced to the harp and sang the goddess's favorite scurrilous songs. Friendly with worshippers, she planned never again to get heart-caught by a man. She gave all her silver to the goddess, keeping enough to buy thin linen dresses.

Then her favorite harpist quit the temple to marry, and she had to find another. Puabi was a little too high-ranked to search herself. The temple servant she sent in her place returned as her dresser brushed her hair at the end of an afternoon.

The smell of the charcoal rose from the dish the crimping tongs lay in; the smell of cedar resin rose from the censer. Puabi rubbed sweat off her forehead with the back of her wrist. "Well, Shiptu?"

"My lady, besides Lu-Nanna—"

"Lu-Nanna is too high and mighty for me."

"There are three in temple besides Lu-Nanna that might please my lady with the harp."

"I would hear them."

"I thought you would say so, my lady. I have brought the first, Iltani."

From behind the servant stepped a young woman in her mid-twenties, holding a lap-harp. A slip of a girl, she wore her long black hair straight, her black eyes deep in kohl.

Their eyes met, and a shiver crossed Puabi's skin.

It caused no comment for a dancer to spend all her time with her harpist. When it became clear their relationship was more than musical, the temple approved. Better to keep your affections within the compound.

After the nobles and princes left Puabi's bed, after the incense sputtered and died in the censer, after the sweeper cleared the courtyard, Iltani lay in Puabi's arms, and nothing was sweeter than that. Her kisses, and her tongue on Puabi's vulva, emotions connecting them as they melded, coming for each other, falling asleep together wrapped in each other's arms.

Those black, black eyes.

Puabi-Ekur shivered, as she had long ago.

Why had they not seen it? So foolish.

It was Jenny.

The threads yanked taut. Though Puabi-Ekur hadn't breathed with their own lungs for centuries, they felt a little breathless.

Chapter 3

$\mathcal{Y}$ou going out tonight?" James asked, in the door of Clayton's dorm room, squinting into the dense, dusty yellow rays of late afternoon.

"No, staying in."

"Oh come on. It's Thursday night."

"I have Water Resource Engineering homework. It's hard to stay caught up with summer classes."

"Duuuuuude. I'm begging you. There are girls to meet." If Clayton hadn't been lying, he might have gone to keep James quiet. He shook his head. "C'mon, I need a wingman."

"You'll do better on your own."

Didn't James have a girlfriend? Even if it was long-distance.

"Meet me at ten o'clock at Earl's?" Clayton recognized the last stand and shook his head. "Dude, I hope your engineering degree is worth it."

The degree was why he was at the university.

He didn't meet his friend's eyes.

At this rate, James was going to flunk Structural Analysis again.

James peeled himself off the door frame, waved at Clayton dismissively, and disappeared.

Clayton sighed. Another friend had asked once why he and James were buddies. That was easy—James knew how to have fun. In other words, James got Clayton into the vicinity of girls, even if James mostly snagged the girls himself.

But tonight Clayton had his own plans.

He waited a few minutes to make sure the coast was clear, then found his bicycle outside, a cheap second-hand road bike for getting around campus. The sun was setting as he reached the motel. His fingers fumbled as he locked up the bike.

At the far end of the motel parking lot, Joanie shut off her car and sat waiting—just sitting, not listening to music, not doing anything. After a moment, she opened the window and let the warm rays of sunset fall on her face, closing her eyes. A breeze flitted about her. It smelled of asphalt from roadwork, but above that floated a hint of flowers.

She was a little early. Usually she had the guy call when he was ten minutes out, but this time she'd just driven to the motel.

It was a chance. This guy could chicken out. So often they did. But she didn't think he would.

She found herself humming.

Her phone rang. "Okay, I'm here," he said. "It's Room 310. I'll meet you in the lobby."

She checked her lipstick in the mirror and climbed out of the car. She wore a new flowered sundress, with a negligée stuffed in her purse. She pushed through the double doors to the lobby, decorated no later than 1975: round mirrors, green patterned wallpaper, tan leatherette couches. Beaming, Clayton leaped from his couch.

Anyone would think they were boyfriend and girlfriend.

While he fired up some weed on the balcony, she changed in the room's bathroom, checking herself out in the mirror. The negligée she put on was new, a deep rose-pink with off-white lace that set off her pale skin.

It made her feel sexy, but more on the erotic side.

Or romantic. Something like that.

It was a job. Two hundred and ten dollars, maybe a bit more.

But she found herself grinning.

Hovering nearby, Puabi-Ekur remembered Iltani—those first days, those first nights.

Puabi had never tried to seduce a woman. Seduction wasn't part of her métier. The man (always a man) put down a token for the goddess, and then she did the goddess's work. She might start with a dance, but then the flutist and drummer would retire. Sometimes she began what followed —touched the man's arm, hiked up his robe—but mostly not.

She and Iltani spent a lot of time together, learning songs. One day, Iltani brought new music she was working on to Puabi, a water-song. As she played it, Puabi improvised a dance, shaking her shawl sewn with beaten-silver lozenges so it sounded like rain.

"You do me proud," Iltani said. Grinning, Puabi made obeisance, then threw herself among the pillows at Iltani's feet.

It was twilight in the courtyard, the edge of the sky stained with crimson and ochre but the zenith cobalt blue. On the air floated the smell of wood smoke from cook-fires and the distant bleat of sheep. A stillness fell.

Puabi reached out, took Iltani's palm in hers, and stroked it. She leaned and put a kiss in Iltani's palm, and looked up.

Those black, black eyes.

Now Puabi-Ekur sat on the bed, in Clayton's body, with Jenny—the three of them, though the boy and girl didn't know that. They'd tossed back the multicolored polyester coverlet and sat wreathed in white sheets.

They could be wrong.

Puabi-Ekur stole out and, lifting Jenny's hand, kissed the palm. Their eyes met. A stillness fell.

They weren't wrong.

They stepped back. Let the boy do this—it was for him, wasn't it?

Because succubi were known for their generosity and thoughtfulness.

The truth was, Puabi-Ekur was scared. They didn't know what reconnecting now meant. People from past lives generally meant trouble.

Clayton took Jenny's shoulders in his hands and drew her toward him.

She shucked off her negligée; he suckled at her breasts, the rose-brown nipples. She stroked his hair, leaning back on the bed and pulling him on top of her. He kissed her, mauling her breasts in his hands, then went down on her, licking, sucking, circling her clit with his tongue till she moaned.

Grabbing a condom from the bedside table, she rubbed the velvety skin of his cock along the shaft. He closed his eyes, then opened them to see her climbing on top of him, her breasts presented to him. Half-sitting up, he mouthed one then the other.

She gently pushed him down and fucked him. He took her hips in his hands, moving her on top of him. She shook him off, searching for her own pleasure, finding it. He closed his eyes and let her ride him.

Harder, harder, faster, till she cried out—just as she did, he came too, as before so intensely that for a moment he lost consciousness. She fell to the bed beside him.

Cool air touched him. He was covered in sweat. He reached out and felt she was too.

Sensation tolled through him like the sound of bells and slowly died away.

She threw away the condom and sat on one elbow, watching him. He lay staring at the beige ceiling.

It couldn't always be this good.

He remembered the girl he'd taken home from the party. That had felt great, but nothing like this.

"Is it always like this, with men?"

"No."

They looked at each other. She shrugged. A lock of dark hair fell across her face; she pushed it behind her ear.

"I guess we're just well-suited," she said. She circled his cock with her fingers, at the base, right above his balls. It stirred. "You've got a great cock, nice and thick. We fit really well physically." She stroked her fingers down his cock lightly; it moved under her hand. She grinned at him. "You should get your money's worth."

This time he was on top. "Try putting my legs over your shoulders—yes—there. Put the pillow under my ass." And then she didn't talk anymore; he drove into her, letting her move him so his cock landed as she wanted it to. Again they came together.

Puabi-Ekur watched—not even doing anything, not anymore.

"Has it been two hours?" Clayton asked.

Joanie started, waking up. "Let me see." Stretching, she reached her phone from the bedside table. "Yeah, it has."

They'd shut the drapes, but through an opening she saw darkness. Below the bedside lamp, golden light pooled.

"Okay," said Clayton. He pulled himself to the edge of the bed and sat a moment, gathering himself to get up, to get the cash he owed her.

She watched him.

Never date a client. Another Tammy rule. But people broke it all the time.

Okay, I'm going to do this.

"I'm hungry. Are you?" she asked.

Dark-blue eyes met hers from under a shock of chestnut hair. "Starving."

He was prettier than he looked at first. Give him a decent haircut, he could be hot.

"Let's settle up, then go find something to eat."

Clayton paused a moment, staring at her.

Suddenly she felt shy. "If you want."

He shrugged. "Sure. I'm on my bike, is all."

"Your bicycle?" He nodded.

She laughed. "Maybe we can fit it into my car."

In the small hours two days later, Joanie sat on Tammy's grey-leather sectional office couch, watching as Tammy worked on the agency website. Now that Joanie had spent a year and a half at the agency, she and Tammy had become friendly, and Joanie occasionally stopped by to drop off the agency commission in person. Along with Hayley, Joanie was one of the agency's mainstays.

"Thursday, where did you go after that one call?" Tammy asked. "I had something to send you on."

"I didn't feel like more work. I should have called and said."

Tammy regarded her over slim-framed glasses. In her fifties, Tammy had kept her looks—long black hair now in a high bun, sweater-dress showing off her considerable bust —and a string of long-term clients.

"You girls. Sometimes—" Something in Joanie's face made Tammy stop the lecture. After a moment, she went back to the computer. "We could've made good money. That's what you're here for, right?"

Joanie made a noncommittal noise.

Nothing to make her critique late-stage capitalism like this type of conversation. Money wasn't everything.

Time to change the subject.

"Hey, I wondered—you know this guy Phil that I've been seeing now for a while?"

Tammy nodded.

"How well do you know him?" Joanie asked.

Tammy stopped typing and glanced over. "Well enough. Why?"

"He's been acting like he's into me, buying me little gifts. He tips like crazy. It's great, but it makes me nervous. Last week, I was waiting for him, and I went into his office to see if he had anything to read. There was a drawer hanging open, so I checked it out. It had a bunch of money in it, and a bunch of BDSM stuff, police handcuffs and videos."

Tammy frowned. "You didn't mess with any of it, did you?"

"Fuck no, I'm not crazy. But I want to know what he's getting up to."

"What kind of BDSM videos were they?"

"Professional ones." She named the makers. "But he's never said a word about anything kinky."

Tammy shrugged. "So he's shy."

The two women stared at each other.

What would get Tammy's attention?

"I don't want the agency to get caught up in anything."

Tammy continued to stare.

She was trying to read Joanie. It was true, Joanie did care about the agency. It'd be a bitch for her and Hayley if things went south.

"I'll ask around," Tammy said finally. "I haven't heard anything. I don't send you girls out if I think it's dangerous."

"I know that."

Tammy went back to typing.

"If you want to concentrate, I can get out of here. But I thought you might want a glass of wine after work." From a bag at her feet, Joanie lifted a bottle of pinot grigio and waggled it.

"Gimme another minute. I want to clean up this page. I asked Donna to do it, but as usual she flaked. We need an IT guy." She flashed Joanie a grin. "There must be someone we can pay in kind."

Joanie half-smiled in response, knowing Tammy didn't mean it. Tammy wouldn't let anyone know about her profession who she wasn't sure of. The therapist friend with whom Tammy shared the office was a former sex worker.

"Okay, done."

Joanie poured out wine in the therapist's coffee cups.
Tammy took off her heavy earrings, rubbing her earlobes.

"What a day! I had to switch gears every fifteen
seconds."

Joanie sipped her cold white wine.

It was an anesthetic, wasn't it?

Everyone was in their own kind of pain.

Chapter 4

On the walls of the spacious basement room hung Indian tapestries, block print on tan background, the printed colors Prussian blue and dark crimson. The overall effect was pink, in part because of a pink-shaded lamp. Incense, sandalwood mixed with other scents, burned in a brass censer in the corner. Pillows and padded mats lay in a rough circle on the floor. Joanie sat on her pillow cross-legged, next to Hayley.

Hayley had found the notice in a small group online. She'd passed the filter of a meetup at All Paths Bookstore, and now they'd been invited to a real Inanna ritual.

After a brief introduction, Sasha, one of the women who led the group, read a hymn: "The pure torch lit in the sky, the heavenly light, the great Queen of Heaven, Inanna I hail!"

The group answered, "Inanna I hail!"

The other leader, Cleo, lit a candle on an altar to one

side, in front of a rounded, smiling statue whose hands cupped full breasts. "Her brilliant coming forth in the evening sky, her lighting the sky, a pure torch, Inanna I hail!"

"Inanna I hail!"

Sasha motioned the group to sit: twelve women ranging in age from eighteen to late fifties, and four men—two bearded hipsters, clearly friends and the boyfriends of two of the women, and two older men.

"Welcome to the Temple of Inanna! I'd like to start out with some gentle meet-and-greet games with our clothes on. Let's break into two circles, one facing inward and one facing outward."

Joanie found herself facing a man in his fifties, the oldest male in the group. Wings of grey led from his temples into wavy brunet hair.

Potential client.

"What do you most want this person to know about you?" the leader said.

Grey-temples smiled. "I really love women. I would call myself a feminist." He clearly considered this a pick-up strategy.

Classic, but not in a good way.

She had to stay courteous—potential client.

Joanie made herself smile invitingly and hinted she had a background doing sex work.

"What do you least want this person to know about you?"

That one was hard. But she wanted to be true to what the group was doing.

"My family's pretty dysfunctional, and my uncle molested me."

"I'm so sorry, my dear." The man leaned forward, stealing a glimpse at her breasts, taking her hand without permission.

Smiling, she retrieved it, wishing they'd had the consent talk up front.

"Is that why you ended up in the sex industry?"

Inwardly she rolled her eyes. It was so cliché. Girls who were molested—everyone thought that was why they did sex work. Girls who weren't molested—everyone thought they were lying.

"No. I did it because it was a job that paid well and fit around my schedule."

He frowned and was about to speak when the leader asked each pair to end their conversation.

She hoped he didn't show up in her inbox. She'd brought some cards to hand out—pointing to a neutral website, not the agency's, a list of erotic bodyworkers. One fear she had was that Tammy would catch her stepping out on the agency.

She flipped the cards over in the pocket of her cardigan.

She didn't have to give them out if she didn't want to.

After the two priestesses led a consent conversation, they all undressed, putting their things to the side of the room. Joanie left on her silver jewelry: a pair of necklaces, hoop earrings, and bangles, lending sheen to her pale skin. A frisson of tension rippled across the gathering as they took off their clothes. The priestesses cued some repetitive, low-tempo trance music, which calmed the energy.

"Let's go with six groups of three. Go ahead and connect with a couple people close by. But if you came here as part of a couple, I'd ask you to separate for this part."

Joanie stood a moment, watching. Hayley was across the room; they'd split up to get a better take on the group. The men separated from one another, and the leaders herded them back. "Would you be comfortable sharing erotic space with a man? If not, that's fine, but one goal of our temple is for all of us to push our boundaries, within the bounds of consent."

The two hipsters eyed each other but joined one group; the older men chose separate ones. Hayley got grey-temples; Joanie angled to catch the other older man.

Sasha briefly described the practice while the co-leader dropped off sheets, cling wrap, bottles of lube, condoms, and gloves. "Please spread the sheets over the mats and tuck them in—we're trying to avoid too much staining. Gloves and condoms are latex-free. I can let you know more details and lube ingredients. Ask if you need to!"

A couple of women went up to Sasha. Joanie looked around.

The two hipsters sat loosely, shoulders relaxed, glancing around quickly, grinning, excited. The women were more circumspect: hands clasped, feet tucked under them or legs crossed, clear boundaries around their energy.

Overall, she was impressed so far. The two priestesses balanced each other and ran the energy easily.

Sasha was in her forties, her wavy dark hair with a few grey streaks caught in a loose ponytail. Slender, pale, with high cheekbones, she radiated warmth. She was casually dressed in a loose singlet over yoga clothes—all of them had been told to dress in loose clothing. The other, Cleo, was younger, in her late twenties or early thirties, mixed-race judging by her skin, hair bound back with a sash. The grin she flashed said playfulness.

Cleo stood out—it was a very white crowd. That wasn't true at the agency, where half the girls were black, Latina, or Asian. Tammy liked to present "a cornucopia of girls, something for every taste." But at best she was businesslike with the black girls, at worst she thought they were on drugs or stealing.

Joanie shook herself mentally and paid attention to the room.

How would the women be without the men? More relaxed. But if it were all-female, she wouldn't have come.

She wanted to do sex ritual, but mostly she wanted clients.

Her date with Clayton had been pretty amazing. It wasn't just his lovely cock—something about his energy. She closed her eyes a moment, imagining his cock inside her: liquid feelings, energy pouring like honey. Hard, masculine hands clamping her thighs.

Opening her eyes, she brought the energy forward to work with.

"All right, let's get started," Sasha said. "Decide among you who goes first. Be sure to be really clear about what you want. You have total permission for that! Talk about which parts of the body are open for touch and which aren't. Talk about what kind of touch you want. And if you change your mind in the middle, that is totally okay." They'd done a demo earlier during the consent talk.

Joanie's group resettled to face each other. Besides herself, it was a woman in her thirties, curvy, self-contained but pleasant, and the second of the middle-aged men: grey frizzy hair in a longish cut, glasses, a quizzical but kind aura, dad bod but not bad.

Cock ordinary. Fine by her. How would he deal with the two women?

He had wit enough to smile at both, not lingering on Joanie. But his gaze stayed on her breasts a split second long.

Uh-huh. I see you, Daddy.

When his eyes came to hers, she blinked slowly in acknowledgement.

He got a card later. If he was good.

"Who wants to go?" he asked. "I'm fine either way."

Joanie turned to the other woman, Zelda. "Do you want to go first?" Their eyes met.

Zelda was wishing Daddy here wasn't there. Did people always have to do this boy-girl objectification dance? Zelda was good-looking—just not top-of-the-bell-curve, every-man-wants-it good-looking.

I'm lucky, I guess.

"I'll go first," Zelda said.

She lay down on the mat, a bit stiffly, arms straight and pinned to her sides—as if laid out for her funeral.

"Have you done this before?" Joanie asked.

"Once, but it was an all-woman group."

Joanie flicked a glance at Daddy. "Jon, how about you?"

He smiled, self-deprecatingly. "I've been here a few times."

"I haven't, but I've done stuff like this before," Joanie said. Turning to Zelda: "We're both here to help you feel safe and protected."

The woman frowned slightly. Clearly she didn't know how easy it was to read her body language.

"What do you want?" Joanie asked.

That proved simple: avoid the sexy parts and do straight massage and sensual touch. Joanie bet that she'd change her mind halfway through.

During the initial massage—basic massage, starting on the long muscles of the arms and legs—Joanie found herself drifting a bit. Her gaze settled on the altar.

Inanna. Queen of Heaven. A goddess of sacred whores —she should get to know her better. She liked a whore goddess who ruled her own city.

The city had come up in the introduction. Joanie had encountered the sacred whore idea before: the ancient class of priestesses, in Sumer and elsewhere, who made love to all comers for the goddess.

Hayley connected more with sexual healing than she did. For her, it was mainly a job. A job she was good at.

She rubbed gently and slowly. Jon was a conscientious masseur and matched her movements, stealing glimpses of her tits and pussy.

Relaxing, eyes shut, Zelda moved under their touch. "Mmm, that's nice. Maybe I'm okay with Joanie touching my breasts and pussy." Jon shot Joanie a look of consternation. Joanie shrugged slightly.

Stay courteous. Potential client.

Closely watching Zelda's face, she lightly stroked her breasts with her fingers. "Okay if I use my mouth?" The woman nodded, biting her lips.

Joanie saw fear but also anticipation.

Leaning over, Joanie tasted her nipples, gently biting, teasing the pretty tits. She bit one red nipple a little harder, the other hand kneading her other breast like dough. The woman squirmed in pleasure, her breath coming fast.

Joanie then moved downward, lightly kissing Zelda's stomach. She stroked her labia. "Okay if I touch inside, with gloves?" The woman agreed, and Joanie put on gloves.

These ladies knew how to put on a sex party. These were quality gloves.

She squirted on a little lube and explored. Continuing to glance at Jon, she whispered in the woman's ear, "What do you like? More inside? Do you want me to lick you?" The woman wriggled, which was hard to interpret. "Should I go down on you?" Zelda nodded vigorously.

Joanie studied the cling wrap and took a deep breath.

She hadn't done this with a barrier before.

You learn something new every day.

She ripped out a long slick sheet, positioned it. Scooting down, she licked and sucked, watching, spreading and respreading the wrap. Zelda's cunt lay like a flower behind glass. She got a good angle, judging by the moans, and kept at it.

She felt the energy click in. Zelda moved like the sea, hips surging. A little more, and she pitched and heaved.

She just had to keep her mouth in place. Okay—there.

Zelda erupted in sobbing cries, the first in the room. Joanie couldn't help being proud of herself.

One for the whores.

Jon looked a little breathless. Hayley caught her eye and grinned. Sasha smiled.

The pretty priestess liked that. Yay.

Zelda sat up, and Joanie hugged her from behind, whispering, "Thank you for that. That was beautiful."

Zelda blinked. "Omigod. I wasn't expecting... thank you."

Across the room, in the low pink light, murmurs and cries rose. They'd broken the ice, and in cascade a series of orgasms rolled across the room. A hot, pink, humid energy flowed in waves, sweet with incense and the smell of human fluids. Sex.

It was like you could smell the oxytocin.

I love this. I was born for this.

Joanie caught her own thought with surprise. For her, sex work had always been a day job. She loved the intricacies of economics and was anticipating getting into chunkier work with her master's, to make a new economics, the economics of democratic socialism. But as gentle cries crossed the room—male, female, it hardly mattered—she felt a deep sense of coming home.

Her glance caught, on the altar, the rounded statue of Inanna.

Smiling, Inanna looked back.

After the closing circle, the party people gathered their things, hugging each other, exchanging a few last phone numbers and emails. Joanie waited for Hayley, who was securing a customer. Joanie had done that already. Jon had her card.

Again the altar drew her eye. The statue called to her. She went over to it.

The altar was simple: a ruffled cloth of pink silk, with apricot rose petals strewn across it, some pink fairy lights, and the statue, emanating... what?

Sasha stepped up beside her. "Joanie. You're Hayley's friend, right?"

"I am."

She was such a pretty woman that it was distracting.

Guys must feel like this a lot.

A few strands of grey streaked Sasha's loose ponytail, which was dark chestnut in pink lamplight. She had lustrous brown eyes and an aura like hot cocoa.

"You have an affinity for Inanna?" she asked Joanie.

"I guess I do."

Sasha met her eyes, questing. Joanie felt a tendril of energy surround her; it was a sexual feeling, and suddenly she was wet. Then Cleo, the other group leader, stepped up and put her hand gently on Sasha's shoulder, leaning to whisper something in her ear. The whisper could have been something prosaic—lost and found, where to put the trash —but the gesture spoke.

They were lovers.

As Cleo stepped away, Sasha watched her a half-moment before turning back to Joanie. "We have devotional circles twice a month. I'd love to have you come to one, if you're so inclined."

Joanie again sensed a wisp of interest from Sasha, like a scent of chocolate. It confused her, but she let herself sink into it. "I'd like that."

Sasha fished a card out of her pocket—colorful, all oranges and purples. She flipped it and wrote a date on the back.

As she did, Hayley stepped up. She looked amazing, blonde hair tousled, shining like a goddess, radiating sexual pleasure. You couldn't help but smile at her, and Sasha did.

"I was saying to Joanie we have devotional circles, the next one in a couple of weeks." A quick scribble, and she handed them both cards with dates on the back. "I hope we see you there! You both seem like the Lady's kind of people."

"I'd be honored," Joanie said, glancing across at Hayley, who nodded with her head and shoulders both.

Chapter 5

Phil leaned over the table, proffering a forkful of steak.

Joanie, fully in Jenny Sex-Kitten mode, bit it off and chewed daintily. Raising her glass of syrah, she sipped, sending a kiss over the rim of the glass. Her stomach was tied in knots, but she kept her face as smooth as cream.

Early training for the win.

She made it through half the steak and the full glass of wine before she called time-out. "Off to the ladies' for a moment," she said, doing her best to convey that she'd masturbate there thinking about him.

They patronized this high-end steak shop often enough that the waiters knew their names and drinks. Low lamps, wood paneling, and candles at the tables set the ambiance. The bathroom went full swank: green marble floor and sink, a green-and-dark-red velvet curtain hung midair.

Entering a stall, she sat. She took three deliberate, deep breaths in through her nose, out through her mouth. Then another three.

She was scared. Her body was scared.

She should've figured out how to deal with Phil before she met him tonight. But she hadn't known she'd feel so different.

Another three breaths, and another, and her body began to respond. Her stomach loosened.

Now, a game plan. She needed a distraction, something new that wouldn't weird him out.

Bring in another girl?

Whatever she did, she'd have to do quickly.

She texted Hayley. <Please come help me with Phil tonight>

Luck: Hayley texted back instantly. <What's up?>

<Dunno. Super nervous. I'll pay your fee if I have to>

<Kk>

Joanie gave Hayley the address and returned to Phil's table. He fed her more steak. "I'm getting kind of full on meat. I feel like dessert." She smiled roguishly. She needed to play this out long enough for Hayley to show up.

As she perused the menu, consciously twirling a lock of dark hair with one finger, a voice called her name. "Jenny!"

"Hollie!" She stood and threw her arms around Hayley. She didn't dare whisper, "Thank the gods you're here," but the glance they shared said it.

Hayley looked stunning—she always did—in a body-conscious dress spangled with pink flowers, golden hair foaming over her shoulders. Phil preferred his girls slim and brunette, but Hayley's curves and genuine sweetness always drew attention. Together with Joanie, she gave a pleasant contrast, bright sun-gold to Joanie's mysterious and dark.

"Phil, I don't think you've met my best friend Hollie. Do you mind if she sits down?" In answer, Phil stood and drew out a chair for Hollie, watching her coolly. But Joanie saw his gaze dip to her cleavage.

Points to her.

They ordered dessert for three, flourless chocolate cake. Hollie applied herself to it. "What do you think?" Joanie whispered in Phil's ear.

"Think about...?"

"Her going to bed with us."

"For a fee?"

Joanie shrugged.

"Okay, I'll bite." He stroked her hair, gazing into her eyes. "I won't tip the same way."

"She won't mind that." She leaned and kissed his cheek. "I thought we could mix it up a little." She put her hand on his knee. "I always love sex with you, but—you know, something different. For special, for you."

Phil stared into her face a moment, and a trickle of fear crossed Joanie's heart. Then he smiled. "That's sweet of you."

∿

"He likes lingerie—did you bring anything?" They were in Phil's big bathroom, with dark-grey walls and big movie-star-style bulbs around a mirror. On the marble tiles, a fluffy white throw rug perched. Air conditioning made it almost too cool.

"I did." Most of the agency girls carried satchel purses that could, in a pinch, carry a chemise or even a pair of heels. Hayley drew on a peach-colored satin teddy with off-white lace that set off her golden skin. Joanie dropped a aubergine slip-dress over her own head.

"Okay, show time."

They'd done three-way scenes before; this would be easy and fun.

What she didn't know was how she'd deal with Phil after this.

Maybe something tonight would help her understand.

They padded into the bedroom. Joanie had snagged the bottle of Laphroaig and three glasses. She didn't plan to drink much, and she knew Hayley wouldn't. But she wanted Phil out for a bit after he came.

"Hi, baby! How do you like your girls?"

The lit bedside lamp showed an expanse of off-white down comforter, topped by six snowy-white pillows. As Joanie and Hayley climbed onto the bed, Phil patted the sheets beside him. They arranged themselves to either side.

Joanie kissed him. Phil hooked her around the neck with one arm and pulled her close. His far hand played in Hayley's hair.

"Kiss my friend," Joanie whispered. "See how pretty she is?"

"She is pretty." He tilted Hayley's chin up and put his mouth to hers.

Go to town, girlie.

He leaned forward into the kiss.

It was working. Good.

She hadn't known if the combination would fly, and she hadn't wanted to pay for it if it didn't. Phil had never been vindictive, but there could always be a first time.

There was something lurking under the surface, with him.

But maybe she was twitchy for no reason.

Sitting up on her haunches, Hayley put Phil's hands to her magnificent breasts: double Ds, with pink nipples on tan skin. Phil squeezed and mauled, enjoying himself. Then, looking up into Hayley's face, he gently licked and then bit the nipples.

Joanie sat behind them, watching.

Nice.

Hayley moved slightly, changing the angle at which she sat. "Let's not forget Jenny!" She leaned over and kissed Joanie lightly; the three of them shared a three-way kiss, all soft liquidness, Hayley's thoughtful tongue questioning and probing. Phil's hand went to his cock; Joanie saw he was getting hard.

"Let me help with that," she said, and knelt to suck him as he kept kissing Hayley, squeezing her generous tits with both hands. In no time, Phil's cock was like rebar.

Sitting up, Joanie whispered in his ear, "You should fuck her." Grabbing the package Hayley'd brought, she put a condom on him. Positioning herself behind Hayley, she propped herself against the stacked pillows as Phil mounted her friend.

It was always sexy, watching. No jealousy—it wasn't like she cared.

Phil made a point of his stamina, so she knew this was going to take a while. As he pumped into Hayley, who filled the room with her cries, she found her mind drifting to… Clayton?

Much less swank, that hotel room where she'd met him. But the warmth of his young body, his shy smile, that magnificent cock that hit just right…

She focused suddenly to see Phil staring at her.

He wanted her to watch him come.

She met his eyes, bringing forward some of the warmth of the memory of Clayton. "Oh, baby, I want to watch you come inside her."

As if her words had triggered him, Phil closed his eyes and cried out, pumping feverishly. After a few moments, he let himself down into Hayley's arms. Joanie stroked his wavy hair, lightly sweaty along the hairline.

Everyone was sweet right after orgasm.

Phil snuggled into Hayley's arms, and in a moment was asleep, snoring. After a moment, Hayley gently rolled herself away.

"If I know him, he'll sleep for half an hour or so. Come with me." Joanie crooked a finger, and they stole out of the room.

In the kitchen, Hayley got herself a glass of filtered water. They sat on two stools by the grey-flecked granite counter. "Do you want to show me the office, where the stuff is?"

"No, that seems too risky. But I wanted to talk without him being right there."

"So, what?"

They'd both been busy with classes, so hadn't talked for a while. But Hayley was her best friend, the only person who knew her whole life, and she'd felt more and more strongly after her conversation with Tammy that she needed someone's advice. Because clearly Tammy wasn't going to help.

"It still bugs me, the stuff in that drawer."

Hayley scratched her cheek. "You know, what seems relatively normal to you and me, the handcuffs and videos, may not seem normal to someone who's older and more in the mainstream. He could be embarrassed. Especially if it's the classic thing, a powerful man who secretly wants to submit."

"True. But the thing about Phil is, for as long as I've known him—I don't really know him. Like Joe, your long-time guy." Joe was a man in his fifties, whom Hayley saw twice a month. "You're not in love with him, sometimes you don't like him, but you know him, know who he is and what he cares about. I don't have that with Phil."

"That is weird. I mean, so many guys are ready to tell their life stories right away."

"I know he's in software, a technical evangelist." She named a prominent local company. "He travels a lot; his region is Australia."

"I'm seeing a couple guys who work there. You want me

to ask them about him? I can say he's someone a friend of mine is dating, like for real dating, so we're not outing him."

"That might help. I'd love to get a little more perspective." A sound of movement came from the bedroom. "Let's see how our victim is."

Chapter 6

Through the window, the sun's last light made a bar of orange on the horizon, fading upward to blue. Clayton had studied all afternoon and felt almost caught up.

He went over the numbers again in his bank's phone app. Somehow he'd ended up with extra cash.

It was almost as if fate was telling him to go see Jenny.

As he thought it, James appeared in his open doorway. They hadn't hung out often so far this summer. Clayton needed to ace his summer classes so couldn't go to the bars much.

He'd noticed too that when he traveled as James's wingman, he almost never picked up a girl. Blond, tan, well-muscled, James looked like the perfect one-night stand. Clayton didn't as much, with his dark shaggy hair and less-cut muscles. Clayton's sport was cross-country, and he still ran, but James spent more time in the gym. Plus, if Clayton had success, James often moved in.

"Whatcha up to?" James asked, enunciating carefully.

Shit—he was drunk already.

"Finishing some homework," Clayton said.

He peered at James.

"Wanna go have a beer? And maybe some pizza? I'll buy."

He wanted to get food into the boy before he became a danger to himself and others.

They ended up at their favorite utilitarian pizza joint, with wood tables shellacked against abuse and kelly-green paint on the walls behind Italian movie posters. They ordered a large pepperoni pizza. James insisted on a pitcher of Rainier—at least it didn't have a high alcohol percentage.

The torrent spilled out.

"Dude—I'm failing again." James sat with his head in his hands. "If I don't turn it around this summer, I'll flunk out of school. Then I'll have to become a barista, or a pizza slinger."

Clayton cast an eye toward the counter, where the brown-pigtailed cashier caught his eye back.

Okay, that was a big tip there.

"Look, dude, keep it down."

"Okay, okay." James could be an asshole, but he wasn't stupid. "Can you help me?"

He took his friend's hands across the table. Bright blue eyes stared into Clayton's brown ones.

Fuck, what was he asking?

Clayton swallowed half a pizza slice to fortify himself.

"Dude, you're in way too deep for me to cheat for you. I'm working pretty hard this quarter myself. I will tutor you, if you want, but you are going to have to do the work. That's my best offer."

James met his eyes.

"Okay. I get it. I need this. You've met my family." James had to become an engineer so he didn't end up running one of his father's restaurants and knuckling under for the rest of his life. "I'll take your offer."

"Okay."

Clayton's stomach released a tight knot—combined worry for his friend and the desire to stand up for himself. He poured himself a pint of Rainier.

A pitcher later, James came up with a way to celebrate his newfound determination for school success. "I'll call Desiree Elite Escorts and see if that Jenny girl's around. You paid for dinner—I'll pay for a hotel room."

"Uh—"

"No, no, don't protest. I know you liked her. Let me do this for you." James jumped up, grabbed his cell phone, and went outside to make the call.

Clayton stared at the empty pizza pan and beer pitcher.

He couldn't run after James. He had to pay.

Maybe he could explain.

They headed for the economy hotel on the outskirts of town where they'd held Rahul's party. Clayton made James let him drive. The summer night was Seattle chilly; he pulled his jacket tight around him.

Inside, he was shaking in fear, his stomach trembling.

He didn't want to screw things up.

He'd understood that going out for dinner with Jenny that Thursday night was a special thing, off the clock, something she'd chosen for herself though he'd paid. For him, it was magic to have a beautiful girl who'd just fucked him, who called him a natural, sitting across from him slurping pho like a human being. When she'd looked at him, he looked away.

He'd also understood it might never happen again. But he wanted at least to preserve it as a fly in amber, untouched, or to screw it up himself. Not have James screw it up for him.

They drove into the hotel parking lot. "You're freaking out, aren't you?" James said. "Why don't I go pay and you sit here and smoke some weed? It worked for you last time. I'll come back with the key."

It was marginally more comfortable to be in the car alone, lighting a bowl. Clayton rolled down the window and let the sweet skunk scent float outward. Haze hid most of the summer stars, but a few winked through. His stomach had begun to settle when he saw James coming back.

Here goes nothing.

It took a half-hour for Jenny to get to the hotel. In the meantime, Clayton smoked James out on the balcony.

Maybe the weed would help with his anxiety.

When the little orange Beetle drove into the lot, he recognized it, but he made no sign.

His bike fit into the trunk, if you bent it just so.

She was never going to talk to him again.

James's phone rang; he shot Clayton a grin, then retreated into the room, leaving Clayton on the balcony. The coming disaster felt inevitable to Clayton, like an avalanche falling toward him.

He should still try to catch her and talk.

He pulled open the balcony's sliding-glass door. Stepping in, he closed it behind him and walked past James to the front of the suite—like Rahul, Clayton had insisted on a suite, though James had grumbled.

"Hey, wait a minute," James said. "She's about to come up."

"I thought I'd greet her," Clayton said, because it was true, and because his brain had stopped and he couldn't think of anything else to say. Stepping out of the suite door, he left James with his mouth hanging open.

In the hallway, he came face to face with Jenny.

She wore college-girl clothes, skinny jeans and a nubbly pale-pink summer sweater. Her face was businesslike.

She glanced up toward him, and her mouth fell open, echoing James's.

James hadn't told her he was the second guy.

"It wasn't my idea," Clayton said quickly. "It was James's. He called before I could stop him. I didn't want to see you—with him..." He trailed off.

How did this make any sense? This was her job. He didn't want to presume there was anything special.

A ghost of a smile crossed Jenny's face, before she hid it. Somehow it gave him hope.

"I think I get it. Do you mind if I go ahead and do the job?"

Yes, he did. But it wouldn't be fair to get in the way.

"Please do. Go ahead."

"How if I do him first, then he sleeps on the couch? Then you can wake him up whenever. The agreement was for two hours." He stared into her face. She sighed. "If you're feeling really broke—I'm willing to negotiate."

"No, it's your livelihood, I don't want—"

"And it's my decision what I do with my time." She gazed up at him, frowning slightly.

It surprised him. He'd almost always just seen her smile.

"Okay. You're driving."

She grinned. "Let me in, then.'"

He grinned back. "I can't. James has the only key."

"You really are a goof." She stepped forward and knocked on the suite door.

After James had finished, Clayton took him out on the balcony and packed him a bowl of some weed he saved for going to sleep, though he didn't tell him that. Then James settled on the couch with his phone, scanning Tinder.

Clayton and Jenny retreated into the bedroom. She went to the bed, shook out the sheets, flipped the pillows over.

He didn't like to think of James with her.

He just wouldn't think about it.

"What's he like in bed?" he blurted.

She rolled her eyes. "Professional courtesy, Clayton."

She propped a couple pillows behind her and patted the bed beside her. "Come sit."

He stared at her a moment longer.

"Oh, honestly—he's fine. He's not you." Something in her inflection made this a compliment. "You can take your clothes off before you sit beside me, if you like." She was back in a slip-dress, this one shiny olive green.

Then he was beside her, and she was kissing him. She tasted minty, like toothpaste. He'd had a vague fear she'd taste of James.

Her clever, nimble tongue darted into his mouth; her hands stroked his hair and shoulders. He gave himself to the kiss, feeling a loosening between them.

She kissed him like she meant it.

"Can this—will you—?" In answer, she pulled the dress over her head. Her tits melted him. Rosy brown nipples erect, her breasts were perfect in shape, perfect in the way they fit into his palms.

He leaned to mouth her nipples. "You can bite a little more. Ah, that's good."

She threw back her head, closing her eyes. "Omigod, that feels good. Put your hand—" she drew his hand to her shaven pussy. He slipped two fingers between her labia.

"Show me what you like," he said.

She screwed up her face and shook her head. "That's fine. This is about you."

"I want you to show me. Show me what you do yourself, then I'll do that."

"Well..." She scooted back along the bed and patted the sheet, to have him sit beside her. "I use two fingers, myself, or sometimes a vibrator. Mostly my fingers, though—it's quieter, and they're always handy. Here." She took his hand and laid it on her pussy, warm under his hand.

He dipped his finger into the wetness. "That's the hood of my clit. Direct sensation is a little intense. Try a little lower—there. Mmm, yes, you've got it."

She felt warm against his finger, her juices like syrup but not sticky. Her breathing sped up. "A little faster, if you can." He obliged. "Put a finger into my vagina—two fingers—curl them—oh never mind..." He wanted to ask what she'd meant, but this wasn't the time. Her breath was coming fast and uneven. His hand was getting tired; he changed his position slightly.

"Don't stop! Keep going!"

He did. She moaned louder, a sound close to sobbing. Her lower body tensed, then rose, pelvis straining toward his hand.

"Oh, yes, yes, yes, omigod, ah—ah!" She cried out wordlessly; then all the tension went out of her body, and she fell limp. But when he tried to move his hand, she held it in place with her own. He could feel tiny tremors going through her pussy.

It was magic, holy.

After a few moments, she opened her eyes and gave a lopsided smile. "Well, thank you. But what about you?" She reached forward and took his penis in her hand, rubbing it gently, moving the outer skin over his hardness.

"I like that you like giving me pleasure. Let me see if I can make myself come again with your cock, shall we?" He made no move. "C'mere, shy boy."

She tugged on his cock, forcing him to move toward her, and slid a condom on him. Leaning back, she positioned his cock, and he shoved himself inside her.

"God, you feel good. You're like the god of cock. Ah!" He liked making her not talk. "Hold on a sec." She moved a pillow under her ass. Clayton took the opportunity to grab that ass with both hands and drag her pelvis toward him.

The feel of her, inside and out.

The globes of her ass, the wet tightness of her cunt. He had to focus not to come immediately.

Pounding into her, he closed on the height. Her groaning and his blended. "Yes, yes, yes—yes!"

Again, they came together. Emotion poured through him—more than the release of fluid. He let himself down on top of her. She wrapped her arms around him and hugged him hard.

It was just sex, but he felt like he could fall for her.

A minute or two passed. He slid off to the side, gently stroked her stomach. She caught his hand and brought it to her mouth, kissed it.

"You seem like a really nice guy, Clayton. Why are you calling me? I mean, you could get a girlfriend."

Sitting up, she grabbed some tissues from beside the bed and wiped herself.

"You can keep paying me for sex, I'm fine with that. I'm just curious."

He sat up, ran a hand through his hair, and pushed himself back against the headboard. She sat cross-legged facing him, naked but utterly self-possessed.

"The first time was for Rahul. The second time I wanted to see if I could replicate the first."

Her black, black eyes bored into his.

"This time it was James."

"Mmm-hmm. And you couldn't stop him."

Was she trying to argue him out of seeing her? That wasn't good business.

"It was awkward. He ran outside, and I needed to pay for our pizza." He frowned. "Are you saying I shouldn't see you?"

"Not at all. But I need you to remember this is a business relationship."

He blurted what he was thinking. "Do you never date your customers?"

"I never have."

At least this was a little less definitive than "never."

"I just want to be sure you're aware." Again she picked up his hand and kissed it. "Let's go check on James."

Puabi-Ekur watched, from their corner of Clayton's mind. Of late, they'd been lazy and hadn't stepped out of their nook.

They needed to be more active.

They needed to figure out this Jenny girl.

Maybe they could come to her in a dream.

The orange Beetle rounded the far corner at the end of the parking lot and disappeared. James and Clayton leaned on James's Chevy, finishing a last bowl, watching it go. Smoke hung in the summer air, the sweetly skunky scent hovering above the smell of shredded bark from the parking island.

James, still staring forward, said, "You've been seeing her, haven't you?" He shifted stance and studied Clayton's face. Clayton nodded slowly.

James handed back the pipe. "Do you think that's wise?"

Clayton knocked out the last ashes and put the pipe in his pocket. "I only did it once."

"It's a great way to spend a lot of money, if you keep it up."

Clayton frowned, staring at his friend.

Could he be more of a hypocrite?

But he didn't want a friendship-ending argument. If he was going to ditch James, he'd rather do it after a summer of helping him. If he'd take the help.

"This wasn't my idea, right?"

James glowered at him a moment, then gazed away, toward the far reaches of the parking lot. Cars passed on the street. A car turned; its headlights cast a moving beam across the asphalt.

James was jealous.

The only woman, ever, who had shown a preference for him over James. And they were paying her. And James was jealous.

Out of the blue, he felt sorry for him.

He'd had no idea how insecure he was until tonight.

"If it helps, Jenny said the same thing to me. I mean, it's

not like I don't realize she's a hooker." He felt the warm glass pipe against his leg. "So I spend my money on weed and prostitutes. It's not what my parents would recommend. But there's worse stuff in the world."

James gave him a long look, and shrugged. "It's your money and your time, dude." Standing, he clicked the key fob, unlocking the car. They got in.

Before James turned the key in the ignition, he shot a glance at Clayton.

"Just let me tell you something I've learned. Don't ever think a whore really likes you."

Chapter 7

It was one a.m. when Joanie got home. Her roommate was asleep. She checked her own stash of weed, decided to save it, and headed for the kitchen. She was in luck; Danielle hadn't finished the big bottle of cheap red wine they'd bought a few nights before.

Joanie poured herself a glass and retreated to her tiny bedroom, cat complaining in her wake. She rewarded him inside the bedroom door with a handful of kibble.

Dropping her clothes, she climbed into bed, dragging her quilt up around her against the chilly Seattle summer night.

She'd done the right thing. The boy had been getting a crush on her.

She wouldn't have cared if it was his dudebro friend. But she liked Clayton. She wanted to be kind to him.

A part of her that she tried to keep hidden, tied up in the

basement of her subconscious, sat up and said: *But what about me?*

Pain rose through her, like a steam of blood snaking through water.

Do I never get what I want?

Her cunt was sore from use, but pleasantly sore, nothing that a day off wouldn't cure. She recalled Clayton pounding into her, and her fingers strayed to her clit.

She'd called him the god of cock. That wasn't very professional. He'd liked it, though.

Unbidden, accusing, the rogue part of herself said: *You made him go away because you like him.*

Oh, shut up, she told herself. She focused on her hand, calling up the lusciousness of that big cock hitting her G-spot.

She rubbed herself for a few minutes, but she was orgasmed out. She fell asleep, her wine untouched.

Those black, black eyes.

Puabi-Ekur had held off from Clayton when Clayton was with Joanie because, frankly, they were frightened.

People from past lives were never good luck. There was always karma involved.

They remembered Iltani.

For the Festival of Waters, Puabi and the other high-ranked dancers together performed a dance about the rivers: women dancing for earth, in browns, stomping the earth in time to the drums; women dancing for water, in silver lozenges, shaking their hips, their arms flowing like water.

Puabi, the lead dancer, had her own solo: the river meets the delta, taking long wide lazy circles, then flows into the sea. At the end, to the sound of flutes, drums, sistrums, and Iltani's harp, she sank into the floor, and applause and praise rolled across the courtyard.

She was surrounded by people. Iltani and the other musicians sat off to the side, also gathering accolades, though not mobbed the same way. Occasionally she glanced over, setting a new person aside—"thank you, the flowers are lovely, Uttu, can you take them?"—sometimes she could see the long straight black hair waving with Iltani's movements.

She could have been a dancer herself, she was so graceful. But then Puabi wouldn't have her harpist.

Then a wave of people separated them.

When she could see Iltani again, the almond-shaped face was frowning. A noble stood by her, judging by his dress, his turban studded with lapis lazuli and gold. He had his hand on her shoulder. Iltani shrugged, knocking the hand off. It was replaced.

A wave of anger and fear went through Puabi. She was a priestess of the goddess; she expressed that through dance and the sexual rites. Though these were her main expressions, she was not without prophesy.

But a new man was before her, someone she'd never seen before, all in dusty brown, a farmer or laborer. As the goddess's representative she needed to be gracious.

It wasn't till the end of the evening that she got to talk to Iltani.

Puabi's fans had insisted she drink beer with them, or at least go out. She owed it to them. But she'd not had more than the usual measure. At a drinking hall in the laborers' district, she was protected by two stalwart carpenters (pretty ones too—she made it clear they should both visit her in the temple). She enjoyed herself. But part of her mind was thinking about Iltani.

Worrying.

Iltani had the right to her own small cubbyhole, but unless a man was with Puabi she lived in Puabi's room.

In the full, black night, stars wavered over a city of rippling lights. Inanna's planet blazed full in the sky through Puabi's window. Puabi lit two wicks on the standing lamp. It was far too late to expect any help from the servants.

Iltani had been waiting, curled up like a cat, asleep. Now she stood, yawning.

"You're back. We're both wearing too many clothes."

The slender slip of a light-brown girl, dropping her dress, shaking out her long hair that fell like a wave of silk. The beauty.

Puabi still wore her dancing costume, a cumbersome combination of light linen and metal, a metal bra and girdle holding up cascades of silver lozenges on light chains.

"Let me help you with that."

"Oh. Ow. Thanks." Pain stung as Iltani lifted away the heavy bodice, which had incised deep lines into Puabi's skin.

"You need a little massage here," Iltani said without inflection. She smoothed the lines with her fingers and hands, then palmed Puabi's breasts, then put her mouth over one and then the other, licking, sucking, mouthing, biting nipples and the pretty roundnesses themselves, till Puabi moaned.

Iltani lifted her mouth away.

"But you still have clothes on."

She unlatched the heavy girdle, letting the skirt fall with a shimmy of bell-sounds to the floor. That left a light under-skirt of unbleached linen; Iltani dropped that over Puabi's hips.

"You should have been a dresser."

Iltani reached between Puabi's legs and impressed her fingers between Puabi's labia, into warm liquid, rubbing.

"You should have been my dresser."

"You'd never get to a dance if I were." Iltani pushed one then two fingers into Puabi, circling them till she hit the spot she knew Puabi favored, then stroking, stroking, stroking. Puabi let go to it, staggering a little as she did.

"Lie down, pretty lady."

She did. A faint scent arose of cardamom and cinnamon, scents Iltani wore, and then Iltani's mouth was on her, teasing, kissing, licking. Iltani's fingers dipped inside her, continuing their stroking. Puabi let her voice go, moaning and whimpering, as Iltani stroked and licked. The feeling rolled through peaks and valleys and then at last released. She cried out, her whole body shaking.

The lamps flickered in the lightest of breezes, carrying the scent of cardamom. Slowly the sensation ebbed.

"Oh, my love, my love," Puabi said. "What about you?"

"You're tired. There's the morning."

"I wanted to ask... " but her brain was shutting down—what did she want to ask? about that noble?

After a few minutes, seeing her lover was asleep, Iltani rose and snuffed the lamp.

That was the advent of Kirkaru, there and then.

They wished they'd stayed awake, spoken up then and there, started fighting him—but you could never know.

Except they had known.

But what did this have to do with here and now? Just because Iltani had returned didn't mean Kirkaru had.

Would they know him if he had?

It was full night. Clayton lay asleep. Puabi-Ekur had released their connection to him and floated to the top of his room. In the silent darkness, the scent of strawberry incense lingered.

What did they want?

Between Clayton and Joanie, Puabi saw the linkage a little frayed.

That James. So jealous.

They could mend things.

But they wanted her too. They wanted to have their own relationship with her. Yet their heart has become engaged with this boy.

Puabi-Ekur had remembrances from many lifetimes, and in many they had been a parent.

They wanted Clayton to succeed as a man with women. They wanted, if it was possible, for him to succeed as a lover of this Joanie, this Iltani.

Far away, Puabi-Ekur felt the tug of right action and selfless love, which even incubi-succubi could feel. Among spirits, they lived as a middle race, fighting on either side of the great spiritual war (or game, for the ever-living). Some incubi-succubi led humans to the divine; some tricked them into spiritual slavery. Puabi-Ekur had for a long time drifted, fighting on neither one side nor the other—merely doing their allotted task, taking seed from men, giving it to women, rolling the dice of the chromosomes, making fate.

Yet there were roles beyond that, to which any spirit could aspire. Spirits like humans could burn off karma and ascend.

They could help Clayton and Joanie. Make positive change.

But did they want that?

In drifting, in not caring, there was safety.

They could put their toe in the water. They could send Joanie a dream.

But what dream?

Chapter 8

Puabi-Ekur tugged at the cord between Clayton and Joanie.

Maybe they could follow it to Joanie.

They took up the thread. It was, in fact, easy to follow—a sensation a little like actual travel through the cool Seattle night, if you could fly by willing yourself forward. The thread led to an older, rambling house, into a first-floor room, to a bed with a quilt. On it lay a curled-up tabby cat, under it a sleeping girl.

Iltani.

As a spirit, Puabi-Ekur had different affordances than a human. It took outsize strength to move matter, but to travel as fast as thought or dip inside a mind was easy.

They sorted downward, through layers like sediment.

Poor girl, she was in a lot of pain. She hadn't been in love for years. She needed this boy Clayton.

There were things as a spirit they couldn't give her.

And yet...

But they should make sure.

Expertly Puabi-Ekur unlocked the closure between life-times and worked into the past, gently, sifting and sorting, till they found what they sought.

Those black, black eyes.

Out the window, framed in painted wood in the mud-brick wall, a palm tree stood, leaves rustling fitfully in a breath of breeze. Puabi woke. Iltani lay asleep with her head on her lover's shoulder.

My love.

The wind pushed at the shutters, banging them, opening one, shaking in a sifting of dust. Gently Puabi shifted the girl's head, settling it onto the bed. She got up, rinsed her face, armpits, and hands, and donned a simple linen day-dress. Still Iltani lay asleep.

She wouldn't see Iltani again till tonight. Puabi faced a long day at the costume-fitters, then her duties at the temple.

She stepped to the edge of the bed and reached down to stroke a wisp of hair from Iltani's forehead. The girl's black eyes opened, and her slow smile spread like water over-flowing from a cup. Iltani's hand went up to clasp Puabi's wrist, and she drew Puabi down onto the bed. Quick as a snake, she legged over Puabi, pressing against her pelvis to pelvis.

They kissed, slowly, lips slicking lips, Iltani's subtle

tongue dipping into Puabi's mouth as into water. Distracting Puabi with a nip on the neck, Iltani let her hand take a long slow slide, fingers searching downward for her lover's cunt. They entered, owning her.

"You are wet, baby-child."

"I was thinking of you."

"Mmm."

The fingers gently pumped, curling to hit Puabi's G-spot. Puabi cried out.

"Oh, you like that?"

Iltani held the nerveless Puabi down on the linen sheets and let her mouth follow her hand, licking and sucking her pretty pussy as the fingers stroked and stroked. Puabi's cries mounted and mounted, mixing with the calls of birds and the sound of Iltani's name.

Puabi-Ekur dropped back into the present. One could do divination from the memory that arose first, but they were too overwhelmed to try.

There were loves every lifetime. Though Puabi-Ekur hadn't donned a body for a thousand years—at least not by the formal route, dying as a spirit to be reborn in human flesh.

But each was unique. There was only one Iltani.

Joanie, now. Jenny, for her whoring. Whoring had changed a lot, in some ways—not in others.

Yet Joanie had found a connection to the goddess that Puabi had worshipped. Inanna.

A host of conflicting desires washed through Puabi-Ekur.

If they were to send her a dream—what dream?

They wanted her back for themself. They wanted to taste the dark wine of her deepest soul. Not to mention the touch of her now-body.

But also they wanted Iltani to be happy as Joanie.

They wanted Clayton to be happy, too. He was a sweet boy, teetering on the brink of love, who'd never loved beyond a school crush.

Being a spirit, Puabi-Ekur could hear the wind of fate whispering, turning corners around them.

If they did the right thing, they could improve their karma.

Did they even care about that?

A pull of emotion came, which an embodied human would experience as love.

All right. They would help Joanie and Clayton.

But they weren't above sneaking in and fucking her every now and then.

Joanie woke up in black dark, the center of the night. After a moment, her eyes adjusted. A little light stole under her door from the hallway.

She'd never had a dream quite like that.

It had felt on purpose. As if someone wanted to tell her something.

In the dream, she'd been in a desert place, a huge mud-brick temple, walls muted shades of red-brown hung with tapestries of griffins and bulls. Outside arch-topped windows, palm trees pasted themselves on an enamel-blue sky. People passed, wearing long linen garments, girls carrying water jugs on their heads. She guessed it was Near Eastern, but ancient—maybe Sumer. She'd glanced down at her own clothes, an off-white shift, maybe linen.

In the dream, she'd been dressed for the time. Had she lived then?

The dream had shifted, and she found herself entering a temple. She came to face a monumental statue, twice as tall as she. A goddess with a smiling face, broad lips, and broad hips held bountiful breasts upward with both hands.

Inanna.

A hush fell in the temple. Though worshippers continued to pray, and priestesses burned incense at a wooden altar before the statue, the layer holding these people blurred and fell away. The room hollowed to a space where there was only her and the goddess.

The statue spoke to her.

"You have come to me at last, little Joanie." The voice held nothing but love.

Full of emotion, Joanie nodded.

"In this time, you are my devotee," the goddess answered. Joanie looked up at the face—white-glazed, big-eyed. The painted lips never moved; the voice came from the ether. "You are a harpist; you play for the dance."

Inanna was the goddess of sacred whores.

"Am I a temple prostitute?"

"No, but the lover of one, the beautiful Puabi, most

famous dancer in Uruk." A breeze smelling of spice circled Joanie and fell away. "She loves you truly. But there is tragedy in this life."

In the hollow space, a sound passed, a distant howling. Joanie felt herself begin to slip away.

The goddess said, "Stay with me a while," and Joanie drew herself again into the goddess's golden presence. "I have a few things to tell you, and a few things to give you. You must know, in your current life, the life where you are Joanie—you are mine there too."

Joanie's mouth dropped open.

I suppose I am.

"You have met some of my worshippers. One or two are not all they seem. Yet engage with them. Many are sincere and will lead you truly." A ripple crossed the air, like a current in water; the image of the goddess shifted, then resettled.

"There is a boy, too, one you have given pleasure."

Clayton.

"He's nothing to me, lady. I sent him away."

The goddess's voice came, gentle with laughter. "Nothing, you say? Remember I am a goddess of love."

The distant howling rose again in the background, and a gust of wind circled Joanie. There was dust in it. It was almost as if hands reached out from it, trying to pull her away from the goddess. She reached forward toward the goddess, but there was nothing to hold onto.

Through the rising howls of wind, she heard the goddess's last words: "Joanie, little Joanie—don't let go of him—"

The grey wind keened louder and louder, rising to a shriek, encompassing her and dragging her away.

Now, in the black night, she reached across to her bedside table, found a lighter, and lit a candle. Flaring up, the warm yellow flame lay cupped in the ivory wax, a little sphere of light reaching to encompass a small, safe space. It was almost as if she still heard the dream-wind howling in the distance.

She'd touched another world. An earlier world, perhaps.

Though she hadn't liked that wind. The howling was like unquiet spirits. For all her witch ways, this wasn't how Joanie usually thought.

But she'd talked to the goddess, who'd said to find her followers.

Joanie reached to the bedside table and after a moment located priestess Sasha's card, purple and orange with flowing script.

Joanie had put off contacting her. Even now she didn't want to upset her own rational apple-cart.

Sasha would think she was crazy, sending email at two a.m.

Oh, who cared.

She dragged herself out of bed, wrapping herself in her quilt—much to the disgust of the cat, who dropped to the floor and stalked off.

Folding her feet under against the Seattle summer chill, Joanie seated herself in front of her computer.

To the tapping of fingers on the keyboard, Puabi-Ekur watched Joanie from the corner of the room.

They'd opened a door they ought not to have opened.

They hadn't expected the djinn.

Long before the coming of cities, the desert wind had personified itself as a tribe of spirits—wind-demons of destruction, turbulent and cruel. Occasionally they took on human form to become some of the psychopaths and narcissists that plagued the human race. As soon as Puabi-Ekur sensed them in Joanie's audience with Inanna, almost without thinking they had stepped into the role of protector.

It was too late not to have their fate caught up with hers. That had happened millennia ago.

What troubled Puabi-Ekur most was that these djinn came in as if they already had an opening. It meant that likely someone in Joanie's life was a djinni in human disguise.

The question was, who?

"When you say you want further training—what do you mean by that?"

Joanie had hoped to meet Sasha, but who sat across

from her was Cleo, hair wrapped high in a turban, nails painted electric orange.

She was so effortlessly beautiful.

Or, well, she didn't know how much effort Cleo put in.

Joanie herself was dressed down, in jeans and a unicorn t-shirt.

They'd met in Joanie's local coffee shop, chocolate-brown walls scattered with mushrooms and ladybugs. Joanie sat in a wooden bench seat, her back to the wall—the gunfighter's seat. Early training had taught her to watch her back. Across from her, Cleo sipped her macchiato, dark-brown doe's eyes blinking.

Joanie had gone over the website that the temple hosted: a careful meet-and-greet site, but Joanie knew the lingo. "Bodywork" or "below-the-neck work" could be massage where the therapist consciously considered how the body holds emotional pain, or it could be Joanie's current work with a layer of therapy thrown in.

There was always therapy thrown in.

"I had a dream about Inanna the other night. It inspired me to get in touch with you."

Cleo's eyebrows went up.

Did Cleo just not think that much of her?

Maybe that was insecurity talking.

Joanie gave a brief synopsis, ending with the wind that had dragged her out of the temple.

"I wished I could've stayed a bit longer in her presence. I felt as if she had more to say to me."

"Have you tried putting up an altar to her?"

Why hadn't she thought of that?

"Not yet. I don't have much space."

Cleo leaned over, her gaze serious. Joanie caught her breath. "It doesn't have to be huge. My simplest altar is just a piece of cloth with a goddess symbol on it, with an offering bowl of spices. The deities need some way to connect to us."

"Yes, I think that's so," Joanie answered, at random.

What did she smell like? Like wildflowers. Like honey.

The electric orange nails tapped on the table a moment, then stopped.

They looked at each other.

"We have a smaller group that meets periodically. Our next meeting is at the Full Moon, seven days from now."

She lay face-down on the down comforter, feeling like a trapped rabbit. A thick-walled glass tumbler sat on the bedside table, empty of Laphroaig. She dared not get more —she didn't want to be drunk when Phil came in.

She couldn't. She couldn't. She had to.

Why did it bother her so much now?

Some deep crevasse in her nature had been touched, and now she'd been swallowed by fear.

Last time she'd avoided him by throwing Hayley in front of her. She couldn't keep doing that.

She had to get her head around this, or stop seeing Phil.

She heard the condo door open.

So tempted just to go elsewhere.

She had perfected that, in her early teens—the ability to

slip out of her body, retreat behind a wall of glass. But she had spent the years since working on being present.

It was too late.

As she heard him enter the bedroom, she sat up, folded herself into a becoming posture leaning on one arm, and put on a smile.

Phil stepped forward, leaned, and kissed her hair. "Honey, I'm starving. Let's go out to eat first, shall we?"

A reprieve. For now.

At dinner Joanie did something that she never did—she drank more than a glass of wine. She had two glasses of wine with dinner, then brandy after dessert. Then espresso after that, to sober up a little. Phil watched her quizzically but said nothing.

It put her in a rarefied place, lifted above the world.

In the world of spirit, she stood out like a beacon, so much so that far away, as Clayton slept, Puabi-Ekur noticed.

She'd made herself vulnerable.

Why had she done that?

About them they sensed a stirring, a twist of unquiet wind.

One of the djinn was near her.

Drawn almost irresistibly, they crossed town to the restaurant where Joanie finished her coffee. But when Puabi-Ekur got there, Phil and Joanie had gone. All that was left was a wisp of wind and a sound of fading laughter.

"Honey, we should leave."

Joanie hung on to the tiny white-china cup, with its last sip of espresso, as if her life depended on it.

"Give me a moment, darling."

Why was he suddenly in a hurry?

I guess I can ride this out.

As they left, the wind whipped up, tossing the long scarf she used as a shawl. In the late twilight, chill as cold water, the wind felt like fall come early. She drew the scarf closer.

A chill and a tingle went through her body. Phil's hand was tight on her wrist as he hailed a cab—they only had a few blocks to go, but he never wanted to walk home from the steakhouse, and he didn't like Uber. She glanced at the tightened hand, and a thrill, half desire and half fear, went through her, harking back to old bad games that her body had imprinted on.

They climbed into the cab; Phil gave the address. Sensing something, he met her eyes, then looked at his hand on her wrist.

"You like that, do you? I didn't know that about you." His smile grew wolfish. "Come here."

He pulled her across the backseat of the cab to him, and kissed her.

There'd never been real heat between them before, but now it flared.

How had they never come to this before? He'd been so careful.

She didn't know if she liked this.

But she could work it.

She made as if to pull back, the frightened bunny. He held her in place with one hand, mouth encompassing hers, teeth biting her lips. The other hand slipped off one strap of her dress, dove into her bra, pulled out her breast. Leaning, he bit her nipple so hard she squealed against his lips. She sensed but couldn't see the cabbie watching them—not to help her, but to get an eyeful.

Omigod I'm so wet.

She pushed her breast against his mouth. "Bite me harder," she breathed.

He chuckled deep in his throat.

She cried out but his mouth was on hers, tongue deep in her throat. When she could breathe, she whispered, "Oh, Phil. Oh, Phil."

Afterward she barely remembered entering the condo. He dragged her to the bedroom and pulled her clothes off, pushing her down onto the bed, pinioning her hands. Her ass in the air, her face in the pillow, she was barely able to breathe.

Condom on, he mounted her from behind—she was so wet there was no need for lube. He slammed into her, pounding at her. Her body gave in, gave way; she was merely prey, an object, a thing, her orgasm climbing.

With one hand, he grabbed her hair and pulled her head back. He hissed into her ear, "My little toy. My little fuck-toy. Mine, all mine."

She came, like a star bursting, harder than she ever had for Phil. Then he came hard, jerking and growling.

She passed out, or fell asleep.

When she woke again, it was the middle of the night. The bedroom door, cracked open, threw a line of light across the floor and onto the rumpled off-white down coverlet and the white sheets. Phil was asleep, snoring, an arm thrown over her.

She smelled like come and felt oddly satisfied.

That had worked.

They'd opened some door, some portal.

Maybe that was okay. She could use him to keep paying her.

Most guys revealed their BDSM on the first date, or the second or third. Phil had been hiring her for months, the whole time carefully controlled—the sex had been so vanilla it squeaked.

Maybe he was just that unsure of himself.

She hadn't dealt with that many men who liked a dominant role, but she'd had her share.

And now, she'd never stayed so late. Carefully she extricated herself from his embrace.

Generally she woke him after a few minutes, went to the bathroom and freshened up, then returned. He'd leave her fee in an envelope on the dresser, in cash, including a hundred percent tip. She'd pick it up and kiss him goodbye.

She wasn't going to charge him extra because she fell asleep, but she had to leave.

She jiggled his shoulder gently. "Phil, honey, wake up. I have to go."

His snoring stopped with a snort, and his eyes blinked open.

"Okay." He gazed up at her with naked longing.

Something had broken open, something had changed.

He reached out, took her hand, squeezed it. "I wish you could stay."

There was no real reason she couldn't, except she didn't want to.

"Don't worry about the extra time spent—that was on me. But I have a ton of studying. I have to get up early and get on it."

She wanted to wake in her own bed, with her own thoughts, with her own life.

"If that's what you want."

"It is." She bit back an apology.

She didn't need to apologize for that.

She left with the envelope and his kiss on her lips.

This night was going to change things.

Clayton was making the As he wanted at last, partly because he'd rather study now than think.

For a week, each day had been black coffee, ten hours of class and studying, cheap beer or weed, then bed.

He couldn't keep doing this forever.

"Don't ever think a whore really likes you." He wouldn't ordinarily take James seriously. He knew too that James was jealous.

But James's opinion was reinforced by Jenny. "I need you to remember this is a business relationship."

One Friday night, having come away from a test that afternoon, he closed the door and ignored James's inevitable five p.m. knock. Let him pick up women on his own.

He broke out the last of his weed and the butt-end of a fifth of whiskey.

Getting wasted alone. Great.

He'd been really depressed beginning of summer quarter. Then briefly he'd been okay.

His mind danced sideways, avoiding thinking this had to do with Jenny.

Now—well.

He lit the strawberry incense, then lit the weed in his pipe.

Puabi-Ekur watched from the corner of the ceiling.

This wasn't working at all. Iltani—Joanie—had gotten whisked away by the djinn, or at least trailed by them, and Clayton was back where he started.

Puabi-Ekur considered their options.

They could push Clayton aside and take over. But that was so complex—get a hotel room, get Joanie over there. Even if they got that far, she might jib.

But the goddess had already told Joanie to keep hold of Clayton. She was ignoring the advice.

Joanie took a couple of calls that Friday night. It was twelve-thirty a.m. by the time she finished the second one. Time to go home.

She drove by the ATM, deposited money, and returned to her apartment as it started to rain. As she opened the door, her cat ran up chattering. She gave him kibble.

She hadn't heard from Phil since their date the night before, but she'd expected that—he generally contacted her once a week.

He might bring up the sugar daddy thing again now.

She'd worry about that when it happened.

She jumped in the shower, then wrapped in a towel padded toward her room, snagging a glass of wine on the way.

One glass—that was all.

What had possessed her to drink so much last night?

Possession—evil influence... she felt off. Maybe it was time for some energy cleansing.

She sat cross-legged on her bed. The cat installed himself on her lap. She grounded, centered, and reached up toward the universe as her first witch-teachers had shown her. She connected with a star and drew star-fire downward and earth-warmth upward, running each through her own energy.

She scrubbed at blockages where her energy stuck. As the sludge moved off, as if it had been hidden underneath, the memory of her dream with the goddess popped up.

"There is a boy, too, one you have given pleasure. Don't let go of him."

But she had let go of him. It was done.

She recalled him taking her brush-off, sitting on the bed in the hotel, the smile on his lips that didn't reach his eyes.

She couldn't lead him on. She was a whore. He was a client. It didn't work. Tammy was right about that.

That cock, though.

When they were together, everything flowed. He was sweet to her, too.

Inanna was a goddess of whores. She must know how they struggled.

Maybe getting rid of Clayton had been dumb.

Joanie reached to the bedside table for her phone and found his number in her contacts.

Before she could stop herself, she typed and sent him a text: <You know, maybe sometime we could have coffee and talk>

As an afterthought: <This is Jenny>

Puabi-Ekur felt proud of themselves.

It had only taken the barest nudge.

The beep from his phone woke Clayton.

He opened his eyes. His head was splitting.

Fucking whiskey.

He wouldn't pick up the phone. It was probably James with some drunken revelation, or god knows what.

A flash of fear passed. It could be his family—someone dead. Mom would likely call, not text. Still…

He grabbed the phone.

Oh.

He fell back on the pillow.

A starburst of joy went through him, like a firework, rising and rising and exploding at the top of the sky.

He'd answer her in the morning, keep his cool.

Oh, fuck it.

<OK>

Incubi-succubi also dream.

Drifting in the ether, lightly tethered to Clayton, Puabi-Ekur floated among stars in the jeweled night, below the mist of the Milky Way.

They arrived at the feet of a darkly shining being. Low red flames erupted around her, as if she sat in a private volcano. To either side of her throne stood torches. On a chain around her neck, she wore a silver key.

Puabi-Ekur shivered with awe. There was no question who this was.

Hekate Soteira. Hekate Savior. To her all spirits owed fealty, from demons to angels; she was called the ruler of the angels. Puabi-Ekur made obeisance, laying themselves prone at the Lady's feet.

But what had the Lady got to do with them?

The silence rang with the Lady's voice.

"The battle is heating, Puabi-Ekur. Some say these are the end times."

The Lady laughed, like silver bells, a laugh like the stars'. If all time is one, there are no end times. And yet time faced forward, and humans traveled forward with it, and spirits such as Puabi-Ekur had to do with humans.

"It is a great game we play, we spirits, and yet it is in deadly earnest. The mortals live and die by it, and return again. Where do you stand, Puabi-Ekur? Even nonaction is an action."

Puabi-Ekur opened their eyes wide.

"You do not need to answer me here and now, Puabi-Ekur. But consider your alliances."

This time she seemed to want a response.

I shall, Lady.

Chapter 9

Hayley fell into the chair at the coffee shop, dropping her backpack on the floor beside her. "Oh, god, what a day."

Joanie looked at her over the edge of her cappuccino cup. She'd taken her favorite wooden bench seat, her back to the wall, to make herself feel protected.

"You were the one who wanted to take summer classes," she said to Hayley. "They're intense."

"Too late to drop them now. I should fill you in—I haven't got much time."

"Mmm?" Hayley hadn't said what she needed to talk about, only that she needed to talk.

"I said I'd talk to my dates about Phil, right? Turns out they do know him." Joanie raised her eyebrows inquiringly. "He's got a good reputation in the field. Smart, friendly, enthusiastic. I told them that a friend was seeing him, on the up-and-up, and I wanted to know if she'd be okay. Unanimously they said my friend was a lucky girl."

"Okay."

She'd seen his enthusiasm when he talked about AI, and just lately when he'd asked her to stay the night. Maybe he just kept himself on a short leash.

"What do you think?" Hayley asked.

Joanie propped her chin on her hand and stared across the coffee shop. A ray of sunlight poured across an empty table.

"I don't know. The other night, I felt like I got to know him a bit better." She described their evening out.

"He could still be embarrassed about BDSM as a dominant," Hayley said. "Lots of mainstream people think it's skeevy."

"He's never talked about his parents, but I got the impression presentation was really important to them." That well-brushed portrait on his mantle.

"Maybe now you'll find out more. Anyway, I gotta run." Hayley leapt up, leaned and gave Joanie a quick hug. "You staying?"

"For a little."

She didn't have to tell Hayley everything that happened.

She wondered if it was the right thing.

But a goddess had told her to do it.

Clayton shaved, looking at himself in the mirror in the dorm bathroom.

He'd have five o'clock shadow by afternoon. Still, not an awful face.

He'd managed to get enough sleep, somehow, despite the stress of the upcoming coffee date with Jenny. He'd planned it on his light day of classes, and he was caught up —there was nothing to worry about.

Except his crushing social anxiety and fear of fucking everything up.

Returning to his room, he rummaged through the pile of clean clothes, still in the basket getting wrinkled. He chose a pair of jeans and one of his many black t-shirts.

Nothing with a snarky comment on it. He had no idea about her politics or opinions. She seemed smart and level-headed, but who knew?

Outside, late summer sunshine bathed Seattle, the day balmy, with a fresh breeze and a few cotton clouds in the blue. After some blocks' walk, he saw the door of the coffee shop propped open, a chocolate brown and pale blue folding sign on the sidewalk in front of it.

He could still cut and run.

He drowned the thought. After the sun outside, the interior of the shop was dark.

There she was.

A half-hour passed, an hour—they talked about movies, school, life. She talked easily, covering his occasional hesitancies. Occasionally she twirled a strand of her long, blunt-cut, dark-brown hair around one finger, which Clayton found adorable.

Finally he got up the courage to ask, "Why did you want to talk?"

In answer, Joanie studied her empty coffee cup, where pale-brown traceries showed the death of bubbles. She was Joanie to him now—she'd dropped the pretense of "Jenny." The loud whirring of the coffee-grinder behind her allowed her to pause and collect herself.

"I don't know," she began. "I guess—" A quick glance up from ink-black eyes. "We got on so well. That doesn't happen a lot. And I liked you. And I said to myself, why not?"

He stared at her, not knowing what to say.

"I mean, Tammy—my boss—says you should never date a client. But I know people who do." She bit her lip, pink and fresh, innocent of lipstick today. It was the first time he'd seen her show any nervousness.

Almost involuntarily, he sat forward, putting his hand over hers.

"I'm not going to hold your work against you. I really don't care." It was strange to hear himself saying it—his parents would have cared—but it was true.

She twitched her hand away. "Okay." He could tell from the way she said it that she didn't believe him and that she wished he hadn't said it.

He didn't know how to salvage the conversation. On a whim, he said, "Do you want to take a walk?"

Her face cleared up. "Sure."

The wind had picked up. They wandered into a neighborhood of student houses, past one painted electric blue, a phalanx of wind chimes hanging from the porch roof, rolling a carillon song across the breeze. They caught each other's eyes and grinned.

At the park, they swung on the swings, till a child and mother appeared and they gave them up. A swell of green grass rose, dotted with a few dandelions. They walked up it, letting their hands fall together and clasp. Somewhere close, someone was mowing; the smell of new-mown grass floated in the air. Almost no one was out—it was Wednesday afternoon.

"I wish we had a picnic," Clayton said.

"I could grab some stuff from my house. It's not far from here."

They climbed the steps to a yellow-painted clapboard house, roof all gables, broken into apartments, a metal box of mail slots by the front door. Down a long beige-painted hallway that smelled faintly of weed, they turned a corner. She took her keys from her purse and opened her door.

"Danielle?" Joanie called.

Her roommate, he presumed. But no one answered.

An abbreviated living room, shades drawn, held a mottled couch facing a TV. A ficus tree pined for light, half its leaves fallen on the floor. Joanie walked straight through to the kitchen. Here the sun shone through a half-open window, breeze fluttering white curtains.

"I could make cheese sandwiches. I have some wine."

"Do you have a blanket or something?"

"I think I have a throw I can use. I need to find it."

He followed her into the narrow bedroom. Its walls were

painted periwinkle. A collection of glass unicorns lined the top shelf of a white bookcase. A queen bed with a patchwork quilt took up most of the space.

He wasn't usually bold, but it was like the next comment in a conversation, or the next phrase in a piece of music. He reached across and took her arm, watching her face as he pulled her down onto the bed.

She lay looking up, mop of dark-brown hair tossed across the pillow.

He sat down beside her, pushing a strand of hair off her forehead. Lowering himself, he kissed her lips: gently, softly, a bare touch; then the kiss went deeper. He kicked off his shoes.

She rolled over on top of him, pinning his wrists to the bed, then leaned and kissed him back. A deep kiss. He freed one hand and snaked it under her t-shirt and bra, finding the warm breast, the erect nipple, tweaking it. She let out a long breath.

Freeing his other arm, he flipped her again, pushed up her t-shirt and bra, and mouthed first one then the other of her breasts, the rosy brown nipples standing to attention. He bit them gently, then a little harder. She moaned.

Slipping down, he unzipped her jeans and pulled them off, with the black panties. Her pubis showed its narrow strip of dark fur. He explored her pussy with his fingers; she was dripping wet. He dipped his fingers in, then slid out and rubbed, like she'd shown him.

She wriggled under his hand, then put her own hand over his. "I want you inside me."

"Okay." He shucked off his jeans, kneeling between her

legs. She grabbed a condom from a package by the bed, put it on, and taking his cock in her hand, guided him in.

The feeling of her was liquid heaven. He began to thrust.

The warm, small room had one small window with an Indian print curtain, a little open so the breeze flitted through. He felt her mattress as it gave under his knees. The quilt rucked up around his legs. Brief impressions, her legs in the air, her arms around his neck, her breathing full of soft moans. He drove into her, seeking the source, the golden light, the red-hot center. He sensed her orgasm building.

As she cried out, he gave way into her, his come spilling, gushing. She pulled him into her arms, tight, folding her legs around his body, so he had no choice but to put his whole weight on her.

They lay there for a minute or two, the soft summer breeze playing with her hair, sending tickling bits into his face. Afterglow washed through him.

"Mmm," she said finally, and he climbed off her, sitting on the edge of the bed. "Hand me a Kleenex or two." He did.

She was wiping herself because he'd made her so wet. It gave him immense satisfaction.

She put her arms around him from behind. He clasped them to him, lifting one of her hands to kiss her fingers.

"So, I don't know. Maybe?"

Midevening Wednesday, Joanie's night off, Hayley had

called her for practical reasons, asking about Tammy. Joanie let her know Tammy was out of town and who was covering —something Joanie did sometimes, but not this week. The conversation had taken a personal turn.

Joanie sat on her bed in tousled covers that still smelled of Clayton, econ books and her laptop in front of her, lamp-light illuminating a yellow arc. Her cat lay at the end of the bed, rolled in a ball. Half a cup of coffee sat on the windowsill in a red mug. She picked it up and drank.

"You're acting weird," Hayley told her. "It's not out of line for you to have a boyfriend. Plenty of us do. It's an advantage that he knows what you do for a living."

"I guess."

"This is a good thing, right?" Joanie didn't reply. "You like him—you wanted this?"

"I guess."

"I don't know the last time you dated someone." Silently, Joanie shook her head. She didn't want to think about it. "I don't think I've ever known you to have a boyfriend."

"I don't know that he's a boyfriend. We just had a date."

"A picnic in the park sounds pretty romantic. And I know you like him in bed. Did you have sex?"

"Mmm-hmm."

"And?"

"It was great. It's always great. We came together. His cock is like my perfect cock. It fits me. He's not super experienced, but it's lovely."

"So why are you being so weird? What's wrong with this picture?"

A memory flared up, from high school, of her mother

kicking some boy out of the house. She didn't even remember what for.

Some Christian reason. She could admire true followers of Christ, but that hadn't been Christianity.

Love just wasn't for her. That made no sense, but it was how she felt.

"I've had such bad luck with relationships."

"Do you feel like you don't deserve them?" Joanie was silent. "Under your tough shell, you're an awesome person. You deserve happiness as much as anyone else."

Did she?

"He sounds sweet, and smart, and he likes you. You like him. Give it a chance."

"I will." But she felt forces arrayed against it, inside and out, like lines of infantry waiting for battle.

She would give it a chance if she could.

Saturday early evening, as dark collected, Clayton studied, bent over equations on his laptop. Puabi-Ekur hovered in a ceiling corner above his bunk.

Consider their alliances, Hekate had said.

They knew to whom they owed fealty. But they didn't know how to go back and make amends.

Incubi-succubi connected to a number of deities. Some had strong alliances, some loose relationships. Many followed Lilith, Lady of Harlotry, their traditional leader. But Puabi-Ekur, born first as Puabi, had grown up serving in Inanna's temple.

But how could they go back after what Inanna had allowed?

Puabi-Ekur flounced, invisibly, spinning in a figure eight. Someone attuned to energy could have felt it. Clayton was engaged and didn't notice.

They couldn't go back, even to follow Joanie.

An hour later, Joanie entered the big tapestried basement room with its pink-shaded lamp. Sandalwood smoke rose from the brass censer. Tonight the pillows and padded mats were absent; this was a ritual without paying guests. Hayley couldn't come—it was Joanie alone.

Sasha read the starting hymn: "The pure torch lit in the sky, the heavenly light, the great Queen of Heaven, Inanna I hail!"

The group answered, "Inanna I hail!" Cleo lit the candle in front of the statue of Inanna. Above hands cupping full breasts, the statue's rounded face smiled.

It was like her dream.

But as in her dream, she felt at the room's edges a flickering, whispering wind that seemed ill-omened.

"This ritual is a full moon devotional to Inanna. We start with traditional prayers. Then everyone can come up and make offerings. If you didn't bring anything yourself, you can offer one of the honey-cakes that Cleo made." Sasha nodded at her lissome assistant, who gestured to a nearby plate.

"After the offering, there's a chance to make individual

prayers to the goddess, and then you can light a tea candle for her. After that, we close."

Sasha, Cleo, and one other woman traded off reading the prayers. Just when these threatened to go on too long—the foreign-cadenced words, the repetition, the ancient flute-music playing behind the words, almost too loud—they were over. They offered the honey-cakes next. Joanie piled hers on the offering plate and stepped back to the circle, licking her fingers.

Under her eyelids, she glanced at Cleo.

She could have sworn Cleo was attracted to her, but maybe not.

Maybe she was just greedy.

Then she stood before the small, rounded statue, searching for words.

"Lady, I owe you an altar." In the flickering candlelight, the goddess's smile moved, reassuring. "Lady, I did what you suggested and contacted Clayton. I guess that was right."

Below and behind threaded the flute-music, sound of a distant past.

Under her breath, not having planned to, she found herself saying, "Please, Lady—bless our relationship. Let it bloom in the right way, whatever that is. I ask your blessing."

She heard the person behind her shift weight. She didn't want to take too much time.

She lit a candle and set it before the goddess. Again in the glimmering light, Inanna smiled.

The group took down the circle. The tea candles sparkled; the pink light shone. The ritual gave way to a party. Most of the other people in the room clearly knew each other. Unsure whether to stay, Joanie drifted to a table of snacks and ate some cheese and crackers.

At her elbow, someone said, "You should have some wine to go with that."

It was Cleo.

"Sure, whatever you say." Several bottles stood open on a nearby table. "What would you recommend?"

"I like this." Cleo poured her some merlot. "I'm glad you didn't leave right away! Are you a student at the university—do I have that right?"

It turned out Cleo was a few years older, a graduate student in anthropology. She'd met Sasha at a lecture on Sumerian anthropology. "It's not my subject, really, but it was an expert whose work I've really liked."

"What is your subject?"

Cleo dimpled at her. "You should never ask a graduate student about their thesis unless you're really serious."

Joanie returned the smile. "Serious enough."

"My work is on perception and creation of race identity, for people who are both Black and Native American."

"Mmm," said Joanie, not sure where to go with this.

With this background, Cleo was bound to be a feminist. Maybe she believed all prostitution was sex trafficking.

"I'm both myself," Cleo said. "Though I grew up mostly with my mother. And honestly, in my stepfather's house in Bellingham, there wasn't even much Black culture. I didn't connect with my biological father's heritage till much later. The work is a homecoming to me of sorts."

"That's cool. My family's mostly German. I'm supposed to be Native American on one side, but I've never traced it."

God, that sounded awful. She didn't want to equate her heritage with Cleo's.

"I'm pretty white bread, I guess. Except for what I do."

What was that about? Some desire to be cool?

Cleo raised her eyebrows. She remembered that look. Cleo didn't suffer fools gladly.

"What do you do?" Cleo asked.

Joanie took a deep breath.

If she wanted to know Cleo better, she needed to tell her the truth.

"I'm a sex worker."

"That's why you're attracted to Inanna, I guess?"

"I guess so. How did you start working with Inanna?"

"Oh, after the lecture I saw some more of Sasha."

Were they lovers, then?

Cleo eyed her as if she knew what Joanie was thinking, but she said only, "We got the idea to start a ritual group centered around worship to Inanna. Sasha comes from the same kind of background you do."

She probably didn't mean German.

"I see."

"She's trying to use it for good. She works with homeless youth, but also she believes strongly in the figure of the sacred whore—the giving of sexual love in the name of the goddess. We started the Inanna shrines together, from that point of view. And for me, Inanna is a woman of color. The people in Sumerian art—those are people of color. "

They looked at each other a long moment, a complicated look. Cleo reached out and touched her wrist with one long finger, this time tipped with fluorescent green.

"You have a strong connection to Inanna." It was a statement, not a question.

Joanie gazed into Cleo's eyes, amber velvet. "I do."

"We should talk."

Joanie waited out the rest of the party. "Do you live here?" she asked Cleo, as the last of the other guests retreated up the stairs. Sasha, whose basement they were in, had excused herself some time ago.

"Me? Oh, no."

Now or never.

"So you and Sasha—?"

Cleo shook her head. "We had a fling a long time ago. We stayed friends." Glancing around, Cleo found a cubbyhole and pulled a few pillows out. At the altar, she relit the candle. "If we're going to talk about the Lady, we might as well bring her here."

Turning to the statue, she said, "Hail, Inanna."

"Hail, Inanna," Joanie echoed.

"So, come, sit." Cleo settled herself among the pillows and gestured to the one next to her. "Tell me about your relationship with Inanna."

Joanie settled herself gently on the paisley pillow, a few inches away from Cleo. From her came the scent of sandalwood and a level stare.

Cleo leaned forward. She kissed Joanie, at first lightly, her lips soft and pillowy.

Then she kissed more deeply, biting a little, her tongue exploring Joanie's mouth. Her hands went to

Joanie's breasts, slipping under her bra, pushing it aside. She leaned down and nipped Joanie's nipple. Joanie moaned.

"Omigod," Cleo whispered, "you're so tasty. Like candy."

In answer, Joanie pulled her t-shirt and bra over her head and leaned toward Cleo, taking in her hands her small breasts through the tank top. Cleo wasn't wearing a bra. Nipples rose against Joanie's palms. She rubbed. Cleo pulled her tank off.

Joanie pushed her down among the pillows, licking and fondling. Cleo was twig-slender, her nipples dark raisins; Joanie admired the lovely flat belly, the protuberant navel. She licked it and got a giggle.

Gently biting Cleo's taut waist, she slid a hand under the waistbands of her broomstick skirt and panties. Cleo was entirely shaved. "Is this okay?"

"Oh yeah."

Joanie pulled skirt and panties off. "Let me get a blanket," Cleo said, and scampered up, digging in a pile of pillows to retrieve a cotton throw patterned with moon-shapes. Joanie stared at her heart-shaped ass.

Saliva filled her mouth, as with literal hunger. She hadn't gone down on a girl for ages—Zelda hardly counted, with the plastic wrap. Girls didn't invoke for her the same constraints boys did. Her family had never considered them romantic options; they were untouched. Cleo tossed the throw across Joanie's jean-clad legs and dropped down again beside her.

For a moment they smiled into each other's faces.

She was so present and happy, like morning sunlight.

Then Joanie took Cleo's hips in her hands, pressed her down among the pillows, and put her tongue to her labia.

Salt, wet, sour. Cleo wriggled and bucked under her hands—Joanie pressed her hips down harder.

Stay still, girl.

Cleo gave soft, breathy moans. Joanie got her rhythm. She could do this forever.

Cleo's labia were fleshy and extravagant, like orchid petals. Her musky scent mixed with the sandalwood perfume.

Like the scent of a temple.

Licking, Joanie got into it, swinging her head, her mouth wet. Cleo was breathing curses below her breath: "Fuck, fuck, fuck..."

She'd never heard a girl curse so much. It was kind of hot.

"Oh—oh—put your fingers inside me—" Joanie did. "Oh, yeah, like that... like that... " Joanie worked it, feeling for the pace, getting tenser herself as Cleo's body tensed.

And then Cleo shrieked—"Oh, my god, oh my god!"— and bucked entirely off the pillow. Joanie caught her around the waist and drew her into a hug, spooning. Cleo's whole body was quivering.

Joanie held her while she quieted, snuggling under the moon-printed throw.

"You came, then."

"Yes! Oh, my god, it's been a while. Oh wow." Cleo reached behind her, at random stroking Joanie's head and hair and shoulders. "Nice, that was nice."

She sat up on one elbow. "Now, what can I do for you?"

Joanie felt suddenly shy, but managed to blurt, "The same. If you want to."

"Oh, I want to."

Joanie lay back on the pillows, gazing at the tented fabric along the ceiling, Prussian blue and dark crimson lotus flowers lapped across pale pink; light flickered gently, from the candles on Inanna's altar. Cleo pulled off Joanie's jeans and kissed and stroked her pubis.

The smell of sandalwood, the light touch of Cleo's hair against her inner thighs, the tongue on her clitoris: the feeling stole up, like the tide coming in, wave by wave by wave. Joanie relaxed into it and let the tide carry her.

At the edge of her consciousness, as if it had been waiting for her loss of focus, a grey wind full of voices rose and whispered around her.

"Here, there's only a sip left in this bottle."

They were standing in Sasha's kitchen. With Joanie's help, Cleo had straightened the room and taken up some glasses to put in the dishwasher.

Joanie took the merlot bottle from Cleo and swigged the last bit. In all of what Cleo was doing was an implied invitation, asking to spend the night together, and she wanted to.

But she had to do the sensible thing sometimes.

"I should probably get home."

"Sure. But you should come over and check out my house sometime. It's an intentional community—we call it

Firebird House, because a lot of the people are fire artists and aerialists. Though I'm not anymore."

"Not anymore?"

"I used to be an aerialist, but now graduate school takes all my time."

Joanie drew close, drinking in the smell of sandalwood, and nestled into Cleo's embrace. "I do want to see more of you," she said.

"Me too you."

A creak sounded on the stairs, and a light flipped on in the hallway. Sasha emerged, hair all directions, eyes blinking, a plastic cup in her hand.

"I didn't realize anyone was still here." She went across the room to the refrigerator and filled her cup from its water spigot.

"We were about to take off," Cleo said to her.

Sasha turned back a moment. "No need. Karen's away. I could put you in her bedroom."

She was okay with their interest in each other. That was good. But Joanie still couldn't.

"I have a lot of homework, I need to get started early," she said.

At the same time Cleo said, "I have to get started by eight a.m. at the latest."

They looked at each other. Cleo laughed.

"I'll probably have time over the weekend, if I get enough done. I'll text you."

Joanie nodded, speechless, hugging it close to herself.

She wants to see me again!

Puabi-Ekur fought the wind.

Wave after wave of grey surged, hitting with weight and force, breaking up, recombining, always coming back, a wall of combat. On this level of the astral, it was like fighting the ocean. Lightning flashed green and orange among sooty clouds. Thunder boomed.

They'd known the djinn were around. Nice of the djinn to come find them!

Puabi-Ekur could be called a djinni themselves, but from a different tribe. Companions to humans age upon age, the incubi-succubi had become humanlike. The others —arisen as challengers, needed spirits of chaos and destruction—could take human form, but their desires and needs were not human at all. Or barely human.

They turned again on Puabi-Ekur, keening like the tempest.

Puabi-Ekur enlarged to the size of a star, made all of gold net, rounding them up like birds, pecking and battering.

I will crush you! Puabi-Ekur cried. The response was hoots and shrieks, the turmoil of a thunderstorm crashing, gliding, splitting.

A blow. The djinn were throwing replicas—seeking to eliminate Puabi-Ekur by creating a perfect double.

A deep rumble. A smash sent Puabi-Ekur flying across the ether.

That had been close.

Closer, larger, a huge crack burst the sky with a shock.

Puabi-Ekur lost consciousness.

"You went out with her, didn't you? You went out with a whore."

Clayton had let it slip by accident. He'd been in a good mood and offered to take James out for pizza and beer, especially since with Clayton's tutoring James had begun to pull himself out of his tailspin at school.

They found a booth, got their pepperoni pizza—Clayton splurged and added sausage—and a pitcher of Rainier. James asked casually, "Where were you last Wednesday?"

Clayton was distracted—he'd taken a sip from his pint and had accidentally spilled beer down his shirt. "I went out. I actually had a date!"

Oh shit.

"With who?"

It was too late to lie.

"With Jenny."

"I can't believe you went out with a whore."

Way too loud. The cashier was watching them.

"Shut up. " James rolled his eyes. "She contacted me."

"You are so naive. She wants to make you some kind of sugar daddy."

"She has the wrong guy. I'm broke."

"Dude. This is a woman who has sex for money. You think she really wants you?"

"Why not? She says the sex is great." Even in Clayton's ears this sounded weak. James grimaced.

"Please. Listen to yourself. She tells all the guys that. She has to be working some angle here."

"I don't get it." Clayton's voice trailed off.

He stared into his beer, then drained the mug and poured another.

James was right. She couldn't possibly want him. There was something he wasn't seeing.

It had seemed so sweet—like music.

James, seeing his glum face, took pity. "Tell you what. Why don't you leave her hanging for a week or so? If she really and truly likes you, she'll contact you again. Wait and see." He finished his own mug and inhaled half a pizza slice. "I'm betting against her, though, dude."

It was never going to happen.

In Joanie's small room, chilly even in summertime, draft seeped in from the windows. She hadn't heard from Clayton or Cleo all week.

Her mother had been right—no one was ever going to want her for herself. She had to package what she had and sell it to the highest bidder. Her mother had meant marriage, but that wasn't how Joanie was doing it.

On her quilt, her cat stood up for a moment, mewing, questioning. She petted him at random. After a few strokes, he curled up again into a warm ball.

She hated feeling like this.

She liked whoring. It was good to bring pleasure to the world. But she hated it when her issues came up.

The grey rose and swallowed her up.

It was never going to happen.

James had been right.

In the stuffy darkness of Clayton's dorm room, late at night under the bluish glow of the desk lamp, he packed the pipe again.

This indica should have been putting him to sleep. But all it was doing was digging him deeper into this hole.

Joanie was so beautiful, why would she care about a schlub like him? She wanted... he didn't know what she wanted. She couldn't be stupid enough to think he had money. But it couldn't be that she just wanted him.

After some time—infinite? small? hard to tell on the astral —Puabi-Ekur popped back into consciousness. Turbulence roiled around them, clouds bubbling.

A wave of black like the night ocean rose to engulf them.

Puabi-Ekur ducked.

The djinn spat insults. "Whoremonger! Pig fucker!"

But Puabi-Ekur's senses twitched.

They felt a tiny change. The djinn's power had lessened.

Thunder sounded, more quietly, timpani farther away. Lightning fireworked in the distance. Slowly, one by one, the djinn wisped away like smoke.

Gone. For now.

Puabi-Ekur let themselves relax, falling into light unconsciousness for healing's sake.

From a distant vantage point, on a throne between two torches, Hekate watched. From her throne, tangling into battles and sucking energy from those who challenged her, ley lines of power ran through the universe.

Chapter 10

In the morning, Clayton woke with one thought clear in his mind.

About this thing with Joanie—he was making up a bunch of shit in his head. Because of James.

When was James ever a good judge of anything?

He needed to text her.

He grabbed his phone before he could talk himself out of it.

<Hi, sorry it's been a while. Want to get some dinner?>

He hesitated, almost added a heart emoji, and decided not to.

He could hear James's comments in his head.

"You know I'm not really kinky, though."

"Of course not," Joanie said.

Everyone was a bit kinky. Why did people draw this huge line? They acted like their kink wasn't really a kink, because they'd read about it in a magazine. Someone else's kink was weird. It was a fetish.

Phil's setup was hardly very kinky by early twenty-first century standards. Since she'd last come over, he'd used black silk rope to tie discreet black-leather fleece-lined handcuffs to the corners of his bed. Standing next to her in the door of the bedroom, he practically vibrated.

"Are you interested—do you want to?"

His voice was a little high, as if his throat was tight. His face was flushed, and the tips of his ears were pink.

She'd never seen him so into anything. Maybe this was a watershed.

Her heart went out to him.

"Sure! I've done this kind of thing before, occasionally."

She'd done it a lot. But it never paid to let a client think you were too out there.

"I'll let you drive," she said.

Stripped bare, she lay down on his bed, snow-white sheets under her ass smooth and slightly cool. She wriggled a little.

She loved how his sheets are always clean. And high thread count.

Leaning over her, he buckled the handcuffs onto her wrists and ankles, tightening the ropes so that she lay spread-eagle facing upward, pussy exposed. Cool air touched her labia. Then his fingers were there.

Gods, I'm wet—oh.

He shoved three fingers in—and they went right in, to the knuckle. She bucked and writhed.

"You like that, don't you? You little slut."

This language was new too. She wasn't sure she liked it.

But a rush of lust overwhelmed her.

He fucked her with his fingers, slowly, slowly, pushing his wet hand in, drawing it out. She smelled the scent of her juices in the air, sweet and heavy, musk. She wriggled.

"Beg for it."

"Give me more."

"Beg harder!"

She pled like a child. "Please, please, please, give me more."

He sped up, bit by bit fucking her harder and deeper with his hand, not quite fisting her. It built quickly—all of a sudden she came hard, her pussy clamping around his hand like a sea creature on its prey.

"Oh, you little bitch." His mouth quirked in a smile. "Who said you could come? Did I say you could come?"

She shook her head slowly, biting her lip, like a little girl, falling into the role.

He put his wet hand to her mouth. "Suck my hand. Suck your slutty juices off my hand." She licked and sucked, feeling the wave of sex coming up in her body, like heat.

"Now I'm going to fuck you." He still wore his peach-colored polo shirt and black jeans. With one hand he unbuckled his belt and unzipped himself, but he didn't pull off the jeans.

He rolled on a condom and shoved himself into her. The zipper from his jeans lacerated her.

Then it overwhelmed her: the cock hitting her G-spot, his kisses that became bites on her mouth and breasts. Her body responded to the predator, desire hot and hard, almost painful, and she came again, her cunt contracting, almost cramping. Then he did too, crying out, face clenched like a fist.

He shoved a few more times, then lay still.

Her pussy stung, ripped by the zipper. She wondered if she were bleeding.

She'd never seen him more into it.

After a minute or two, he got up, pulled off the rubber, grabbed some tissues, and cleaned himself up. Standing over the bed, he stared at her a moment, zipping up his jeans.

Turning, he walked away.

She heard his footsteps cross the kitchen tile, then the front door open and click shut.

She tested the cuffs and rope, but they held.

That was an old trick.

But he was paying for the time.

"How long did he leave you there?" Hayley asked.

They were back at the coffee shop the morning after Joanie's Phil date. Sunlight angled in. Around them, murmuring talk rose and fell amid the smell of fresh coffee.

"Maybe a half-hour?"

"How much did he tip?"

"Two hundred percent. He gave me four hundred and fifty dollars."

"Shit."

"I know."

Joanie took a mouthful of cappuccino. Almost too hot, it warmed and grounded her. That, the sunlight of the day, and the warmth of the wooden bench under her helped bring her present.

"It really frightened you, didn't it." Hayley made it a statement, not a question.

It wasn't just new fear; it was new fear built on old fear.

Being trapped, locked in a small space. The closet. Trapped with the smell of her own sweat, with the smell of ancient cat pee. Trancing out, going far away.

"It frightened me. But I have to admit, it got me off hard."

"There's that." Hayley idly stirred her Frappucino with a spoon, flattening its foam bit by bit.

"I mean, I was never into it with him before, really. But now I halfway want to see him."

Blue eyes met ink-black. "I suppose that's a good thing...? I have to say, my dom would never do something like that without talking to me, not in scene but beforehand. He had me fill out a questionnaire. It sounds clunky, but it works." Hayley and her dom had been together nearly a year.

"How dangerous do you think this is, with Phil?"

Hayley shrugged. She twirled the liquid in her cup, then took a mouthful. "Not too dangerous, I think. I mean,

Tammy knows where you are, right? Phil doesn't sound like a guy who wants to get caught."

Joanie looked into Hayley's clear blue eyes. "You're right about that."

Her body settled.

She hadn't known how anxious she was.

"You could bring it up and tell him what works and doesn't work for you."

"I suppose." It'd be hard enough to do that with a boyfriend, let alone a client.

Hayley raised an eyebrow. "It's your life. What about that Clayton boy? Did he get in touch with you?"

"He finally did."

"That took a while."

"He apologized, at least."

"Are you seeing him again?"

"Next week." Joanie stared off across the coffee shop, shaking her head. In the fall of sunlight, dust motes floated.

"You're into him, aren't you?"

"Too into him."

"Silly. Being into it is the fun part."

"If you say so. It feels like torture to me."

Hayley laughed. "I though you liked torture."

That afternoon, Cleo texted Joanie out of the blue. They were both on campus. Cleo had a favorite Indian restaurant on the main drag, a hole-in-the-wall painted orange, pink, and yellow. The smell of spices hit Joanie on entrance. It felt like comfort.

Now they were bonding over samosas and mango lassis. A hollow sucking sound said Cleo had reached the bottom of her glass, the inside furred with pale-orange foam.

"Tell me about your relationship with Inanna," she said to Joanie.

"She was the first goddess I ever learned much about. Of course I ran into 'The Descent of Inanna' first. I loved that she had it all, in a way—a goddess of the heavens who was unafraid to go to the Great Below."

"To her sister Ereshkigal. What do you see their relationship being like?"

"I don't see them as rivals, or enemies. I see them as being—well, really, twins. Twins with different gifts, different places to rule, but twins nevertheless."

"When Inanna goes to the Great Below, and she's stripped of all the attributes of rule—what then?"

"It's a process she has to go through. She has to face her depths to have the right to rule."

"So it's psychological?"

Joanie knew to be careful here. Whether the deities were archetypes or real was a perennial argument in pagan and polytheist circles.

"I wouldn't say psychological, exactly." She turned the myth over in her mind. "She is the queen—she carries governance and sovereignty with her."

"She's stripped of it as she goes."

"She has to renew herself."

"Why does she go to the Great Below, then?"

Cleo was really catechizing her. Why so much, why now?

"If I recall, in the earliest version she goes because she wants to. She sets her ear to the Great Below."

Cleo grinned.

"Yes, doesn't she? Why does heaven have to go to hell, do you think?"

Puabi-Ekur had beaten the djinn back, but they knew the djinn would return.

A wall of cloud, massed like a thunderstorm, hung at the edge of the astral horizon. Occasionally red lightning illuminated the cloud bank for a moment.

They'd had some help in that fight. Who it was, they could figure out later.

They thought they knew which of Joanie's humans were djinn. But they had to be sure before they acted.

They might try diplomacy first.

Late summer was the only reliable stretch of warm and dry weather Seattle ever got. In the tall blue sky, fluffy cumulus clouds swam, stately in their crossing. The smell of the ocean floated up from the Sound.

<Do you want to go get some coffee?> Clayton texted.

<Sure>

Midmorning, Joanie, newly awake and still a little

blurry, sat in front of him. That perfect oval face, slightly chapped lips barely pink; the curves of her, her breasts under a tank-top, her nipples—his hands always longed to touch her, but he was careful, maybe too careful, as if she were a breakable thing.

They'd begun to tell each other about their pasts, bit by bit, no long confessions. Joanie had skated quickly over her abuse, but it was on the table. Clayton's own past was relentlessly normal; his parents had wrapped themselves in a blanket of normalcy. Even now, he was the overachiever he was, periodically, between bouts of depression, because of the picture his parents had painted, not in words but in unspoken expectations.

"Do you talk to your mother at all?" he asked Joanie.

"Sometimes. I went back last Thanksgiving."

"How was that?"

Joanie laughed. "A fiasco." Her mother's latest boyfriend had shown up drunk and made lewd remarks about Joanie, who'd left abruptly before dessert. "She called and cried about it. She apologized."

"Did you end up forgiving her?"

"I guess so. It's more like numbness than forgiveness."

Despite his caution, Clayton reached across and took her hand, kissing her knuckles. "Oh, sweetheart."

She gave him half a smile.

He walked her to her econ lab, but lab was canceled, the teaching assistant sick. It was Clayton's short day; he'd already had his one class.

He should study. But he wasn't going to.

"Do you want to do something? Go on a hike maybe?"

"I'd have to find my boots. Can't hike in these." She gestured to her flip-flops.

They wandered back to her apartment, to her narrow periwinkle room. The cat jumped onto the bed and meowed inquiringly. Joanie set him on the floor. Clayton gave the cat's chin a rub; he twined around Clayton's ankles and was gone.

Clayton smoothed the faded pastels of her quilt with his palm. "Tell me about the signature on this corner."

"My Aunt Marie made the quilt for me. She was one of the few bright spots in my childhood. She listened about my uncle—she even told my mom. But my mom refused to hear it."

"I'm sorry."

Joanie shrugged. "It was a long time ago."

They lay down, him spooned behind her. Their weight crushed a scent of incense out of the quilt. Her mood felt uncertain; he didn't want to push.

But with that glorious ass poured into tight jeans against his crotch, he couldn't help getting hard, and she felt it. She picked up his hand, laid the base of his thumb against her lips and kissed. Reaching back, she massaged his cock, then flipped around and unzipped him.

Her lips surrounded his penis. He closed his eyes. She fondled his balls, stroking his perineum. She sucked and milked his cock, stroking the base with her hand as her mouth pulled lovingly at the top half.

He moved his hips under her, groaning.

He wanted it to be for her too.

"Do you want to fuck?"

She lifted her mouth away. "You could talk me into it."

In answer, he sat up, unzipped her jeans and pulled them off, taking her cotton panties with them. Pushing up her tank top and bra, he put his mouth to her warm nipple, licking and sucking, as he fondled the other breast with the other hand.

Sliding down, he put his mouth to her pussy, found her clit, and focused there. She tasted salt and sweet, like salmon. She moaned, and after a few minutes pulled at his hair.

"Get up here and fuck me."

He kissed his way up her flat belly, across her breasts, gently tongued and nipped her nipples, kissed her mouth. Her pussy juices were still on his lips as he explored her mouth. Her hands caught his cock, covered and guided him, planting him firmly inside her.

The climbing glory, the beauty of it engulfed him. Her cries rang like birdsong. She came, and he felt her cunt contract around his cock. Then he came too: a small, white explosion in his mind, a moment of blankness.

He let himself down on top of her gently. Her arms enfolded him. She stroked his back. He kissed her face, her cheeks, her mouth: sweet and soft. Sliding off, he nestled by her side and fell asleep.

Incense smoke rose from the brass censer in the corner of Sasha's basement room. Crimson lotuses floated on the tented fabric of the ceiling and walls. Half-kneeling on a paisley pillow, Joanie wore her professional smile. For the evening, she was Jenny.

Cleo had made clear this temple was Sasha's gig. But Cleo had set up the connection for Joanie, and it was trust in Cleo that had gotten Joanie there.

This was the longer, more expensive Inanna temple, for which the small bedrooms down the hall were opened. The group was smaller than for the earlier temple—three women, five men. As they completed the call to Inanna, Joanie felt the goddess come in, hovering, protective.

At Sasha's gesture, the three women went to stand before the altar. Each wore lingerie or was naked except for jewelry, makeup, and perfume. Joanie wore a filmy pink-flowered teddy and for scent a dense jasmine. For the evening, she had dedicated the perfume, and herself, to Inanna.

It was a pop-up bordello.

The men had seated themselves among the pillows. An older gentlemen, in his sixties by Joanie's guess, stood and went to Sasha, clearly her client for the evening.

"Choose your preferred partner," she told the other men. "I know two of you put in a bid to be first in ritual." Sasha meant they'd offered more money, but she never talked about money directly.

A man strolled over to Joanie. He was tall, over six feet, with the build of a runner and a big hooked nose. "Hi," he said. "I'm George."

"I'm Jenny." Smiling, she stood on tiptoes and kissed his lips. He responded by grabbing her ass, firmly enough that she squealed.

This date with him would only take so long.

Joanie knew that upstairs drinking coffee sat a friend of Sasha's, Paulo, a big, slab-muscled martial artist with dreads who served as her bouncer. He could control George if necessary.

She led George to a room down the hall, decorated like the main basement room with a tented Indian print of elephants. A stick of sandalwood incense dropped ashes on an altar in the corner.

George wrinkled his nose. "Awfully smoky," he said. "Can you put it out?" She stubbed it out.

The corner of the coverlet had been drawn down, and next to the bed a small table held condoms, lube, gloves, and a few silicon plugs that Joanie knew had been well-boiled. She sat down on the sheet and patted the space beside her. George sat down, stroked her hair, and looked into her eyes.

His were quick and dark. She didn't know what he was searching for.

"I want your ass. That's what I paid for."

"I can do that!"

Early in Joanie's career as Jenny, she'd had a client who loved fucking her ass. She'd sized up from butt plug to butt plug so she could take his considerable member. She wasn't frightened when she unzipped George, half-tumescent, and found something huge.

"Can you take it?"

"I think so."

She knelt to suck him, mouthing just the tip, circumcised and an angry purple. Warming to her work, she worshipped it with her tongue.

She loved cock.

When she'd been looking at a communications degree, no one had ever said, "You love writing, but why do it for money? You'd be a word whore."

She loved sex. She loved sex with different people. Even the so-so times could be fascinating.

Her client's hand rested gently on the crown of her head, bobbing as her head bobbed. "Pretty girl," he crooned. "I don't want to come in your mouth, though."

Obediently she stopped sucking, continuing to pump him with her hand. He looked at her meaningfully. She spun around, pulled off her filmy teddy, and squatted on all fours on the bed with her ass in the air.

"You're clean?"

"Of course." She managed to make it sound not annoyed but professional, like a hotel clerk saying the minibar was full.

"Do you want a cock in there?"

She nodded, making her blunt-cut hair swing.

She wanted it done with. But she couldn't say that.

He was a gentleman inserting himself, rolling on the condom, adding plenty of lube, after entering slowly, letting her sphincter adjust. Bit by bit, he begin to thrust.

"Oh yeah," she said. "You can do what you want, baby."

He began to fuck her hard. She propped herself on the bed, elbows and head making a tripod base against his force.

In, in, in. The motion went all through her pelvis.

It put her in sub space.

After all, it's where the term bottoming comes from.

George noticed. He grabbed a hank of her hair, jerking her head up. "You like having that sweet hot ass of yours fucked, don't you?" With his other hand, he pawed her pussy, slick with juices. "You're wet. You really like this. Mmm-hmm, you—" he continued to thrust, his breathing getting ragged, his words breaking up—"you bitch, you whore, you hot—you hot little slut—you—" then just wordless grunts, till he cried out. His body shook with the force of his orgasm.

A few last thrusts, and he went limp. Catching the edge of his condom, he slid himself out and gave her ass a slap.

He disposed of the condom—she took professional pride that it was clean outside.

Told you, George.

They lay down next to each other. Waves of sweet oxytocin reverberated through the room. "My wife—there's no way she'd ever consider that."

"I'm sorry."

Who knew if he'd even asked? But he was paying for her time.

"You're a hot little number. I wouldn't mind fucking that ass of yours again sometime."

Bingo! Her own, separate client. With no Tammy percentage to pay.

"I have a card I can give you."

The second guy also took a card, so Joanie called the evening well-spent. She'd made nearly as much money as on a Desiree Elite Escorts night, in less time with less driving.

After the men left, the women took down the circle. Joanie felt the presence of the goddess retreat, like a wave going down the beach. On the way out, Sasha stood by the door, radiating pleasure like a scent. Joanie hugged her, and Sasha responded with a kiss on the lips.

Joanie took Sasha's head in her hands and gave her a deep tongue-kiss.

Now she'd remember her.

"Did you like your experience, then?" Sasha said, a bit breathlessly. "Would you consider coming back?"

"I would!"

Sasha studied her a moment, her gaze lascivious but somehow chilly. Joanie blinked and stepped away.

She didn't know if that was how she wanted to mix business with pleasure. She should ask Cleo about her.

Sasha did take cash from the men and pay up front. That was a plus.

The evening looked forward to fall, gusty, wind snapping the tree branches back and forth. A few leaves fell. It recalled the grey wind around the edges of Sasha's Inanna rituals, which rose and dropped with a faint air of menace.

Maybe it was always like that in ritual. She didn't have a lot of experience.

Back home, she felt a residue of erotic energy. With two fingers she explored her still-juicy cunt, settling her index and second finger on her clit, rubbing in a repeated circle.

The membranes under her fingers reminded her of something. The texture of a peach?

A fantasy arose, Sasha as a lamia, beautiful but cruel, with scales the color of her chestnut hair. Sasha's snake body twined around Joanie squeezing as the forked tongue licked her. She came so hard it hurt.

Chapter 11

In the whirling wind, pillowy black-blue clouds circled, a whirlpool, a nemesis. Rain crashed like surf. Occasionally the clouds parted to show a dark scarlet flare of sunset. A hint of froth below showed the sea.

Puabi-Ekur was waiting.

There was no time in this place that was not a place, so it was both a short and an infinite time they waited.

Puabi-Ekur hated being kept waiting.

The first one arrived whistling. Because whistling was one of the most obnoxious things anyone could do.

It hopped bobbing through the air and appeared as if sliced in half: half a head, half a body, one arm, one leg. It came up beside Puabi-Ekur, out of arms' reach of Puabi-Ekur's form, of a giant, blue-skinned man.

Something to show they did not want to be fucked with.

"They'll be along directly," this one said.

Puabi-Ekur shrugged. They kept their own backup a

quarter-dimension away, all dark, winged bodies and impressively sharp teeth, along with a few who presented in human form, or mostly. Tessa loved her black, mandarin-collared business suit, and the forked tail only added to the look.

The smaller folk trickled in, presenting as dogs, jackals, and snakes, or zombie-like. Then larger ones appeared, water-people and a troop of seductive females. The last showed up as fire. They entered with a flare and a sound of wind, as if they burned the air itself.

Puabi-Ekur yawned a little and called in Sabit and Aea to flank them. That was scary enough for them.

The largest ball of fire floated forward. In a roaring voice, like a bonfire talking, it said on the interior plane: YOU WISHED TO SPEAK

I did. I want a cease-fire.

WHY ARE YOU TAKING TROUBLE FOR THIS

Because I know where this goes.

The ball of fire flared and crackled to itself for a few nonmoments.

YOU ARE A SENTIMENTAL DREAMER

How many are in place, at least? Tell me that.

HUNDREDS OF THOUSANDS

On the mundane plane?

A steady sound of the whispering, muttering, and popping of flames: a nonanswer.

I see what you're planning. It's too hard.

WE HAVE MORE FAITH IN HER THAN YOU DO PUABI

No deal?

NO DEAL

The challengers slid, walked, hobbled, and apported away. Sabit and Aea nodded goodbye and popped to another dimension.

Once Puabi-Ekur was alone, Tessa appeared. Brushing off a volcanic rock, she seated herself. Her red-scaled tail flicked from one side to another. In her purr of a voice she said, "You know they're right, Puabi-Ekur."

Puabi-Ekur shot her a glare.

"You've loved her for four thousand years, and you still don't think she's equal to an ifrit or two? You're being over-protective."

Puabi-Ekur stared out over the boiling mass of clouds, to a split that showed a tendril of ocean. "You don't understand."

"I've been in love. We all have."

"But I remember it."

The red tail twitched back and forth. "No need to be insulting."

She cocked her head to one side, studying Puabi-Ekur, then took pity on them. "The ifrit are challenging her. It's what they're supposed to do."

Puabi-Ekur met her eyes with a level gaze.

Tessa shrugged her shoulders. "I shouldn't expect a succubus to listen to reason."

The night wind nudged at the shutters, which rattled and creaked. The sound woke Puabi.

The room was not completely dark. At the corner altar to Inanna with its thumb-sized statue of the goddess, the oil-lamp was burning. Before the altar, Iltani sat.

The slender body, the breasts, each like the bowl of a shallow goblet; the flamelike form, the person sitting there, her narrow passionate soul like an oasis in the desert, all bound up with her music.

A cord drew back her dark hair, leaving one strand hanging. Puabi wanted to go and stroke the hair back from her forehead, kiss her forehead, but she gave in to quietude and the desire to watch her lover in silence.

Iltani sat, legs folded under her, focused on the goddess statue, whispering under her breath.

Puabi wondered what she was praying for. She listened hard, but all she heard was sibilance, and the shutter kept creaking, making it hard to hear. Finally she sat up.

"Iltani."

The girl's head turned. She had a hunted look.

Maybe she shouldn't ask. But she had to ask.

"What are you praying about?"

Iltani just stared.

"Come to bed."

The next few weeks were a kind of cat-and-mouse: silent or not-so-silent pressure from Puabi, retreat and evasion from her lover. Finally Puabi lost her temper one evening after a rehearsal.

"Iltani, I love you, and in the end you're free to do anything you like. But I won't have this barrier between us. Tell me, or—" she broke off. "Or I guess things will have to change between us."

The golden light of late afternoon, toward twilight, cast itself across the courtyard, which was slightly less like an oven that it would have been an hour before. Blue shadows flowed over the mud-brick cobbles, eating half the courtyard; flies made angled patterns by the potted palms. Puabi wiped her forehead with the back of her arm; she'd been dancing. She stood above Iltani, who sat with her back to a column, harp lying against her body.

It really was time they talked.

Iltani frowned and sighed, settling back on her heels. She set aside her lap-harp. She had a new one, dark-varnished wood inlaid with silver. Puabi assumed some admirer had given it to her. She never concerned herself with things like that. Iltani, like Puabi herself, was an artist; she had aficionados, even patrons.

"It's that noble. Kirkaru."

"Kirkaru?"

Iltani shrugged, resettling herself into a position with crossed legs. She picked up a dusty palm frond from the cobbles, laid it across a dip between two mud bricks, letting an ant cross it like a bridge. "He came when you danced at the Festival of Waters. He's a music-lover. Or so he says."

"And?"

Iltani met Puabi's eyes and looked back down again. "He's been sending me presents."

"Like this new harp."

"Yes."

Puabi turned this over in her mind.

Iltani hadn't been out late, or at all. Puabi knew where she was nearly every minute of the day. She betrayed no excitement when she said his name. As far as Puabi could tell, she only desired women. Puabi had no need for jealousy here. And yet...

"It's bothering you, isn't it?"

Iltani shrugged, not looking up.

"It is, I can tell."

Iltani glanced up, then away.

"I can go talk to the hierarchy about it. Get him to go away."

Iltani shrugged one shoulder again.

This girl! Frustrated, Puabi sat down beside her.

"I know you had a hard time in your childhood, before you came to the temple. But here in the temple, the priestesses and priests are good. They want the best for us. We are a community, all devoted to our goddess."

"Sure. We'll see."

The long table sat in a room with a frieze of bas-relief, Inanna accepting gifts from her worshippers. Inanna stared forward, her face a mask; she seemed unhappy with what was offered her. Puabi found her expression unsettling.

Along the long table sat the priests and priestesses who ran the temple. Today was the day of the week that they heard petitions from within.

The chief scribe studied her down his long nose.

"And what is your petition, Lady Puabi?"

"My lord." Technically she didn't have to call him that, but it kept him sweet. "There has been a noble, the Lord

Kirkaru, giving my harpist Iltani gifts. They make her uncomfortable."

"Does Lady Iltani say so herself?"

Puabi nudged Iltani hard with one elbow. This was why she'd made her attend.

"Lord Shulgi, I do."

"I see." The chief scribe exchanged a glance with the chief Inanna priestess present. She was a woman in her late forties, high-born and a bit snobbish, but she and Puabi had always gotten along. She regarded Puabi as an ornament of temple. But now she gave Puabi a long, measuring look that Puabi couldn't interpret.

"Lady Iltani," the chief scribe said, "why do the gifts make you uncomfortable?"

Iltani stared at the mud-brick floor. Puabi had foreseen this question and had coached her.

"I believe he is trying to buy my favors."

"But you are a priestess of Inanna, are you not? Is lying down for the goddess not one of a priestess's duties?"

"It is not my path. I am a harpist. I have never lain with a man."

Again a look was exchanged along the table, and a murmur of talk.

Puabi wished she hadn't said it like that. They could interpret it as an offense against the goddess.

The murmur died. The chief scribe turned back to Puabi and Iltani, now holding hands, their hands clutched tight.

"What would you have us do?" the chief scribe asked.

"I would like my harpist not to be troubled. We are one

of the temple's greatest assets—when I dance, the silver runs. You know that." Puabi scanned up and down the table, catching the eyes of each one there. "I call on you to protect this child of Inanna."

The chief scribe nodded gravely.

The gifts stopped, for a time.

Chapter 12

"It's been a while since we talked," Tammy said.

In the small hours of a late-summer night, Joanie sat on Tammy's office couch, watching as Tammy finished some accounting in a spreadsheet.

"It has."

She'd poured herself and Tammy a glass of pinot grigio each and sat with her feet tucked under her. Tammy was click-clicking away on the keyboard, despite her long red nails.

Joanie didn't see how she worked around them. Maybe she was just used to it.

Joanie took a mouthful of white wine. She'd bought it chilled, and it felt good in her mouth and throat. Though she'd made a lot of money, it had been a long night.

"So you're doing Inanna shrines at that woman Sasha's house, huh?"

Joanie froze.

How had Tammy found out?

Tammy looked over as if she'd read Joanie's mind. "I have my spies."

It must have been one of the men. Though she hadn't recognized them. Hayley wouldn't tell Tammy anything.

"What do you think of her setup?" Tammy focused now on the screen, blue light painting her well-made-up face.

Did Tammy really not care?

Something in her boss's fixity of pose spoke.

No, she was pissed.

Joanie provided a rambling description of the Inanna shrines and the setup in the rooms. "I don't make as much money as here, but she doesn't care if I see clients outside. At least I don't think she does."

"Mmm." Tammy focused on her screen another moment, then shot Joanie a sideways glance. "I would watch out for that Sasha. She's not some goddess-worshipping cream-puff, like you think she is. She's got a profit motive, and then some."

Joanie made a face. "Don't you? Doesn't everyone?"

Tammy turned toward her, face clenched. "I sure do, honey. I hope you do, too."

"Honey"—that wasn't good.

"You're mad at me," Joanie said, flatly.

"What did you expect?"

Joanie sighed.

She'd expected more time moonlighting before Tammy found out.

"I appreciate that you helped me get into the business.

But I haven't signed a contract with you. I can't. You can't sign a contract to perform an illegal act."

Tammy stared at Joanie over her slim-framed glasses. A strand of long black hair had slipped out of her bun; she pushed it away from her face.

"Whatever. You owe me one."

No, she didn't. But she didn't want Tammy making trouble for her.

"What do you need?" Joanie asked, cautiously.

Tammy turned back to the keyboard. Joanie knew she was purposely keeping her waiting. Tammy typed a while, studied her work, then pushed the keyboard away. Swiveling her body toward Joanie, she stared at her.

Tammy was trying to freak her out. Joanie met her eyes, displaying no emotion.

"You're a cool cucumber, aren't you?" said Tammy. "What I want is not that big a deal. I'm going out of town for three weeks, and I need you and Hayley to cover the office. Set up the outcalls, track everything. But I need you to be the one in charge."

"Me?"

"No one I trust will be here the whole time except you two. And Hayley's a smart kid, but you worry more. I need a worrier to do this job."

Joanie stared into Tammy's eyes. Tammy didn't blink.

She'd done it before, for a shorter period of time. It was a calculated risk. If Joanie set up calls, legally it was promoting prostitution.

A core of tension coalesced at the pit of her stomach.

"Okay."

Tammy's vacation lay a few weeks out yet. The upcoming week, Clayton had finals—Joanie had taken only one summer class, so didn't have much concern about acing the paper and test remaining.

It was time to make some money.

"Three tonight, and three tomorrow night?" Tammy asked her that Thursday.

"You'd better believe it."

"What about Phil? He still calling you?" Tammy loved that Phil was a solid money-maker.

"He's in Australia." Australia was his region. Every month to six weeks, he traveled there for a week or two.

She assume he had a girl, or girls, out there. No skin off her back. She halfway wished he'd stay in Australia.

The BDSM they were experimenting with engaged her attention. She didn't go on autopilot as often as before. But she still sensed dark fish swimming on the lower levels of Phil's psyche.

She could probably avoid them, though. Avoidance and denial had carried Joanie through many bad situations.

Her third date began at midnight, at a hotel in Kent she'd seen the inside of a few times. It was where she'd met Clayton, which made her smile. She'd also had a few business-guy dates there, and one she'd bailed out of fast, with some meth heads suddenly in the money. You had to keep your intuition running in this business.

She pulled into the parking lot, shut off her music, took

a deep breath, and called the number she had for the guy. Joe.

Not his real name, she was sure.

"I'm here."

"Come to Room 214."

She grabbed her bag (with the babydoll tucked inside it) and headed into the hotel. She smiled at the front desk clerk, who smiled back, and aimed for the steps.

Nothing about her said whore. She was just a pretty young lady, probably a college student. She *was* a college student.

She knocked on the door. The shadow of an eye crossed the peephole. Was he expecting someone else?

The door opened. There stood James: all of his six-foot-two self, his blond hair newly cut high-and-tight, with his two-thousand-watt grin and tight, well-muscled body. Efficient in bed, a little bitey. Fond of doggy style.

She did not step into the room.

"Hi, James."

"Come inside."

She stayed in the hallway. "I don't know what game you're playing, but I don't like it."

"I'm not playing a game. I just want to spend some time with you." She appreciated that, being in semi-public, he didn't call her names or say what he planned to do with the time.

There was nothing particularly aggressive about his stance. But she didn't like it.

He gave her puppy-dog eyes. "Come inside."

Her intuition was running the police siren. "I have the right to refuse service, James."

"I know that. That's okay." Still with the puppy-dog eyes. "Come on. If you really want, you can leave after we talk. But... " he frowned, the frown of someone who didn't really understand himself what he was about. "I honestly just wanted to see you."

And fuck her. For money. To prove he could, and to hurt his friend. He wasn't opaque to her.

But her intuition had stood down over the last exchange. She was no longer scoping the area for places to run and for available weapons (her purse held pepper spray and a flashlight to strengthen a punch).

"Okay."

The room was a smaller version of the suite where she'd met him the first time, all in tan and olive. Narrow, long, it was dominated by two queen beds next to each other— queen by courtesy, more like double beds plus. By a stream- lined desk sat a chair, padded seat covered in olive-and- black vines. She sat there. James pouted a moment, then sat on one of the beds.

She wriggled in the chair, swiveling it on its base, and crossed her legs. He might never get at this pussy again.

"James, what do you want?"

He grinned. "I think it's obvious." He leered. She frowned.

"You want to hurt Clayton. You want to break us up."

"Maybe." His face went serious. "Maybe I'm here for my friend. Maybe I wanted to see what you would do. Not everyone wants their best friend dating a whore."

"Oh, please." She probed the psyche behind the bright blue eyes.

Like all arrogant boys, he had a chip on his shoulder. She wondered where that came from. But that was just curiosity—she didn't care. This exchange hadn't made her like James worse, but it hadn't made her like him better.

"Clayton's your prop, your wingman. You mostly care because he's getting something you're not."

James shrugged and grinned again. "That too."

Joanie frowned. "Do you really care about him?"

"Do you really care about him?"

He was trying to turn the tables and take power. She wouldn't let him.

"I do." She set her bag on the floor and grabbed her phone. "And I'm going to call him right now."

"Don't!" James leaped off the bed, moved as if to snatch the phone, but was locked in place by her glare.

"You touch me, James, and I'll blow this whole thing apart, so help me God." Seattle had recently gone to a Nordic-style legal approach for prostitution, which targeted the johns, so James was as likely to go to jail as she was. She saw in his eyes that he knew this. Most frequent flyers did.

The phone rang. And rang. And rang.

No answer.

They stared at each other.

"He's not picking up," Joanie said, to buy time.

She didn't plan to lose the power position here. But what did she want?

"I don't mind fucking you. But I'm going to tell Clayton

as soon as I get a hold of him, and if he says not to do it again, I won't."

"Oh, Jenny." James put his well-coiffed head in his hands, shaking it, gazing at the floor. "Don't do that."

It registered, with a small note of pleasure, that Clayton hadn't told James her real name.

It was tempting to play with James here. But she didn't.

"Or you can walk out of here right now. You can keep your money. I won't keep your secret; I'll still tell him. But if you want, I'll tell him you had second thoughts and wanted to preserve your friendship."

James looked up at this. They locked eyes again. Blue flame ignited in his.

"Leave this room without fucking you, when I'll probably never get to again? Not a chance."

"I'm going to tell him first thing tomorrow," she said.

"I don't care. I'll make it right. Or maybe I won't. I'm not going to leave this room without fucking you."

Oh, really?

"Since you said that was okay."

He was willing to burn his bridges with Clayton for one night with her.

This touched some small, dark part of her.

Because she was the shit. She was the real thing.

Watching her, he stood and stepped forward. "I want you like crazy. Feel that." He put her hand on his crotch. "I'm rock-hard for you."

He had a pretty nice cock. It wasn't Clayton's, but it was nice.

She squeezed gently. He closed his eyes.

"Okay," she said, standing. He leaned and kissed her, a kiss full of sexual hunger. She kissed back, becoming another self: not the girl who loved Clayton, but a woman who knew sex as a territory and a skill.

"I bought some champagne," James said.

"Awesome."

She slipped into the bathroom and put on her new babydoll, dark scarlet with a deep black-lace border. In the spotlit mirror, she took a moment to touch up her lipstick, which matched the babydoll.

Vanity, vanity.

She looked amazing.

When she emerged, James had poured them each champagne in hotel plastic cups. He lifted his cup to hers wordlessly. In silence, they toasted and sipped. Then he reached over, took her glass out of her hand, and drew her toward him.

They kissed again, deep and then shallow, playing. Clearly he liked to kiss. He drew the straps of her gown off her shoulders, so it fell half-off, and cupped her breasts, then leaned down and kissed one, then the other, then took one in his mouth and gently suckled, biting a little. His other hand went to her cunt.

She felt him grin as they continued to kiss.

Because she was sopping wet.

His fingers slid into her liquid, rubbed her clit, thrust into her vagina, exploring, claiming. Curving, they found her G-spot.

Oh God.

Oh, right there.

She shut her eyes. Her babydoll fell to the floor.

He wasn't a talker, but his eyes noted he'd connected. He continued stroking her. Her eyelids fluttered.

"Don't or I'll come. I want to come when you're fucking me."

"Sounds good to me." Leading her by the hand, he threw back the covers on the nearest queen and swung her down onto it. He shucked jeans and shirt in a moment, leapt onto the bed, and placed himself between her legs.

She lifted her head. "Condom."

"Yeah, yeah." He leaned over to the bedside table, took and opened a shiny package, rolled the condom on.

He pushed two fingers inside her. "Don't think we need lube."

She wriggled a little, reached out, and guided his cock in. He began to pound at her.

Mostly her eyes were shut, focusing on the sensations in her own body. She wanted to come for him; it was her parlor trick. Occasionally she'd open her eyes and glimpse him.

He had a pretty body. All those abs.

He put her hands on her hips, pulled her up with her ass in the air.

Her head went into the pillow. He mounted from behind, his cock hitting her G-spot. *Oh God.* The feeling rose faster than she expected, suddenly peaking; she came. Then he came, brought on by her orgasm: he cried out, and she felt him shudder.

After a moment, he let himself down, weighting her

body down onto the bed. She moved her head so she could breathe.

She let him lie there a few minutes, then wriggled. "Don't crush the merchandise."

"What? Oh, sorry." He rolled off, lay beside her. She watched him out of the corner of her eye, not sure what he planned next. He took the condom off his now-limp cock.

Was he done now?

She maneuvered to the edge of the bed, found her champagne cup, sat up, and sipped.

"Hey, Jenny." Not done. "Could you suck it, please? I'd like to go again."

He wanted his money's worth. And who could blame him?

"Sure." She downed her champagne, then wiggled over and took his cock in her mouth. It tasted like latex and dribbled with come.

It was a job.

"You did what?"

"Last night, my final date was James."

Clayton and Joanie had met for coffee, at her favorite coffee shop. She'd said she had something to tell him. She'd said it so neutrally he'd had no idea what it would be.

What she said now didn't make sense.

Clayton had one final left. It was late August; full summer had settled on Seattle, a golden thickness of sun. He'd been thinking of asking Joanie to go to the beach for a weekend, if they could find something cheap in Ocean Shores. But now...

"You went ahead with it?"

She sat facing him, her back to the wall, on a wooden bench in her favorite booth, sun glinting on her brunette hair.

So beautiful.

How could she not understand?

"I needed to make money. It was my last gig of the night. Does it really bother you that much? I won't do it again."

How could she?

Part of him wanted to turn and run. Part of him wanted to pick up his scorching-hot latte and throw it in her face. Part of him wanted to cry.

But he didn't want to break this thing they had. It was precious to him.

Gently, tentatively, she put her hand over his on the table. With some effort of will, he kept his hand where it was, didn't slide it away. A ray of sun glinted off stray hairs on his fingers. Her fingers were like dark ivory.

"I can see it bothers you. I'm really sorry."

He heard it in her voice.

She was sad; she regretted it.

"I didn't realize it would bother you this much."

Maybe there was something broken in her, from her background of abuse, that doesn't understand why it bugged him. A blind spot, a not-understanding.

He could see this, in his mind's eye, from far away, as from an airplane a city might read like markings on a map. But his heart and his gut felt something else.

How could she have not known that she was betraying him?

"Clayton, look at me."

He did. He was close to crying, but he was not going to do that in a coffee shop.

"I'm really, really sorry. I'll never do it again. Okay?"

He met her eyes.

No, it's not okay.

He couldn't let her see that—he couldn't let her hear that.

He hated to see her unhappy.

"It's okay."

She lay on her bed, on top of her quilt, curled in a fetal ball. She'd finished her last exam, she'd handed in her last paper, and she'd been able to escape home.

How could she have been so stupid?

She should have sent James packing. A few hundred dollars wasn't worth it.

Her small altar was at the edge of her sight.

Please, Inanna. Please let it work out okay.

Chapter 13

In the middle of the night, Puabi returned to the bedroom she shared with Iltani. The room lay dark and silent, Iltani asleep, the only illumination the lamp Puabi held in her hand.

Puabi had been called to the temple to dance for a high-born lord. He'd asked for a dance to the flute, so Iltani had taken the night off.

The affair was formal, with a high-born group gathered to watch. In the audience, Puabi had seen her prince of long ago. He was still beautiful, but he looked worn: heavy, with a face burnt dark by sun and wind and deep circles under his eyes. She had heard his marriage wasn't happy.

After her dance, she had a moment alone, drinking a cup of black beer her attendant brought her. She gazed across at her prince, and her heart shivered, as if she were nearing the edge of a precipice.

She'd shaken it off, but now it came back to her.

Foolishness.

She set down the lamp and took off her clothes.

Iltani stirred in the darkness. "Is that you, Puabi?"

"Myself, baby-child. Who else comes to see you, this late at night?"

"No one," Iltani's voice sounded unaccountably sad.

"Do you wish someone besides me would come?" asked Puabi, jokingly.

"No." Her voice sounded desolate. Dropping her belled skirt with a jingle, Puabi sat on the bed.

"What's wrong?"

"The gifts are back." Iltani gestured with her hand. On the windowsill sat a vase of cut flowers, lilies from someone's hothouse.

Puabi strode across the room, opened the shutter, and pushed the vase out the window.

They heard the vase shatter on the mud bricks below.

They listened to hear a reaction from the temple, but there was none. It was the middle of the night; the only ones awake were cats and lovers.

Iltani sighed. "It doesn't go away that easy, Puabi. You know it doesn't."

Puabi and Iltani returned to the temple council when they sat again at the long table, below the bas-relief of Inanna accepting her worshippers' gifts. "What is your petition, Lady Puabi?" the chief scribe asked her.

His eyes flickered to the chief Inanna priestess.

They knew.

"My lord. We asked that the Lord Kirkaru stop troubling

my harpist, the Lady Iltani, with his attentions. For a time, he ceased. But now he has begun again."

"I see," said the chief scribe. He and the chief Inanna priestess exchanged another look.

"I have asked you to protect this child of Inanna," Puabi said, grabbing and clutching Iltani's hand.

"Indeed," said the chief scribe. "And may she be protected."

Puabi stared at the chief scribe, who returned her stare unblinking.

This was all she was getting.

The gifts didn't stop.

Puabi-Ekur hovered over Clayton as he slept.

Puabi-Ekur considered Iltani desolate, Joanie crying herself to sleep.

If he dared, the boy would cry himself to sleep as well.

Was there some karmic debt these children needed to pay? Were rival divine influences fighting?

No—they saw no particular debt. The gods diced with each other, but it was just a game.

Still, people got hurt. They received happiness briefly, only to have it ripped away.

Puabi-Ekur suspected that Hekate had helped them in their battle with the djinn. Hekate wanted them to consider their alliances.

What did they owe these deities who toyed with humans?

Puabi-Ekur knew that they struggled with questions as old as embodied spirit. But the ifrit had challenged them.

If they acted, if they changed Joanie's karma, they took away her challenge.

What was love if it could not act?

The first few days of Tammy's vacation were uneventful. Joanie kept the books; the girls handed over their commissions. Everything went like clockwork.

Monday evening, usually a slow night, Phil called the business phone. "Jenny, is that you?" Clearly he'd expected to get Tammy. She explained.

"Are you still doing calls?" He sounded worried.

"Of course!" They set one up for the following Friday.

"I wish she didn't have you working the phone, honey."

Why did he care?

"It's not a big deal. I've done it before." He signed off, and she set down the phone, frowning.

Something was up. She didn't get it.

She wasn't going to worry about it.

But the call from Phil set the tone for the evening. Only a few minutes later, she got a call that felt off from the start. That it was a call was the first tip-off; they did almost all their work by email.

"Hello, Desiree Elite Escorts, the most beautiful girls in the city. May I help you?"

The man on the other end cleared his throat.

He was nervous. They mostly were.

"Hi. I was interested in seeing one of your girls this evening. Would she come to me, or would I come to her?"

Jenny explained the agency did only outcalls. "But I don't have anywhere to meet her," he said.

"If you want to have one of our intimate dances"—the cover fiction for the standard hookup was "lingerie dances"—"a lot of customers rent a hotel room."

"Is it possible for me to come to you?"

"I'm sorry, sir, the agency isn't set up for that."

"Okay." He hung up.

Right after that, she got the email:

Hi, this is Tom. I'm interested in seeing one of your girls tonight. Nothing fancy.

Joanie grabbed the standard screening email. Tammy asked for ID of some kind, a LinkedIn or some other online identification to prove the client was real. Tom replied:

I'd rather not do that. Can I meet one of the girls for coffee somewhere?

This was a pretty standard request—with the recent changes in policing, targeting the johns rather than the girls, a lot of men were understandably nervous. Joanie wrote back:

Do you want to do that tonight, or later? I'll send one of the girls. Do you have a favorite?

Pictures of most of the latest girls were online, and she had gotten pretty expert at talking guys into one of the others if need be.

Tom wrote back:

Whoever's available.

As it happened, everyone was out on calls. Hayley

would be coming in to cover the office for the end of the night.

She wondered if she should take it. She could use the money.

It was a line Tammy never wanted her girls to cross—never set up your own dates. But Tammy was dire about a lot of things, some of which made sense and some of which didn't. Joanie had set up a few freelance dates. The procedure was the same.

Proper screening was important. But it wasn't rocket science.

They made a date for eleven-thirty p.m. at a Denny's in a mall near the office.

Hayley rolled in a bit before eleven. Joanie filled her in on the evening, including the upcoming coffee date.

"Are you sure you want to do that?" Hayley asked. "Better send one of the other girls. It makes it easier to do the, 'I don't know what you're talking about! I'm an exotic dancer!' thing."

Maybe Hayley was right.

But Joanie had been doing this as long as Hayley had.

"I can take care of myself. I'll check his ID; I'll talk to him. I know the ropes."

Hayley shrugged. "If you say so."

The nighttime Denny's could have been anywhere: burnt-orange vinyl booths, cylindrical Seventies light fixtures, Moons Over My Hammy on the menu. A bit too much AC pumped out for the sundress Joanie was wearing; she kept her jean jacket on. She ordered decaf coffee and a side of eggs.

It would have been nice to eat anything she wanted. But she was a girl.

When the heavy-set man with black-rimmed glasses walked in, she knew instantly it was him, and waved.

At a guess, his wife hadn't had sex with him in months.

He sat across from her in the orange-vinyl booth.

"Happy to meet you!" she said. She watched him taking her in. She'd dressed college-girl style, as she usually did: a clingy knit tank-dress, but nothing she wouldn't wear out with friends.

She could be his daughter. But she wasn't.

The waitress materialized, and he ordered coffee. When he turned back to Joanie, it suddenly hit her.

He seemed like a decent guy. But he could be a cop.

"I totally get that you might not want to go into details in email or on the phone. But we need a little information about you."

"Is this enough?" As the waitress set down his coffee, he flipped open his wallet and showed his driver's license.

"May I?" He handed her the wallet. She slid out the license. She fingered the laminated plastic and studied the photo, the signature, Mount Rainier ghosted in the back.

It looked legit.

Thomas Moreno. What kind of name was Moreno? He didn't look Italian. But plenty of people didn't match the ethnicity of their names.

Her intuition sent up a distress signal, but nothing she understood.

Still, there was something up. She needed to be careful.

The waitress returned. "Do you want anything to eat?"

Tom asked Joanie. She shook her head. Tom turned to the waitress. "I think coffee's it for me, then."

The waitress nodded. "Here's your check!"

Tom checked the tally. Then, giving Joanie a significant glance, he put a ten dollar bill down on the table.

He was trying to tell her he tipped well.

"What kind of girl are you looking for? Have you gotten a chance to go over the website?"

He leaned across the table and put his hand over hers.

"I like you."

She felt it too, a solid manly lust. It wasn't exactly her taste, but it was like being offered milk chocolate when you preferred dark. It was still chocolate.

Compared to a lot of them, Tom seemed like a pretty solid guy.

"Tell me a little bit about yourself," she said.

He said he was a businessman who ran a string of parking-lot espresso stands at the edges of the Seattle metro area. He gave her his card.

She fingered it: good cardstock, printed somewhere, not cheap. It seemed legit.

Competing impulses warred within her.

She was always broke between quarters—too much stuff to spend money on. It'd be dumb to set herself up. But she could use the money.

A lull fell in the conversation. Pointedly he smoothed the wrinkles out of the ten dollar bill. "If it's money," he said, "I have it." Retrieving his wallet, he showed her a thick stack of bills within. As she watched, he thumbed out one then another. They were all twenties; there was no fake she could see.

"I have to ask: Are you with the police?"

He shook his head, looking shocked and mildly disgusted. It seemed genuine.

He could be acting. But if so, he was pretty good.

Okay, she'd bite.

"You seem like you'd be a great agency client, honestly."

"Can we go to your place?"

"I'd recommend a hotel."

Danielle would kill her if she saw clients at their apartment. She had to figure a way to move out. If she went independent, she needed to see people from her place.

She gave him directions to her preferred hotel. She let him buy her the eggs and decaf. They parted in the parking lot, yellow light from the restaurant windows streaming across the asphalt. The air smelled like eggs and cheese.

"See you there!"

She let him get ahead of her—he would check in, then have her come directly to his door. It was a motel, with outdoor steps and doors facing directly outside. She wouldn't have to deal with the front desk.

By now it was twelve-thirty. Her time of night.

She drove through Seattle's northern outskirts, low strip malls alternating with small one-family houses covered in clapboard or vinyl siding. A particular shade of aqua said some houses and owners had been there since the 1960s. The yards had trimmed grass, juniper or mountain-laurel hedges, hydrangeas ranging blue to purple, and fir or cedar trees.

The streets held an openness and a sadness under the blue-tinged streetlights. Through her open car window came the scent of conifers. The sky was overcast, clouds scudding over breaks to show a few stars.

When she was halfway there, he texted her the room number.

Usually she felt a little nervous on the way to a new customer, tonight especially so.

Her stomach was in knots.

What was with that? It was a regular date. It'd be fine.

She drove into the parking lot. The wind had a smell of rain in it. She sat a moment in her car, then taking a deep breath, got out.

By the nondescript door, a cold breeze insinuated itself under her skirt. She knocked.

Her stomach tied itself tighter.

He answered. In the doorway, she poured herself upward toward him and kissed him on the lips. He smelled like aftershave and a little of sweat, but not in a nasty way.

"Why don't you get comfortable?" she said. "I'm going to go change."

When she came out of the bathroom in her lavender teddy, he was sitting on one of the double beds, in boxer shorts, hunched over, forearms on his thighs. He still had black polyester socks on, mid-calf length.

He gazed up at her, face dejected. "How do we do this?"

He hadn't done this before. Or he was trying to trap her.

Still she didn't give anything away. "Well, I do my stuff, then I freshen up and you leave the money on the dresser."

"Okay. One-fifty an hour."

"Yes."

They froze a moment, her staring at him, him staring back. She stepped forward, stroked his hair.

"Can we start with a blowjob?" he asked.

"Of course!"

Finally, it had gotten started. He'd been making her nervous.

She knelt between his open knees, reached a gentle hand into the fly of his boxer shorts, stroked the soft penis.

She looked up. "Could you take your boxers off?"

"Sure." He stood, peeled them off, and sat down again.

She put her mouth to his penis, licked it, and drew it into her mouth, hand on his balls.

"Miss," he said gently, "you're under arrest."

It was a punch to the gut.

Goddammit. Fuck it, fuck it, fuck it.

She sat back on her heels, staring at his heavy face, the blue of five-o'-clock-shadow coming up through the skin of his cheeks.

"Show me the fucking badge, if I'm under arrest."

"Okay." He grabbed his boxers off the floor, stood and put them on, then reached over to his dad-jeans and got a second wallet out of his back pocket. Meanwhile she stood up. He flipped it open to his badge.

Sitting down on the corner of the bed, she took it, studying it as she had his driver's license.

She couldn't tell if it was fake. But it wasn't.

As she stared at it, he recited her Miranda rights. She'd read they only did that if they were going to try to get you to self-incriminate.

"You have the right to remain silent... "

Once he was finished, he sat down next to her on the bed, six inches between them, with the same pose as before—hunched over, forearms on his thighs.

"The Desiree Elite agency doesn't belong to you. We know that. We have reason to believe it belongs to Tamera Jenson. Do you know her?"

Joanie heaved an angry sigh and said nothing.

"Here's her picture." He pulled a photo out of the second wallet.

She wished she'd noticed that before. She'd been too interested in the money.

I am so dumb.

Tammy must have been ten years younger in the picture, but it was her.

"I can tell you recognize her."

Joanie said nothing. She looked past the photo at the multicolored bedspread, in faded paisley. The room smelled faintly of chlorine bleach.

"You have a choice here. I can take you in both for prostitution and for promoting prostitution. You probably know promoting prostitution has a fine of up to ten thousand dollars. Or you can get up to five years in prison, or you can get both."

Joanie nodded.

Part of her mind was trying to think her way out of this, but most of it was running around in circles like a rat in a cage.

Shit, shit, shit.

"But we both know it's not your agency. I want to pick up your boss, not you."

Fuck me.

"We have reason to believe she's been coercing people into prostitution."

Joanie gave him a dirty look.

Maybe? She didn't think so.

That just didn't seem like Tammy. She'd checked her out pretty thoroughly before she started.

"Desiree Elite isn't her only business. We have reason to believe she has businesses that promote underage prostitution as well. Sexual slavery."

Maybe?

How well did she know Tammy?

"You'd be making the world a better place if you helped us out."

He hadn't said how, and he hadn't made any promises. Cops did whatever they wanted.

He leaned a little closer. "Come on, honey. You know Tammy would sell you out in a heartbeat."

She said nothing, only tried to kill him with a glare. If she really fully were a witch, she could.

"All right. We'll see how you feel after a night in jail."

Chapter 14

The cell's pale yellow-green walls were the color of baby puke. The space had a metal toilet and two metal shelves for beds, one above the other. Each shelf held a mattress pad covered with green vinyl, with a built-in pillow. The room smelled like piss.

The door clanged shut.

Joanie and the other woman in the cell, a tall busty woman in a red dress and matching fishnet stockings, eyed each other.

She had to be a hooker too.

"I've got the top bunk," her cellmate informed her.

Joanie shrugged and climbed onto the bottom metal shelf, huddled into herself.

She'd see a judge tomorrow to set bail. It could've been worse—it could've been the weekend.

She meditated a while, then curled into a fetal ball and tried to sleep. After an hour or so, she succeeded.

In the red-mud-brick temple, a broad altar lay at the central point, on it a shining copper dish where incense burned. Through the door to the shrine, Joanie saw the white-gypsum statue of the goddess with its huge lapis-blue eyes. Inanna smiled at Joanie, holding forward in her two hands her bountiful breasts, symbol of succor and release.

A wind rose, full of red dust. The temple drew away from Joanie as if it could move on its own. The curtain of dust shimmied and thickened, hiding the statue of the goddess.

A woman's voice whispered, "Oh, my love, my love, my love."

Her heart felt sad to breaking.

She woke up with tears in her eyes, in unfamiliar darkness, on a mattress pad that smelled of bleach and piss. She stared into the darkness a long time before falling back asleep.

"It says he wants me to meet him."

The boy who'd brought the tablet had disappeared, or Puabi would have given him the back of her hand.

At their temple lodging, just past dawn, the sky past the open shutters lay a lambent, saturated blue. A soft wind soughed in the potted palms that dotted the courtyard. They'd planned today to be quiet, to practice a new song and its dance, maybe stroll out into the city or among the gardens. But the tablet had banished all that.

"I don't want you to meet him."

From where she sat on the bed, Iltani looked up at Puabi, her eyes black as water at the bottom of a well. "Please, don't make trouble. I can do it."

"Why are they doing this to us?"

"His caravans are more and more successful. He has given the temple several large gifts. All he wants is some time with me. Why not?"

Because you don't want it, and I don't want it, and it is a violation.

Puabi had given her life to sexual service, and yet it was a promise of the goddess that her servants would not be forced. Iltani shouldn't be pressured like some maidservant cornered by a soldier.

But Kirkaru had given baskets of silver, enough for a new wing of the temple. Someone like Puabi, the most famous dancer in Uruk, had friends who would bring her these tales.

"I can meet him," Iltani repeated.

"I wish you wouldn't."

"I have to."

This was news.

Puabi stroked the long black hair, shining like a polished curtain of basalt, softer to the touch than delicate linen.

"Who has been pressuring you?"

Iltani moved gently under Puabi's stroking hand.

"Oh, Puabi. Who hasn't been?"

Puabi-Ekur hovered over Joanie in the darkness, thinking of the past.

A memory like this was like a burn. If you touched the burned area, you felt a twinge. If you pressed the burned area, you cried.

The woman in the top bunk shifted in her sleep. Puabi-Ekur gave way briefly to paging through her memories, easy for a spirit such as they.

The self that didn't sleep muttered to itself. "Goddammit, Tre, why did you have to attract attention? If you weren't such a nuisance I wouldn't be here."

Puabi-Ekur was inclined to agree.

Humans didn't know how to run these lives. They were made of god-stuff. But they brought themselves such suffering.

If Puabi-Ekur had known how quickly everything would break apart, they would have spent every minute of every day in bed with Iltani. They wouldn't have gotten up to dance, or to eat. They would have wasted away, a wraith of love.

How they'd loved her.

Joanie woke again.

She knew this time there was no going back to sleep. Her internal clock said it was sometime before seven a.m., which was when she usually tore herself out of bed to the soft chiming of her phone alarm.

In the darkness, she heard the breathing of her cellmate, still asleep.

She felt so dumb. She'd known it was coming, and she'd still let it happen. She'd wanted the money too much.

Now she needed to get out of this mess.

A week ago at home, she'd finally found some red-pink cloth, printed out a picture from the internet, made a makeshift matte, set cloth and picture on a windowsill, and given Inanna a glass of beer—knowing from her reading that Sumerians brewed beer.

Now, in her mind's eye, she conjured up that small altar.

Lady Inanna. Please help me.

Words came to her, words that she knew were right: *I dedicate my life to your service. You know I do.*

Please get me out of here, in the best way. Whatever that way is.

In the darkness, for some reason, she caught a wave of scent: the smell of piss.

Oh, Lady, please.

The security guard ushered Joanie into a small, white-painted room dominated by a video screen. The judge quickly found her a court date about a month out, and Joanie got the name of a public defender. Because she was charged with a felony, her bail was set at five thousand dollars.

"Now what?" she asked the security guard who returned her to the common room. Among orange plastic chairs and faux wood tables, women milled about, eying each other. No one fought overtly. Everyone wanted to keep their heads down and get out.

The heavyset woman gave her a long look. "New at this, huh? Call someone to make bail for you." She gestured to a phone in the common room.

"Do I just get one call?"

"Call as many people as you like."

Joanie swallowed hard, staring at the phone.

She wouldn't call her family. She'd rather spend a month in jail than tell them about this.

She wasn't sure where Tammy was. Nowhere handy for bail. Clayton'd do it, but he was broke. Hayley, Danielle, same deal.

But she knew someone who did have money, who knew she was a whore.

Phil.

When Phil picked her up, it was sunny out, still full summer Seattle-style. The detention center was downtown, in a landscape of moving cars, concrete, sun. Reflections off windows caught the dark azure of the sky. She caught a whiff of the ocean coming up from the Sound.

Phil led her to his BMW, parked a few blocks away. She still had her brief tank-dress on, and she'd redone her makeup. She caught the eye of several men as she walked.

Phil noticed, but it seemed to make him no happier. Usually he liked her as arm candy.

"I had to take a half-day off work for this."

That sounded extreme, and entirely his own decision.

"You've got half a day left! I'm sure you can still get a lot done."

He gave her a glance under his eyebrows.

Ah, she was supposed to act grateful.

"I'm sure I can show my appreciation somehow."

He grinned. "That's more like it."

She spent the first half-hour in his shower, washing off the stink of her fear. Clean, wrapped in his fluffy white robe, she let him feed her chardonnay and lead her to the bedroom.

As she stood inside the bedroom door, she dropped the robe. He smiled to see her. "Such a beautiful girl."

Still fully clothed, he threw himself onto the bed, rolling over on his back on the white down comforter, inviting her to climb on top of him. She did, slipping on the persona of Jenny Sex-Kitten. (He now knew her real name. He continued to call her Jenny.) She tongue-kissed him, playing at being so horny she could practically eat him. And she was horny.

She kissed and bit his neck, pulling off his sage-green polo shirt. He had a lovely torso, tan and hard. She stroked and licked her way down it, unbuckling his belt, tugging off his chinos. His hard cock made a tent in his blue-and-white cotton briefs.

She took them off and mouthed his cock, licking and sucking the tip, rubbing him with her hand.

He sat up, pushing himself back against the headboard. "That's right, baby, give me a proper blowjob."

She sat back on her heels and pouted a little. "Not a fuck?"

He shook his head smiling. "You're going to have to work your way back to that." His hand shot out, grabbed her long, dark hair, wrapped his fist in it, tugged down quickly so her head hit the comforter, her face fully planted in its folds. She wondered if he planned to smother her but found a little air.

"You owe me. You'll owe me more before this is done."

"Mmmph?"

"I'm going to get you an excellent lawyer. You'll get probation at most. He's going to charge me top dollar. And you're going to pay me back in sex."

She looked up, her eyes round.

He chuckled a little. "Do you have any choice in the matter?"

Her dark eyes met his pale-blue ones.

She could refuse his deal.

But she really didn't want five years in jail and a ten thousand dollar fine.

She shook her head. "No."

He grinned. "Say no, Daddy."

"No, Daddy."

Part of her seethed in shock and rage. But—her saving grace, her downfall?—part of her filled instantly with helpless lust.

"Suck my cock, little girl."

She crawled up along the bed, knelt in front of him, and

took his cock in her mouth. The cop's flaccid cock leaped to mind. She set the image away.

After a few strokes, his hand fell on top of her head, pushing her to go faster. She almost gagged before she caught herself; then she released her throat and got into the rhythm. She let herself go mindless, a cock-sucking machine. He positioned both hands on her head, shoving her up and down like a piston, till he filled her throat with come.

Hayley, in the meantime, had done the necessary and shut up shop till Tammy's return, sending Tammy as cryptic a note as possible to let her know something was up, something bad.

Wednesday late afternoon, Hayley rendezvoused with Joanie in the coffee shop. It had been a broken-up day, some cloud, some sun, distant thunder occasionally—storm weather, rare for Seattle.

"Triple cappuccino, eh?" she said, as Joanie picked up her order. It was nearly four p.m.

"I need something to finish off this day with." It was the break between quarters, with nearly nothing going on. But once she'd returned from Phil's, the stress of her last couple days had broken to pure exhaustion.

Too bad she couldn't sleep for a week.

"So, tell all." Joanie filled her in, holding nothing back, including her dedication to Inanna and her interaction with Phil.

"Wow. What an asshole."

"Well, he's a professional techbro. But, yeah."

"Are you going to do it? You do have a choice—he can't make you use his lawyer."

"I know that."

The shop door was open, letting in a breeze, which curled around her legs like a cat. Her roommate had fed her cat while she was gone and had asked no questions. Danielle knew what Joanie did for a living and didn't care, though once after a half-dozen gin gimlets she expressed the fear that Joanie would "steal all my dates with your whore ways." But after a tearful reconciliation, nothing more was said.

"I think I will take his offer, though."

"Really? Sexual indentured servitude?"

Joanie shrugged. "I've thought all around it. I want to be sure I get no more than probation. This is the best way to do that."

"But you only make half as much an hour as a lawyer does."

"I guess." Joanie wondered how tips figured in. "I can make a spreadsheet." She met Hayley's blue, blue eyes.

Her eyes were soft, somehow. They conveyed warmth. Unlike Phil's, which made Joanie think of marbles.

"I have to admit, something about it makes me crazy horny. As indentured servitude goes, it has its perks."

"I guess." Hayley scratched a mosquito bite on her leg, a fine long leg with an even golden tan. "You may think this guy's a dom, but he isn't in my book."

"Oh?"

"No. I told you, my dom and I negotiated about what would work for me. Has Phil ever done that for you?" Joanie shook her head. "Maybe he's inexperienced, but he sounds like a narcissist or sociopath to me. Someone who really doesn't care about you, who's using you like a thing, like a toy."

"I guess you could see it like that."

But that was the sexy part.

Hayley frowned a little, leaning forward over the pockmarked, lacquered wooden table. Joanie caught the scent of her perfume, lily of the valley.

"Someone who is looking out for your best interests will ask a bunch of questions. They don't want to trigger you. He sounds... careless at best."

It was Joanie's gig. Did Hayley think she was stupid?

"I only have so many options. So far I've been able to handle it okay."

"Yeah, well, you're venturing into darker territory, right?" Joanie had to nod. "I didn't like when he tied you up and left you. He had no idea if that would trigger you—he never checked. Did it?"

Joanie looked aside.

"It did, didn't it? I have the sense to ask, because I'm your friend."

"Hayley, yes, you're right, but Jesus." Joanie pushed the hair back from her forehead. Between the coffee and the heat of the day, she had sweat along her hairline. "I have to get through this somehow. Don't dismantle my denial."

Hayley gave her the side-eye. "Joanie, I don't care about your denial. I don't want you dead."

After Hayley left, Joanie stayed a while longer, nursing her cappuccino. Returning home felt like diving back into life, something she didn't want to do. She found an issue of *The Stranger,* the local weekly indie rag, and paged through it.

Hayley thought Phil might kill her. She was pretty sure he didn't have it in him.

But part of her wondered. She still didn't claim to understand him.

On her phone, she opened her email program. No emails from prospective indie clients.

She hadn't heard from Clayton for nearly a week. That was unlike him. Usually he texted her every two or three days.

She rarely texted him, less so lately. Her reluctance to do so wasn't something she had looked at hard.

It was still so new, between them. And they weren't in that great a place.

She was afraid. She hated admitting it, but she was.

She hated to get rejected, like everyone else.

Before the bust, he'd sent "Hi" and an emoji heart, and she'd replied in kind. Nothing had come since.

He probably was still smarting from James. Though to her that felt like a century ago.

She hoped the bust didn't freak him out. You never knew, with guys.

Fall quarter, she'd briefly dated a guy who liked the idea that she'd be doing him "like a pro." But when he realized how many of her Friday and Saturday nights were booked, and when it sunk in how many cocks had been in her mouth, her pussy, her ass—even with condoms, even with regular testing—he quailed.

She hoped Clayton wasn't like that.

If it did fall apart, it was her fault. Because of James.

Okay, here goes.

<Hi! It's been a little while. I'd love to see you! <3 >

What a cop-out, what a fail a heart emoji was.

She'd never told him she loved him.

One night, the middle of a night he slept over, she thought she'd heard him whisper it into her hair. It was hard to tell if he was sleep-talking, though.

Did she love him?

A wave of sorrow broke over her, so much she felt tears in her eyes.

She never cried. But she cried over him.

Clayton had gone home for part of the break, but by the time he got Joanie's text he was on a Greyhound returning. The bus was half-empty, and no one sat next to him on the polyester-fuzz seat. The weird, packaged, almost-floral smell of the toilet hung in the air. He had an engineering book—he'd planned to try to get ahead for the coming quarter.

But that was never going to happen.

When he got Joanie's text, he was staring out the window. The bus was on I-5 heading past Fife, a wasteland of electronic signs. The part-shaded windows made the sprawl distant, as if he watched an alien planet from a landing craft.

Humanity deserved to be wiped off the map, if Fife was any indication.

His phone beeped, and he glanced down.

Oh. Joanie.

Almost he wanted to delete the text without reading it.

The conversation about her sleeping with James had put him in a frozen state. He didn't see how to go on. And yet part of him clung to her desperately.

He did care for her. Her beauty, and the beautiful sex—how could he not?

<On my way back from the parents'. Will get in late. How about tomorrow night?>

She texted back nearly instantly: <Sure!>

Chapter 15

On a whim, before stopping by her place, he bought a bouquet from the grocery store. The Gerbera daisies shone as if they had their own interior light, orange, yellow, and hot pink. At the apartment house door, the doorbell long since dead, he leaned on the porch railing and texted her. <Here.>

She came to the door, hand visored against the sun, in a tight-fitting sundress with a smocked top of blue and purple paisley.

He wondered how many men she'd taken that off for.

He was twisting the knife in his own wound. But the pain was dull. He knew she was a whore when he met her. He met her because she was a whore. He didn't care.

But the talk they'd had about James, when she'd so misunderstood his pain, made him wary.

"Oh, thank you for these!" She stood on tiptoes and kissed his cheek. "Let me put them in water."

He followed her into the apartment, through the shadowy living room to the white-curtained kitchen bright with indirect light. At another time, he might have gotten close and found a way to kiss her. Now he stood watching her trim the ends of the flower stems and find a vase.

"They're so pretty," she said.

Now he should kiss her.

He crossed over to her and took her slender body in his arms. Bones like a bird's. Gently he covered her mouth with his.

The magic took hold. She smelled like jasmine. Kissing her was like fire and wine. Her arms around his neck felt like love. Her breasts pressed his chest and he pulled her ass against him with both hands—her sweet ass, the best in the world. She kissed him like she cared.

Fuck James. He didn't care what James thought.

He considered taking her to the bedroom. But with James in his head, he felt shy. They headed for the door.

Outside, it was twilight, the light an even lavender. She walked swinging her purse. They had planned to go to an Indian restaurant.

He took her hand and kissed it.

Fuck James. He didn't care.

They sat in a booth, red hangings spangled with bits of mirror. They shared palak paneer and tikka masala. He bought them both Indian beer; they split a mango lassi. They went beyond his budget, but he decided he didn't care.

They didn't talk much. Finally, he said, "What have you been up to?"

She sighed. "I got busted."

Part of him was scared. Part of him was relieved. "Tell me about it."

She did, at length, but her story tailed off toward the end. "So—are you getting a lawyer?"

She stared down into her lap.

"A friend of mine is hiring a lawyer for me."

A friend, huh?

"You mean a customer, don't you?"

She looked up. The black eyes seemed hot—if black could be a color of fire. "I do. If you have a problem with that, you're probably with the wrong person."

Her anger hit his pain.

"Maybe I am with the wrong person! I don't care what you do with your time, or your body, but I do care that you feel like it has no effect on me!"

Instantly part of him told himself to shut up, not least because they were in a crowded restaurant. A quick glance around showed that no one was paying attention. But they'd pay attention soon enough if he and Joanie kept it up.

He closed his eyes, negotiating with his temper.

Joanie was staring at him. Before she opened her mouth to speak, he said, "Look, I'm sorry. I just—look, we need to talk, but not here. I'm sorry. I don't want to say anything hurtful."

She continued to stare at him, then after a moment took a deep breath. "Okay. Okay, I hear you."

He got the check—too much, oh well—and they walked back to her apartment in silence. The lavender had faded to a deep cobalt blue, and a chilly breeze was up. He put his arm around her, and she snuggled into his armpit.

If only they could never talk. If only they didn't have to think about past or future but could just be in the moment forever.

It sounded very Zen. But life didn't work like that.

In her kitchen, she turned on the stove light—the fluorescent overhead was oppressive—and retrieved a bottle of white wine. He let her pour him a glass without comment.

Liquor would help this conversation, absolutely.

They sat at the kitchen table, which had a checkered blue-and-white cloth. The kitchen smelled faintly of curry. The wine was cold, astringent, and numbing on his tongue. Danielle, the roommate, came in, nodded at them, and retreated to her room.

He drew a finger around the top of his wineglass, making a ringing sound.

"I'm sorry. I didn't mean to be insulting. I'm aware of what you do, and I don't intellectually have a problem with it. I guess I didn't foresee how it might play out."

She nodded, gazing into her wineglass.

A tear rolled down her cheek.

"Oh, Joanie. Oh, honey." He set down his glass, stepped around the table, and hugged her from behind. Her cheek against his shirt, she sobbed. He kissed her hair at random, kissed the salty tears. "What would help?"

She shook her head.

He knelt on the floor and held her while she cried.

After a while she stopped. "I'm going to go wash my face," she said, and disappeared into the bathroom. He heard the water running in the sink—an ordinary sound, a domestic sound.

When she returned, she said nothing but took him by the hand and led him to the bedroom, as if her only form of communication was with her body.

That wasn't so. She was a smart girl. She was going to be an economist. She was a witch as well. He eyed what looked like a small altar.

Following his eyes, she said, "It's for Inanna. She's the goddess of sacred whores, from ancient Sumer."

He nodded, accepting the strangeness, in a state of pause.

She lit a candle on the windowsill. Shadows crossed the walls as she stroked his hair and kissed him deeply, her clever, slender tongue exploring, bringing him the taste of wine. She unbuckled his belt, knelt between his knees, and took his cock in her mouth. It felt instantaneous, how he rose to her attention. Smiling, she sat up, took a mouthful of wine, and knelt again to his cock, enfolding it in her lips —the chill of the wine and the warmth of her tongue merged to something exquisite. He threw his head back, watching the flicker of candlelight and shadow on the ceiling.

A moment before he thought he'd orgasm, she drew away, slipped off her dress and panties, put a condom on him, and mounted him, riding him so his cock angled as it most pleased her. She moaned, and he took her hips in his hands and flipped her so he was on top. He drove into her, again and again, eyes closed, everything red behind his lids. Then first she, and a moment later he, gave a final cry.

He jerked and twitched, spurting into her. It felt like a huge amount of come—cups, quarts, gallons—as the spasms thrilled through him. But a lot of juice came from her.

He rolled off and got rid of the condom. They lay in each other's embrace, sweating, the air cooling them off. They had to move to avoid the wet spot. She gazed across to him, face flushed.

"I think I squirted. I don't often do that."

"Cool! What makes that happen?"

She shook her head. "I don't know. I think you hit me just right."

"What's it like?"

"It's a really strong orgasm. I can really feel the contractions."

"Huh." He wrapped her tightly in his arms. "I'm glad I could make you do that."

Curled together, they fell asleep.

In the middle of the night, he woke. The pillar candle was still burning. Stealthily he lifted himself—she stayed asleep—and leaning over blew it out.

The wax had entirely filled the saucer that held the candle and begun to spill. Idly, with the nail of his thumb, he scraped it off the windowsill.

They hadn't talked.

Maybe that was good. But they couldn't go without talking forever.

This was hard. He didn't know where to go with this

relationship. Joanie should get to do what she wanted to for money.

It wasn't the thought of guys in general that bothered him. It was when specific ones came up—when James came up—that it got dicey.

Well, they couldn't talk now.

He lay back down beside her, taking her in his arms. In moments, he was asleep.

Chapter 16

The legal office was in one of the older buildings downtown, its two-story lobby full of white-painted plaster columns and exposed brick. A phalanx of mixed-color chrysanthemums stood in vases along the windowsill.

The lawyer came out smiling and shook her hand. Joanie scoped him in a glance: high-polished brogues, three-piece suit, and aviator glasses. He ushered her into his office, with wall-to-ceiling windows overlooking the street, grey except for the red flash of the streetlight. The sky was overcast, and a light tracing of rain dotted the window.

He sat her in a well-padded rolling chair facing his desk, and propped himself on the desk corner.

"I've been looking at your case. Based on what we know, I'm pretty sure we can get you down to misdemeanor prostitution and two years' probation. You'd have to plead nolo contendere."

"Okay."

"We should be able to get your record cleared after the two years, assuming you don't violate probation."

"Sure."

It sounded like the best she could do. She'd known what she was doing was illegal. Though it shouldn't be.

"What do you need from me otherwise?" she asked.

"Show up at the court date in September. It should be cut-and-dried. I gather you don't want to tell the police anything about the agency owner...?"

She shook her head.

He leaned forward. "Anything you say here is covered by attorney-client privilege, so you can tell me. I'd like to know a little bit about what was going on. Why were you running the phones that night?"

I guess I can tell him.

"Tammy was out of town. In fact, she still is."

"What did the cop tell you when he picked you up?" Joanie filled him in. "As he was hinting, the cops think that Tammy's associated with a ring that traffics underage girls. Do you know anything about that?"

Joanie shook her head. "That really doesn't seem like Tammy. She thinks of herself as empowering women to make money. She's not interested in sex trafficking. She's said so."

She caught his eyes. "You do realize, a lot of prostitution isn't human trafficking, right? I went into this with my eyes open. I don't think it should be illegal."

The lawyer nodded affably. "I understand. Are there any questions you have for me?"

Joanie shook her head.

Then she was done, at loose ends in downtown Seattle in the middle of the day. Long shadows of skyscrapers crossed the wide street. In the other direction, the Space Needle stood out against mottled grey clouds.

If she didn't have the agency anymore, she needed to think about how to make money. She could get a day job.

Or she could check in on the Inanna temples.

She wondered how safe that was.

In the days and weeks following the reappearance of Kirkaru's gifts, Puabi saw less and less of Iltani.

She was always there for the big productions, the dances before the temple hierarchy and for the nobles and rulers. She was in their bed most nights—and then fewer and fewer. She had friends among the temple musicians, many places she could sleep—and yet Puabi wondered if she had another lover. But Iltani acted as loving as ever and denied any other connection.

The temple presented another dance, in the great court-yard, torches illuminating the coda as Puabi sunk to the ground, a woman mourning the loss of her lover. The last of the bells on her girdle fell silent with the last pluck of Iltani's harp.

The nobles politely clapped and finger-snapped their appreciation. Puabi rose and took Iltani's hand, and the two made obeisance to show their gratitude.

Then out of the crowd, his turban studded with lapis

lazuli and gold, came Kirkaru. "My dear Lady Puabi! As always, a brilliant performance." But his black eyes narrowed above his smile.

He moved toward Iltani. "My dear Lady Iltani. Your things are packed?" Iltani said nothing. "You come with me tonight."

The words turned Puabi into a pillar of stone.

"What?!" She spun to face Iltani.

Iltani stepped forward, took Puabi's hands in her own. "There was no good way to tell you. I tried—but—"

"What's going on?!" Puabi looked from her to Kirkaru and back, then dropped Iltani's hands as if they burned her.

Kirkaru stepped up. "The Lady Iltani is coming to live at my compound. She will no longer be your harpist, but rather grace my dwelling as my chief concubine and musician."

"She what?!"

Iltani stepped up, between the two. "Puabi. Kiss me as if you might never kiss me again."

Puabi heard the death-knell in her tone and took Iltani in her arms.

"I don't know how long this will be," Iltani whispered. "Perhaps I can get away. But, as you foresaw, the temple hierarchy sold me."

Puabi was about to say something furious, but Iltani put two fingers over her lips.

"We cannot fix this now. We may never be able to. So kiss me, and tell me you love me. I love you with all my heart, and I will never love another."

Puabi held Iltani in the shelter of her arms and kissed

her as if they were alone: her forehead, her cheeks, her earlobes, her neck, and finally her lips, probing her lover's mouth with her tongue. Iltani kissed back with hunger.

Kirkaru cleared his throat, and Iltani stepped away.

"Goodbye, Puabi."

"Goodbye." Puabi saw out of the corner of her eye a number of former audience members watching. This scene had to be worth double the price of the performance.

Holding her head high, she ignored these people, though she couldn't stop tears falling.

Kirkaru took Iltani by the wrist and led her away.

Puabi never saw her again.

Chapter 17

$\mathcal{M}$eet me at the Denny's near the office," Tammy told Joanie over the phone.

Joanie got there at eleven-thirty at night. Tammy hours. She beat Tammy to Denny's—her boss usually ran late, except when meeting a client. Grabbing a faux-wooden table, she ordered decaf coffee and a plate of fries.

The last time she'd been there was with Tom the cop.

Mixed with the thought of jail, the memory made her want to take a shower.

Outside the window, a line of cars was parked. It had rained, which gave luster to the golden reflection of restaurant lights on the car windows.

The door opened, and Tammy walked in, her black hair up in a bun. She wore new sunglasses with gold rims—not feeling like dealing with the hoi polloi, apparently.

Joanie waved her over and stood to hug her, but Tammy's embrace was brief.

"Let me get something to eat before we talk," she said. "I'm starving." Sitting, Joanie pushed the plate of fries over, and Tammy started work on it.

Joanie told her tale, broken up by Tammy ordering a cheeseburger. "The bust was entirely my fault, and I take full responsibility."

"You should," Tammy said. She habitually came down hard on the girls as part of their "learning the ropes." Then she shrugged. "Really, though, this has been coming a long time."

A rush of fear swept through Joanie. What if the stories about human trafficking had been true?

Tammy eyed her. "If you think I'm into human trafficking, no. You should know me better than that. But there are people in this city who do something like that. Closer to you than you think. They're no friends of mine—in fact, I'm pretty sure they tipped off the cops."

"Tipped off the cops?"

"Your cop Tom told you they were on the tail of a human trafficking ring. So did your lawyer." Joanie nodded. "Sometimes cops nail things by their own work, but pretty often it's a tip-off from some enemy."

"Why don't you tip them off right back, if you know what's going on? It sounds like nasty stuff."

"It is nasty stuff, done by nasty people. If they found out I led the cops to them—well, I don't know if they'd kill me, but they might. And they would find out I told the cops. I figure let the police do their own work. I don't have to take the fall."

She popped the last bite of her cheeseburger into her mouth. "I've got some money saved. I'm outta here."

"Really? Okay." Joanie twirled a french fry in a puddle of ketchup, trying to take it in.

Her livelihood, the whole agency, blown up in a few minutes. Not even a blowjob's worth of time.

Tammy watched her. "Don't take it hard. You did me a favor. It's just luck the cops called when you were there. If they'd caught me, I'd've been in jail a while. Or I'd have to rat on some people who, like I say, would show their lack of appreciation. This is easier."

"Tell me about these human trafficking people. At the very least, I want to avoid them."

Tammy took a sip of her water. "I should've gotten a Coke. The human traffickers? If you want to call it that. Yeah, you should avoid them. They—whoops, I'm getting a phone call." She glanced at the number. "I need to take this outside."

It had to be a client. "Okay, I'll wait."

As she'd expected, the call took several minutes.

Tammy was making a last date. Because Tammy would always take the money.

I'll miss her, the git.

Tammy came back in looking flustered. "It's my regular, Sam. He's in a real hurry. I gotta go."

"But you were going to tell me about the human traffickers!"

"We'll get another chance. Gimme a hug." Joanie stood up and hugged her. Tammy hugged back, hard, then stood away from Joanie a little, her hands on Joanie's shoulders.

"I'll miss you, girlie. You've got a real head on your shoulders. You can make a go of this if you want—just listen to your intuition about cops! Jesus! Anyway." She put a twenty dollar bill on the table to cover dinner, gave Joanie another hug, and left.

Joanie stared at the door, glass in a metal frame, slowly closing.

She wondered if she'd ever see her again.

Her next lazy morning, Joanie didn't go to the coffee shop. She'd made her own coffee, in a blue china cup, sat sipping it in the sunlight that fell across her kitchen and pooled on her blue-and-white checkered tablecloth. She had to save money.

She could contact Sasha. But she'd rather talk to Cleo. They were between school quarters. Maybe she could actually see her.

Gathering her courage, she wrote: <Hey, what's up? You around? I'd love to see you.>

Cleo replied right away. <I was just thinking about you! What does your afternoon look like?>

When Cleo invited her to her house, Joanie knew what would happen.

This so works for me.

At the address she found a hippie house, the garage facing the street painted bright medium blue with a moon, sun, and stars in yellow. Prayer flags festooned the small yard, connected between branches of two massive cedar trees. She walked up the concrete steps and brought her hand up to knock at the flimsy screen door, then saw Cleo beyond, sitting at a table. She pushed through, and then she was in Cleo's arms.

"You want to come upstairs?"

Joanie nodded.

In Cleo's bedroom, the window was open a margin of an inch. The scent of mowed grass floated through. The room was tiny, just a bed, a dresser, and an alcove where dresses and skirts hung. She had an Indian sari tented above her bed, orange, yellow, and magenta with shining gold thread.

When Joanie sat on the bed, the comforter released a scent of floral incense, maybe rose. It felt like a century since they'd been together.

Cleo kissed her. Her lips were soft, like ripe fruit, and tasted faintly sweet, like honey—lip balm? honey from her tea? Joanie surrendered, as she rarely surrendered, and Cleo filled her mouth with a questing tongue, one hand cupping and squeezing Joanie's breast.

"You're so pretty. You're like sweetness itself. You're like candy."

Joanie drew away, her face quizzical. "The last time I saw you, you only wanted to talk."

"Sasha wanted me to vet you. It wasn't a date."

"Is this a date?"

Cleo shrugged. "Depends on what you mean by a date."

She pushed Joanie back onto her pillows—half a dozen, Indian patterns in orange, yellow, magenta, with gilt thread and mirrors. Against Joanie's sundress-exposed bare shoulders, the pillows were scratchy. Cleo climbed on top of her and pumped her pelvis against Joanie's, rocking her gently.

"I'm fine with dates that are just sex," Joanie said.

Cleo gave a Cheshire-cat grin and tugged her sundress over her head. Underneath she wore nothing. Her middle-brown skin had undertones of yellow ochre, tonal with Joanie's lighter olives, different versions of the same palette.

In Joanie's head, there were no words, just a rushing like the sea.

She pulled off her clothes. The slender belly, the protuberant navel—Joanie stroked these, gently, not slowly, on the way downward. Cleo's shaved pubis was completely smooth. Had she shaved for her?

She cupped Cleo's pussy with her hand and slicked her fingertips in Cleo's juices. Cleo closed her eyes. Joanie quested with her fingers.

Here? Where? What do you desire?

She slid out from under Cleo and sat up, gently pushing Cleo back onto the pillows, and slipped two fingers inside the warm, wet cave of Cleo's pussy. Heaven.

She flipped her hand to curl her fingertips against where she hoped Cleo's G-spot was, and put her mouth to Cleo's clit. Cleo bucked and heaved, and Joanie put her free hand firmly on Cleo's hip to hold her down.

She got into the rhythm, moving her mouth and hand together. "Fuck, fuck, fuck, omigod, omigod, omigod," Cleo said, writhing against Joanie's hold. Joanie could feel the energy building, like a trapped animal running around a cage, running, rising—

"Oh my god!" Cleo shouted. She cried out and fell

back among the pillows. Joanie felt her pussy contracting around her hand, and the warm wash of energy pouring out of her. And she felt a caress from her goddess. On top of her dresser—Joanie had been seeing but not seeing it—was an altar with a statue of Inanna.

Cleo lay motionless, eyes closed, a few moments, then opened her eyes. "I'm seeing stars, I swear."

"For real?"

Cleo grinned. "No, not quite, but that was... intense. I'd sit up, but I don't know if I can." She flapped her hand, beckoning Joanie. "Come over here."

Joanie crawled into Cleo's armpit.

It was like coming home.

After a minute or two, Cleo rallied. "So what can I do for you? What do you like, lady?"

"Oh, more or less the same thing."

"How would you feel about... " Cleo reached across the bed to the dresser, and from the bottom drawer produced a glass dildo, with red and orange marbling on a white base. She wiggled it in her hand invitingly. "Don't worry—it's clean!"

It looked like some species of candy cane. Cleo gazed at it, lips pursed thoughtfully. "I have to say, it's one of my favorite things."

"I'll give it a try."

Joanie lay back, closing her eyes. Cleo's hands touched her, soft fingertips crossing her nipples; then Cleo's mouth was there, biting.

"You can bite harder." Cleo did.

Joanie wriggled. Cleo stroked her with the lightest of touches, sometimes just moving the air above her skin.

"Soft," she whispered. "You're so soft."

Down the landing strip to her labia, between her waiting lips. "So wet." As she stroked her clit, Cleo worked the dildo into her cunt. "Like it?"

"Yes. Oh, yes."

"Good." Carefully, watching her face, Cleo continued. Everything she did was good.

The cool of the glass inside Joanie warmed. The head was shaped perfectly, like the head of a cock, but solid and hard. Cleo got the angle so it got her G-spot, still rubbing Joanie's clit.

Joanie's gaze flickered, eyes open then shut. The tent of sari above her glittered as it moved in a hint of air from the window. The scent of mown grass mixed with a scent of incense, currents separate in the air.

Like a garden. Paradise as a garden.

Then all she had room for was sensation. She cried out, losing herself in a burst of orgasm that shook her body. Keeping her hands in place, still moving gently, Cleo watched her face.

After a time, Cleo lay down beside her.

They fell asleep.

A half-hour later, Joanie woke to Cleo rolling over beside her.

She came to slowly. The sun had climbed onto the bed, making the mirrors on the pillows flash.

"Did you have lunch?" Cleo asked. "Do you want lunch? I made some hummus yesterday. I'm really proud of myself! But it's pretty garlicky."

"I don't mind."

In the bottle-green kitchen, roommates wandering in and out, they shared hummus and vegetables and talked. Joanie filled Cleo in on her brush with the law.

"Are the Inanna shrines still a thing? I haven't seen any emails recently."

"I thought you weren't interested in the Inanna shrines anymore."

"Who told you that? I am. Particularly now."

Cleo raised an eyebrow. "If I were you I'd lie low right now."

"Sure. I guess. But I don't have any income. I have some savings, not a lot."

Cleo shrugged. "Well, it's no harm to us, I think." She studied Joanie's face, and pursed her lips. "I'll make sure you're back on the mailing list, if you like."

"That would be great. Now, tell me a little more about your community." She'd read a bit about intentional community and was curious.

Cleo grinned. "Sure, I can talk all day. But you should see it in action. We have a community open house once a month—why don't you come to that? Our next one is in September."

Chapter 18

***

*C*layton lay back on his bunk, letting the engineering book slide from his fingers, and returned to his usual reverie.

He should text her.

She was probably busy.

If he saw her again, they'd have to figure out what they were doing. He should figure out what he wanted first.

James appeared in the doorway, sunlight framing him, gilding his hair. "You look like a man who needs a beer."

Clayton heaved himself off his bunk. "You're on."

As they strolled down the U District's main drag, James said casually, "I can't stay too late. I have a Tinder hookup at ten."

In as level a voice as he could muster, Clayton said, "At her house? Or are you having her come to the dorm?"

James would do anything. They'd established that.

"Fuck off, Clayton," James said without any heat. "As if I'd have a Tinder date over to that rathole."

"Have you gotten your final grades back?"

"I did. All As except one B. But I passed everything."

He didn't sound very excited, considering the hard work it had taken on both their parts.

In a lisping little girl's voice, Clayton said, "And that's why I'm buying Clayton as many beers as he wants tonight."

"Okay, dude, whatever."

Petulant, were we? As long as Clayton got the beer.

Puabi-Ekur watched Clayton, back in his bunk. When Puabi-Ekur cared to, they could read Clayton's mind, and they did so now.

His thoughts still revolved around Joanie. He was just a lot more drunk.

Puabi-Ekur dropped back, plane by plane, to where they could see Clayton's and Joanie's lives as threads, now caught on each other.

They could still be disentangled without much damage to either.

Puabi-Ekur had seen a potential of deep connection. But they hadn't created it yet. They were only half-connected, betwixt and between.

Surprising. Maybe Puabi-Ekur needed more perspective.

They put another layer of distance between themselves

and the tangled life-threads. A few hundred universes should do the trick.

From that vantage point, the cause was obvious, a scattering of dust left by a billowing grey wind.

The djinn. They should have known.

Anger blew up inside Puabi-Ekur, and just as quickly, Puabi-Ekur put it away.

The djinn were just doing their job. And look—new patterns arose.

Almost Puabi-Ekur was entranced by the new beauty the universe wove—each time the djinn blasted some carefully contrived pattern, the universal spirit created something new.

Often the universe created something traveling spirits would never have considered. They were just meddlers.

Though maybe Puabi-Ekur should meddle more.

A twinge caught them, an echo of a lifetime long ago.

There had been times when they should have acted and did not.

"No message, then, from Lady Iltani."

"None, my lady."

"Very well." Puabi gifted the child with a bit of silver. He ran away.

She sat in the courtyard at the end of the heat of the day. Shadows fell across her chair; her youngest student fanned her with a palm-leaf fan. When Puabi waved a hand, the student gave her a cup of well-water flavored with mint.

Whenever anyone went to a particular river crossing where a set of wide fields spread, irrigated by canals, there was a standing order to stop in and greet the Lady Iltani. Sometimes Puabi sent songs or new instruments. Occasionally she got a reply.

Many of my messages were intercepted, she guessed. But some weren't.

Over time, her pain had dulled. She found a new harpist; she took students of the dance. Time and again, she had a chance to take a trip to that river crossing, and she didn't. She didn't want to give Kirkaru the satisfaction. Plus he might not let her see Iltani.

The chief scribe stepped out of the shadow of the temple.

"I can tell you why you got no message, Lady Puabi." His bald head and long nose somehow seemed different, as if something hung on his flesh, making him look older. Lack of sleep?

He knelt beside her chair, and then she knew something was wrong. "What is it?"

"The Lady Iltani is dead. She fell down a well."

Puabi leapt to standing, glaring down at him.

"No one falls down a well! You mean she threw herself down it!"

Slowly he stood, wincing—his joints were arthritic. She felt a flare of empathy, which she snuffed out.

"It gives me no joy to tell you this."

"You killed her! You know that!"

He shook his head. "Not me alone."

They stared at each other.

Puabi could have visited her. Perhaps over time she could have gotten her back.

She'd let her pride stop her.

By necessity, Joanie had given Phil her cell number. She'd been a little afraid he'd bother her, but he'd just texted her once. <Can you come by on Thursday?>

<Sure! 7 p.m.?>

<OK>

On Thursday, she'd half thought he'd be there waiting for her, but it was the same as ever. Letting herself in with the hidden key, she passed into the kitchen, running her fingers over the grey-flecked granite counter.

"Phil? You here?" No answer.

In the bathroom, she changed into a slip, chocolate satin with olive-green lace trim and ribbons. She trimmed a hangnail and reapplied her mascara, staring at the mirror.

Stepping back a moment, she took a more general view. Long dark hair, blunt-cut, shiny, slim olive-skinned body. She liked how the ribbon harmonized with her skin.

Maybe the circles under her eyes were darker. Stress. School was about to start again—that wouldn't help.

Still, the package worked. She looked good. She blew a kiss at her reflection.

She helped herself to Laphroaig, no more than usual. She didn't want to become an alcoholic, the family curse.

On the California king, Phil had the comforter folded back to show pewter-colored sheets. She lay down on them, wriggling a little. High-thread-count Egyptian cotton—it was like silk, but better, not as rough.

She didn't love Phil, but she loved his things. Was that wrong? At least she didn't love beautiful things more than people. Wasn't everyone attracted to beauty?

She heard the door open, and let herself sink into Jenny Sex-Kitten mode, posing seductively on the bed.

He came in, glanced at her, and smiled. "There's my girl."

He pulled his shirt over his head, displaying his impeccable abs, slid off his chinos and briefs. His hard-on popped to attention.

"Do you want me to suck your cock, Daddy?"

"Uh-huh." He stepped to the edge of the bed.

She slid forward, kneeling obediently put her mouth on his cock, pumping the shaft with her hand, settling into the rhythm. "Deep-throat it, baby." She complied, releasing her throat, taking his cock in till she could almost touch his pubic area with her lips, continuing to suck. He threw his head back.

Did he want her to just suck him off?

She unmouthed him for a moment. "Daddy—do you want to fuck me?"

Glazed, dreamy eyes met hers. "Yes, I do," he said after a moment.

He reached forward, grabbed her slip, and yanked forward—she heard a seam rip.

Fuck.

There went seventy-five dollars. Oh well.

Then it came off, over her head.

She reached to the bedside table and grabbed a condom. At least he was a stickler for these. Phil was germophobic and afraid of sexually transmitted infections.

She batted her eyes at him, radiating little girl. "May I put it on you, Daddy?" He nodded. She did.

Grabbing her elbows, he tipped her backward and mounted her, sliding himself into her in one motion.

There. Yeah.

"You like that, don't you? Uh-huh. Pretty baby. Tell me what you're thinking about."

That was new, him wanting her to talk.

"Daddy's—unh—huge, hard—cock inside me."

"Good girl. Now I want you to come for me."

Joanie focused on the cock inside her, moving so it hit her just right, riding it from below.

She'd make it happen.

She missed Clayton's cock.

There, there, there... inevitability took over, and the orgasm spilled out across her body. She gave way to the rush of feeling. A few moments later, Phil came. She could tell from a characteristic moan and a wriggle he gave, a thrill through his body. He let himself down on top of her and lay there, not moving, pushing her into the mattress.

Though it was outside her range of vision, she could tell from his movements he was checking his phone.

He lay on top of her perhaps five minutes. She got used to it, though her breathing was constricted.

If this was what he liked, it was easy enough.

After a time, he got up. "Dinner?"

"Sure." She sat up, stretching.

Now or never.

"I thought we could talk about compensation."

He was putting on his polo shirt. He turned around, frowning.

"Compensation?"

"It's my understanding that Johnson's office charges about three hundred an hour, on average. I'm a hundred-fifty an hour before tip. So it's about two of his hours for every one of mine. Has he billed you yet?"

Phil shook his head. His frown got deeper.

She was going to need to ask the lawyer to send her copies of the bills. Or keep a running estimate.

"So—this deal—I wasn't planning on doing this indefinitely."

"Maybe you should."

She started mapping exit routes out of the apartment. "Let's talk about it over dinner."

Out, among people, where she could run away if she needed to.

He stared at her another moment, his eyes like blue marbles.

"Okay."

She had a Manhattan, which took the edge of her tension. That, the candle flames, the wood paneling, the highlights off glasses and mirrors, and a dark-red velvet curtain by the bar combined themselves into sensual pleasure.

Phil took another bite of his steak. "I'm sorry," he said, "I didn't mean that like it sounded."

I don't believe you.

"Mmm?" she said, politely.

"What I meant was, I think you should move in with me. Or, even better, have your own apartment in the same building."

She grimaced, cutting into her steak. "Can you afford that?"

"Yes, I can. Pretty easily, at this point."

Really? She wondered how he did it. She let him sit a moment before answering.

"Thanks for the offer, Phil. I really appreciate it."

A flat gaze at her. "In other words, no."

"It would be great to have my own apartment. Though it's further from school, as far as it goes—"

"It could be someplace closer to campus. I don't care about that."

"Are you saying you want me to be your sugar baby?"

"I'm thinking about that, yeah."

If he could afford that... hmm. Interesting.

But she just didn't know him that well. She didn't know things she'd like to know about him, if she took that step. And Hayley had made a good point about his dom approach. Though she thought she could handle him—she had so far.

Like Hayley said, she could ask for what she wanted.

He moved a little closer around the curve of the half-circle booth. "We could negotiate the details. Anything you like. But all this has me thinking."

He put his hand over hers, hard, pressing it against the tablecloth.

More quietly, he said, "I really like where things have been going, baby. I'd pay a lot to make you all mine."

His hand moved to clamp her wrist, painfully. His other hand reached under the table for her crotch, under her panties. He pressed his fingers to her wet vulva, then curved them, shoving two fingers inside her.

"All mine," he whispered again.

The tablecloth hid everything. At least she thought it did.

In her mind, she saw the dwindling level of her bank account.

She didn't trust him fully, but then who did she trust? Danielle? She wished Danielle would pay rent on time just once. It would mean a lot not to have to worry about money.

She smiled, batting her eyes at him, in full-on sex kitten mode.

"Maybe."

The quarter had started, and suddenly the coffee shop was full of laptops. Joanie's was open to her econ workbook, but she glanced up and waved when Sasha arrived.

Moving through sunlight into shade, Sasha tinkled gently as she walked. She looked the complete high priestess in a full, tiered red-pink skirt, tie-dyed rainbow wrap shirt, three necklaces, and chandelier earrings.

Joanie sensed around her what she often sensed now

around Phil, a grey mist—like at the edges of the Inanna temples, a fog. It made her uneasy.

Sasha set down a cup of herbal tea, folded her skirt under her, and sat.

"I felt like this was a better conversation to have in person than in email, you know?"

Since what they were talking about was technically illegal. Joanie nodded.

"I'll come right to the point. I don't think the Inanna temples are a good place for you right now."

Fear tightened Joanie's belly. "Yes? Why not?"

"I heard about your little... mishap." From Cleo? She didn't believe it. "I knew you were working for Desiree Elite." Had Cleo even known that? It wasn't Cleo who told. "It's not at all personal. But I have to be careful."

Joanie held her breath and counted to ten, staring into her cappuccino cup.

"Do you think the police are tailing me or something?"
You're crazy, lady.

"I think it's a lot more complicated than that. I think Tammy was in over her head, and there are things going on you don't know about. I don't want a connection between Desiree Elite and what I'm doing."

"You mean the human trafficking that the cops are investigating?" A membrane went down over Sasha's eyes, and Joanie knew she had hit a nerve. "I know all about that."

"Do you." Sasha's tone was flat.

On the astral, the fog was as thick as a wall.

Joanie shouldn't have said that.

"Well, I don't know everything."

Sasha began to say something, paused, and sighed. "I like you a lot, personally." She flicked her gaze down Joanie's form, pausing at her lips and tits.

Sasha wanted to have sex with her.

"Let's just let this blow over, and I'd be very happy to have you back. Just not right now."

Sasha wanted her. She could work with that.

"Okay."

Sasha rose and exited, earrings jingling, leaving her tea. Joanie imagined a snake's tail slithering after her.

Until this blew over, as Sasha put it, Joanie had next to no money coming in.

Chapter 19

*P*inning both Joanie's hands on the bed above her head with one hand, with the other Phil repositioned her hips, pulling them up and back. Fingering her pussy, plunging his fingers into her juices, from behind he re-entered her, shoving into her again and again and again.

Joanie could feel her inner walls chafing. Dammit! She didn't want to get sore.

It was a job.

"My little girl, my sweet little bitch."

"Oh, Daddy. Omigod! "

"Tell me to hurt you, baby."

"Oh—oh—hurt me, Daddy!"

He slapped her ass hard, so it stung, then shoved into her one more time with a yelp and relaxed. He must have come.

His body collapsed, her under it. He was done.

Thank everything holy.

But she felt unholy. She hadn't talked to Inanna lately.

Around her, thick as fog, on the astral she saw the grey mist she associated with Phil. As he'd often done recently, he lay on top of her several minutes, so she could barely move and had to find room to breathe. This time he didn't look at his phone.

"You are such a sweet piece of ass, baby. Fucking you is one of my best things. I want to own you."

Own her?

"Sure, Daddy. I love that you want that."

"I'll get you a nice apartment by the college. I'll give you an allowance. I'll pay what you need me to pay. It's cheap at the price to have your hot little cunt all mine."

"Mmm, Daddy. That sounds good!" She wriggled a little underneath him, to show appreciation.

It was starting to sound good. Especially with the Inanna temples not an option. She'd had a few former customers contact her, but hardly enough to support her. In the past, she'd made her living through the agency.

She was never going to be all his, but they could negotiate that.

She had four classes that quarter, none of them easy. She made that her excuse a couple of times, putting Clayton off.

But she had to face him sometime.

A sunny day in early September, it didn't feel like fall yet. She perched at the base of a Douglas fir by the swing set in the park and got her laptop out of her bag, aiming to do some classwork on microeconomics.

But the sun's angle made seeing the screen hard. After shifting a couple of times she let herself close her eyes and bask in the sunlight.

She didn't want to see him.

She still liked him. It was just hard.

Relationships—wasn't it easier to go it alone? She had an image of herself as a relationship buccaneer, in a soiled poet's shirt and tricorn hat. But that was just a romantic face on her fears.

She saw him before he saw her, crossing the wide swell of low grassy hill, and her heart lit up. The shaggy dark hair, the quietly fine form. Not super-ripped, like James, a little soft-edged, but nice, with muscular shoulders and arms. Pale skin. He'd stayed in all summer doing homework.

She didn't want to break up with him.

She wished she hadn't done James that one time. She hadn't seen what would come of it.

She wouldn't care if Clayton fucked Hayley. But Hayley wouldn't do it to compete with her.

She waved, conscious of the image she projected, a pretty girl in a flowered sundress. She had indulged herself, bringing her floppy-brimmed straw hat, bordered with dark-rose grosgrain ribbon. It lay on the grass by her thong-sandaled feet.

He saw her across the park, before she saw him, and looked away.

Too pretty. So pretty it hurt.

He had thought a long time about what she meant to him, and what being with her meant.

He didn't have to be with her. He liked her a lot. He was a little bit in love with her. She was pretty, and smart. His parents would like her, if they never found out what she did for money.

But he had to get his head around it. She was a whore. She'd gotten picked up by the police for prostitution.

She'd fucked James.

She saw him now, so he couldn't run away.

He came forward. It was a gorgeous day, the air perfect, sunny but the shade cool, a little bit of breeze. It wasn't a day to break up with someone.

She gazed up at him, shading her eyes. Something about the curve of her arm drew him in, the shadow along the muscle and the smooth pale-olive skin. He threw himself down on the grass beside her. He smelled jasmine, with a musky bit of sweat.

He was still hers.

She stroked his shoulder and hair, then leaning down kissed him.

If only they could never talk.

They played Frisbee for a while—she'd brought the Frisbee—then made their way to her apartment. She led him by the hand to the bedroom and flicked on the fan. She sat on the edge of the bed.

He sat beside her, kissed her shoulder blades and neck,

and slid the straps of her sundress off. The long dark hair fell over her shoulders like a waterfall. He put his hands on her breasts, cupping them and squeezing them. Her rose-tinged brown nipples looked like exotic candy. She moaned as he licked and bit her. He pushed her back onto the bed, fingering her wet labia.

Pushing back her skirt, he kissed his way down her pubis and put his tongue on her clit. She tangled her hands in his hair. On either side of his head, her thighs squeezed and pressed. He shook his head a little to gain himself room.

"Yes," she said. "Yes, oh yes..."

Then she only moaned and cooed. He spread her legs a little with his hands. She tried to pull him upward, tugging at his hair. But he wanted to make her come.

He shook his head and continued, licking the slick flesh, slightly bitter, scented with musk. She bucked and he stayed with her, keeping up the steady, gentle licking. She cried out, and her whole body shook. Reaching for his hand, she grabbed it.

He could feel the energy pouring out of her, wave after wave of pure, raw life.

"So good. Come up here and fuck me."

Standing, he shucked his clothes, climbed between her legs, and slid on a condom. He fingered her pussy, sloppy wet. With her help, he shoved himself in.

She locked her ankles at the small of his back as he rode her, then put her legs over his shoulders. He drove into her, seeking that receding goal, the ever-better feeling, a high, brightly lit place. Pictures flashed before his eyes: a forest glade, a mud-brick temple under a flat blue sky.

Then he came, and everything went white for a moment as he pumped himself out. He lay down on her, breathless, as gently as he could. She stroked his sweaty hair.

After a few moments, he sat up. She shook her head and drew him down, his head on her shoulder. The fan blew wind over both of them, and slowly his sweat dried.

"So what do you want from this?" she asked. "It's up to you."

He started to speak, and stopped himself.

What did he want?

"It's hard for me," he said. "The James thing."

"I didn't realize how much that would hurt you. I'm really sorry."

"I know. Let's—" He sat up, looked into her face. Indirect light made her skin glow like gold. "I love you."

Almost he wished he didn't, but he did.

She stroked his face. "I love you too."

"Let's see how it goes. I'm not totally sure I can hack this, but I'm willing to try."

She pushed a hank of hair back from his forehead.

"That's about all anyone can say."

*S*he sat three rows back, on a long wooden bench shaped like a pew. The pale blue-green fluorescent lighting made everyone look washed-out.

It was interesting what people wore to court.

Clean hoodies and jeans, or polo shirts and chinos, was the uniform for half the people on the benches. A few people dressed professionally, as she did—she wore a charcoal-pinstriped pencil skirt and a white dress blouse. She got that it was classist, but today she wanted to look more like the lawyers than the hoodie kids.

Breezing in, her lawyer found a seat next to her just before the judge entered. "You doing okay?"

Joanie nodded.

"This should be a cakewalk. This judge is lenient with first offenders. You'll do fine."

Joanie swallowed hard.

The prosecution had agreed to the plea bargain,

knocking her felony promotion of prostitution charge down to misdemeanor prostitution. The clerk called her case. "City of Seattle v. MacEwan."

She stepped forward with her lawyer to stand by the judge's lectern. The judge read out the charge, and her lawyer put forward her plea of nolo contendere.

The judge glanced over her glasses at Joanie. "You understand this means you're not contesting this charge?"

Joanie nodded. The judge let her gaze rest on Joanie another moment, then moved it back to her lawyer. He made his argument that she get a reduced sentence. "Your honor, my client is a college student in economics, with a bright future ahead of her."

"Mmm-hmm," said the judge. "Young lady, I trust you've learned your lesson through these proceedings."

"Yes, Your Honor, I have." Her voice shook.

"I'm going to waive the fines and give you two years probation. I don't want to see you in this courtroom again."

"Yes, Ma'am."

"Pay court costs on the way out."

As they left the courtroom, Phil sauntered up the long marble-floored hallway. "Did I miss the action?"

"It worked like we thought it would. Two years' probation."

"Awesome!" Phil was beaming. He turned to Joanie. "Let's pay up, and I'll take you out to lunch!"

"Great," the lawyer said. "I'll leave you two here." He gave Phil a manly half-hug then ran down the courthouse steps.

Phil covered court costs, a few hundred dollars. "Where do you want to go for lunch?" he asked.

"I don't care." She hadn't expected him to show up.

"There's an English pub down the street, if you like bangers and mash and shepherd's pie." He leaned close to her and said conspiratorially. "Then you can come over and play."

She put on a sparkling smile. "I'd love that, Daddy."

The condo was air-conditioned against the late-summer heat. He'd kept the white down comforter, folded to show pewter-colored sheets.

"Take your clothes off, baby."

She peeled out of everything, the pool of black hose falling to her feet, and folded things neatly—he liked that. Facing him, she arched her back to present her breasts.

"Am I going to get your big cock, Daddy?"

"Not yet, baby. You have to take your punishment." He gestured to the bed, and she climbed on top on her hands and knees. To her wrists and ankles, he buckled new dark-rose suede cuffs, knotted to the bedposts with black silk rope.

In another situation, this might have been hot. But she wasn't sure she could trust him.

"These came new in the mail for you today, baby."

This visit was about the new cuffs, not a celebration.

"You've been a very bad girl. You know you have."

"I'm sorry, Daddy!"

"Sorry isn't good enough. You're going to have to pay." Testing the ropes, making sure she was firmly attached, he slipped from a drawer a new flogger: black leather, with flails that each ended in a point. It was going to be wicked.

Reaching forward, he pushed his fingers between her labia.

"Nice and wet. You like this, don't you?"

"Yes!" There was no other answer. "But I'm scared, Daddy!"

"You should be, baby." He laid a hard smack across her buttocks.

He should've warmed her up first. Oh, well.

He struck again, again, and again. She wondered if he wanted her to make noise.

"Count for me, baby." She counted up to ten. "But you missed the ones before." He laid down a hard smack.

That was getting to be a bit much.

"Sorry, Daddy."

"Am I beginning to hurt you?" She nodded. "Ten more. Count them."

She did. Each was harder than the last.

They really hurt. She hadn't thought he had it in him.

The final blow felt like a spray of molten fire, and she cried out, falling forward with the force of it. Instantly, he was on her, massaging her rump with his hands, pulling her hips forward, fondling her dripping pussy. "So wet. What a good girl."

Scrabbling in the bedside drawer, he found the condoms. He poked at her with his cock and found his way in, mounting her. As he thrust, reaching under he hit and pinched her breasts with his hands.

"God I love your hot little cunt. Tell me you love it, baby."

"Oh, Daddy! I love—unh—your cock in me."

"You do, don't you? What a hot little fuck you are." Then there was no more talking, just the slap of his thighs against hers. She ground against him, seeking her own pleasure, but he came first, pushing her down into the mattress.

On top of her, cock still inserted, he fell asleep.

She wriggled a little, trying to find room to breathe.

Afterward, in the blood-orange kitchen, he poured her a glass of prosecco as she perched at the counter.

"So how much do I owe you?" she asked.

"About three thousand dollars," he said casually.

About twenty hours. That wasn't bad.

"You'll be paid up pretty soon. But I'm worried what you're going to do now."

"How do you mean?"

"You're not working anymore."

She nodded slowly.

"I want you to seriously consider my offer. I get you an apartment or condo, whatever works best, by the U, give you an allowance, set you up."

She sipped the prosecco, gazing at him. It was an attractive idea.

"You don't want me to see anyone else," she said. "I'm not sure I can do that. I'm seeing a couple of people."

"Oh, baby, I don't care if you see your friends."

She cleared her throat. "Not friends. I have two lovers. A guy and a girl."

"Do you? Is your friend I met, Hollie—is she your lover?"

She could see the fantasy as if it was projected in the air.

"You want her to come over again?" she asked.

"Is it her?" She shook her head. "Tell me about your girl lover."

She described Cleo, though it felt dirty and not in a good way.

"Mmm, baby, that's nice. Would she go to bed with us?"

Never.

"I don't know. I can ask her."

"You can see her. I don't want you seeing any guys."

It fell into place like a deadbolt. They met each other's eyes.

She needed the money, when it came down to it. The rest was details.

She could live with this. At least till she had some savings. For the entire two years' probation would be safest.

She'd have Cleo, or other girls if not her.

She had to see Clayton one last time.

Chapter 21

Two weeks into the quarter, Seattle put on Indian summer. The color of the days had changed, a little more golden and elegiac. The first sugar maples—aliens from the Northeast, planted for color—were turning, tipped at the tops with red, then yellow, then green, like a paintbrush dipped in three colors.

It was Clayton's last year. He had taken the GRE and was planning his moves on graduate programs in a desultory way. He'd reviewed them all—the ones he hoped for, the obvious ones, and the fallbacks. He had a guarded confidence. The boss at his last internship and most of his professors loved him.

But he didn't know what he wanted.

Everything was hazed over with a grey smut—like a desert wind had dropped dust from a storm.

He hadn't heard from Joanie in a couple weeks. He knew something was wrong—he knew it in his body. He told himself that she was busy, that she'd had her court date, that he shouldn't bug her.

Finally he broke down and texted her. It was Thursday night. He'd almost fallen asleep in his bunk in the dorm, the concrete box where he'd lived for three years, smelling as usual of dirty socks. Around midnight, she texted back.

<Sorry. I do want to see you.>

He texted back an emoticon heart.

She replied: <What are you doing right now?>

<Nothing>

<Can you come over?>

<Sure. Be there in a half-hour.>

He took a five-minute shower, threw on the clothes he'd worn that day, and found his bike at the rack.

The chilly dark smelled of rain. He sped up to the yellow house with the roof all gables, locked up his bike, and leaning on the porch railing called her. "I'll come get you," she said.

She appeared in the darkened doorway. Her hair was stacked in a bun, stray strands wisping from it. He met her eyes like ink drops. She smelled of jasmine. He folded her in his arms.

It was like coming home.

"Come inside."

The living room was half-full of boxes, taped and labeled: Kitchen. Bedroom. "Is Danielle moving out?" Danielle had threatened a few times to move in with her boyfriend.

Maybe he could move in. Though it was too early.

"No, I am." She threw herself on the couch with an

audible thump, reached over, and lit a big candle on the side table. "Come sit by me."

When he did, she clambered onto his lap like a child and kissed his face all over. Something wet touched his cheek.

She was crying.

"What's up? What's wrong?"

"I think I told you about my regular date, Phil? Who helped me with the legal costs?"

"You did. By the way, your court date—"

"Let me finish. Phil wants to be my sugar daddy, and he made me an offer I can't refuse. An apartment, an allowance, paying my tuition—the full deal. Considering I can't really work for two years, I gotta do it."

There was a shoe that hadn't dropped. "And?"

"He doesn't care if I date women, but he doesn't want me dating other men."

"Oh."

She spoke all in a rush: "I have to. It's the security I need. I need to finish school. I can't—" He laid his finger on her lips.

Then they were both crying.

"I'm sorry, honey." She pulled back his head by his hair and kissed his face again and again. "I love you. I wanted— it doesn't matter what I wanted. You deserve someone better than me."

"Don't say that shit." She started to speak and he kissed her again—then picked her up (so small, so slender, like a bird) and carried her into the bedroom.

He kissed her face, kissed her neck, slipped off her tank

top, and kissed her breasts as if he worshipped her. He did worship her.

"Please fuck me. I'm going to die if you don't fuck me. Your cock is like God's."

Shucking his clothes, he took off her shorts and panties. "Hurry." He grabbed a condom and shoved himself inside.

A pause, a moment of stillness, then he moved. She moved with him, her legs latched behind his back. The room was dark, the only light the faint trace of candlelight from the living room. His eyes adjusted, but mostly he went by feel: her smooth skin, the slickness of her cunt enveloping him. He thrust and thrust.

She called out, sobbing. A moment later he came.

He let himself down gently onto her body. "Don't slide out."

"I'll try not." A wash of emotion passed through them, like a wave. He imagined himself on the dark ocean—the black sea, the pale, shadowed foam.

She did love him. And he loved her.

"Can I see you as a friend? I don't care if I fuck you."

"Hush." She nudged herself out from under him, pushed him to one side, and slid down his body. Her lips touched his cock.

"Hey, wait." She made a questioning noise. "Can we have some more light?"

Sitting up, she lit the purple candle on the windowsill.

"I want your cock again. I want your cock a million times over."

He half-laughed. "Probably not a million times."

"Let me try."

She descended to his cock and took him in her mouth.

"Oh God." Within moments he was hard again.

"Let me do the work this time." She rolled a condom onto his stiff cock and mounted him.

Candlelight fell across her moving torso, her pretty olive-skinned breasts. He took them in his palms, squeezing and kneading them. Her breath came faster. "Pinch me." He pinched her nipples between finger and thumb. "Harder." He got his nails in. She gave a happy sigh. "That's good."

He felt the energy rising. Her riding him, moving to find the right spot, the exquisite sensation of her on his cock—these pulled him in. The feel of her breasts in his hands. She didn't care how hard he squeezed and pinched her. He leaned up to bite her, and she leaned down, her long black hair tickling across his face and chest like a rain of silk.

"I'm almost there," she breathed. Then she cried out, once, then again and again. The energy splashed through her, to him, and he came, harder than he expected. A flash of white obliterated the world. She lay down on top of him, damp with sweat, and he held her.

If he just didn't let go.

They woke late. Danielle hadn't made it home—she'd probably spent the night at her boyfriend's. She'd talked him into moving in so Joanie could break the lease, and she'd agreed to keep Joanie's cat.

Joanie made espresso in a stovetop pot. Wan sunlight fell across the blue-and-white checkered tablecloth, filtered by clouds. Wind outside shook the trees. A few yellow leaves spun downward.

"You want a latte?"

"Sure. Do you want to go out for breakfast? I can miss my early class, but not my twelve-thirty."

She shook her head. "I can make eggs, if you want. I don't want to be around people."

She sat down across the table from him. The circles under her eyes meant she hadn't slept well, but the worn look made him love her more.

"I didn't see this coming," she said. "I'm sorry."

"Can I see you?"

"Not for a bit, at least. I need to see the lay of the land first."

"Okay." It was all he could say.

"I'll text you."

She might. It was possible.

She scrambled eggs with cheese and salsa. He made toast. The smell of food sent him into a brief fantasy.

Imagine, five years from now, them living together, with their own kitchen.

It was ridiculous.

He hadn't done this right.

He pushed eggs around his plate with a fork. "Look, the whole James thing, I was stupid about it. I wish I hadn't wasted so much time."

She put her hand over his. "It's fine. I was stupid to sleep with him. I just—I don't know. I don't think it means the same thing to me, because of who I am and what I do."

He needed to be gentle. This was no time to fight.

"It was me. I shouldn't have gotten so butt-hurt. I'm sorry."

She gave him half a smile. "Apology accepted. But it was me too."

"It's okay. It's done now."

Now when everything could be right, chances were he'd never see her again.

Chapter 22

The day Joanie moved was overcast, with an intermittent wind full of grit.

It came from all the construction, all the slick high-rise apartments going up, like the one she moving into, the older buildings with character torn down. She couldn't summon the energy to care about that.

The move took only a few hours on her half-day, after classes. Phil had paid for movers, two sunburnt men who smelled of weed. Her furniture and boxes barely half-filled their truck.

Like Phil's condo, her apartment shone with newness, full of sleek white modern cabinetry and stainless steel in the kitchen, elsewhere pale maple floors and earthy green accent walls. He'd bought her furniture, including a king-sized bed and high-thread-count sheets, and brought over items for decor, including his faux-bronze urn full of alder sticks. He'd given her a credit card, and she charged the move to it.

The movers cleared out, and she was there, amid her boxes, alone.

It didn't feel like her place. She'd never been this person.

But it was what he wanted, and he was paying. At least she wouldn't see him till the following week. He was in Australia again.

She could call Cleo. But Cleo wouldn't understand.

She opened her first kitchen box, pulling out spatulas, spoons, and forks. Rough-edged, unmatched, they looked weird in the space. She found herself going slower and slower, till she sat perched on the high stainless-steel-legged barstool, elbows propped on the counter, a pile of silverware in front of her.

Fuck it.

She could use some of her fine, fine cash from Daddy Phil.

Throwing on her jean jacket, she went a couple blocks to the nearest grocery and bought a bottle of white wine.

Pinot grigio, in honor of Tammy, wherever she was. Another person she'd lost.

By the time she got out of the store, it was early twilight, the blue-lavender sky smudged with grey. She walked the two blocks back, passing other students who barely registered her, the gritty wind circling and enveloping her.

She drank herself to sleep.

Now she was his, Phil came to see her more often. He had a key to the apartment. He surprised her by being there one afternoon when she returned from class.

"Hi, baby," he said, standing up from the overstuffed chair, earth-green to match the accent wall. "Glad to see me?"

"Of course!"

He moved into her bubble of space. Putting his hands around her waist, he kissed her hungrily. He tugged her skirt up with one hand, pushed her panties aside, and plunged two fingers into her cunt. She closed her eyes and humped his hand—like the next step in a dance, which you do even if you don't like your partner.

Part of her liked it.

"So wet. That's nice, baby. I want to fuck you, but before that I want to hurt you."

"Anything you want, Daddy!"

He grinned. Walking her backward through the open door, he threw her onto the down coverlet, identical to his. Thank the gods, the bed was made—he hated things messy.

She lay face up, quivering. He lay down on top of her and kissed her. She could feel his hard-on through his chinos. He pushed up her tank top and bra and bit her nipple savagely, so hard she cried out.

He put a hand over her mouth. "No noise, baby." The other hand went to her cunt and delved into it, fucking two and then three fingers inside.

"My wet, hot baby. You know I own you."

She nodded vigorously.

"I want to beat your ass, baby, and then I want to fuck it."

He got out the stingy flogger he'd used before, which now lived at her apartment. From his messenger bag, he pulled a leather tawse—two layers of leather sewn together at the handle, with a split working end. With it, he caressed her ass.

"Are you clean down there?"

"May I check, Daddy?"

"Don't take too long!"

She hurried to the bathroom, started the shower, and got on the toilet.

If he'd given her notice—but, whatever. Now she was his, or so he thought.

Done on the toilet, she dropped her clothes and leapt into the shower. She had to move quickly. He wasn't very patient.

When she came out, he looked a little white around the lips. "Sorry, Daddy!"

She scampered naked to the bed, and he tossed her the dark-rose suede cuffs. "Put 'em on, baby."

Obediently she buckled them onto her ankles and wrists. "Put this towel under you." He threw her a fluffy white hand towel. He connected the cuffs by carabiners to black-silk ropes tied to the bed, leaving her spread-eagle, bottom up.

Leather whistled through the air to sting her naked, raised ass. He alternated the tawse and the flogger. She breathed deeply and grounded, sending an energetic cord deep into the earth.

But he didn't work her up at all, just pounded her with two kinds of leather, again and again. It hurt.

"Ow, Daddy!"

"You took too long in the shower, baby. I'm sorry."

She settled in to endure, but it was past her ability to do that and stay present as a good whore should.

"That hurts, Daddy!"

"I'm punishing you, baby. You shouldn't take too long."

That had drawn blood. And that.

This was too much.

"Don't, Daddy! Please stop."

"Twenty more. Count them."

But he didn't use the flogger or tawse. She heard a new sound in the air, a whooshing, and glanced over her shoulder. From the urn behind the door, he'd grabbed an alder switch.

"Daddy!" There was real fear in her voice, and he smiled beatifically.

"I said I was going to hurt you, baby. I'm really going to hurt you. Now start counting."

Each blow burned like fire. She could feel how welts crossed her flesh. She counted.

"Nineteen. Twenty."

"And one to grow on." He threw back his arm and hit again, with no mercy.

She was crying.

"Now I'm going to fuck that pretty butt of yours." Lifting her bleeding ass, he stuffed a pillow under her and dropped his chinos. He grabbed condom and lube, slicked himself, and drove into her.

Pain seared her, like he'd shoved in a red-hot poker, and she screamed. Pulling out, he shoved her face into the pillow with one hand.

"No screaming, Jenny. No screaming ever. Or you'll stop screaming."

He held her face down, into the pillow.

Things went black and white.

The moment before she passed out, he let her up, dragging her head up by the hair.

"No screaming, baby. Do you understand?"

She nodded.

"Now I'm going to fuck that pretty, bleeding ass of yours. And do anything else to your body I want. I own you." He slipped his free hand under and grabbed her breast, taking it whole in his hand, and twisted, leaning to watch her face. The pain was amazing, but she bit her tongue, only letting her eyes go wide.

"Better." He dropped her head, repositioned himself, and drove his cock into her ass.

It hurt like fire. She could feel him damaging her. But she didn't make a sound.

Nowadays Puabi-Ekur stayed outside Clayton's body nearly all the time.

It was lovely to have a body. When the boy fucked the girl who was Iltani, it was hard to stay away. But all those emotions! It was better to float among the stars. How beautiful the nebulae were, pink and blue, shining with the light of a thousand suns.

All those emotions.

They remembered being Puabi, holding Iltani in the shelter of her arms and kissing her, that last time.

There were times they should have acted and did not.

This sudden affection for nebulae was just fear.

Puabi-Ekur had checked in on Joanie at her new place—checked in and run away.

Joanie might not be equal to her challenge. Like her friend Hayley, Puabi-Ekur was afraid.

Maybe it was time to create a little karma.

Hekate was right. They needed allies. And to do some research.

Till now, Puabi-Ekur had avoided the smoky grey wisps the djinn left in their wake. Now it was time to follow them to their source.

A curl of smoke rose. In a brown room lit by candles, in the smallest bedroom of a subdivision duplex, a circle of five teenage girls passed around a bit of foil covered with brown paste. One by one, they heated it from below and sucked the smoke from brown-fogged tubes.

A sound of coughing came from another bedroom.

"Kayla's been sick," one girl said. "We should cover for her."

"Okay. If we can," said a second girl.

"We need to figure it out. She's coming over soon."

"Who?" asked the newest one. The other girls rolled their eyes at her.

"She's going to expect rent," said the first girl.

"I thought she was helping us out?" asked the newest one.

The first girl shrugged. "I guess. It's better than the streets."

"Is it?"

"I wouldn't get on her bad side. Now come on, she'll be here any moment." Hurriedly, the other four found bills in pockets and purses and put them in the first girl's outstretched hand.

As they finished, the front door opened. A big, slab-muscled man with dreads entered. The five girls ran downstairs.

"Hi, girls," he said. The first speaker darted forward and put the collected money in his hand.

"This is what we got for the week," she said.

He settled onto the couch by the beaten-up coffee table. Slowly, as if he had all the time in the world, he counted out the money. Then he turned his gaze on each girl, one after the other.

"What about Kayla?" he asked.

"She's got the flu. Her takings are there."

He looked at the first girl steadily a moment, then shrugged. "It's not me you have to worry about. I'll let you know if there's a problem."

He stood ponderously. The others drew back, leaving the newest one up front.

From behind her, the first girl whispered, "Sorry, Tildy."

He met Tildy's eyes and held out his hand. She trembled, but she put her hand in his. He led her upstairs.

Puabi-Ekur stepped back from the room into the ether.

If their work shook up the djinn, the girls would be freed.

But what was the connection?

A grey wind whipped up, blowing Puabi-Ekur back out among the stars.

Ah—the circle of girls, that was easy. The connection was hard.

Chapter 23

Across campus, the maple leaves turned red and yellow and began to fall. Joanie had two years left of school, and two years left of probation. Some days, completing that span looked possible, if not easy.

Some days, it looked like an eternity of hell.

She and Hayley still met at the coffee shop. Now the winy smell of fall floated through the doorway on a cold breeze. Joanie hadn't given up her sundresses, but she wore cardigans over them.

The cardigans covered her new bruises. Phil was getting more and more ambitious with her pain tolerance. At least he mostly left marks in hard-to-see places.

Sitting in her favorite booth, face warm in the sun, she pulled down her sleeves to cover the raw marks the suede cuffs had made the day before. She'd struggled unsuccessfully to avoid the blows of an alder switch.

Hayley sat down in the place across from her. "How are you liking your new classes?"

Joanie shrugged. "They're okay. I had hopes for the Honors Research Seminar, but I'm really not liking the professor. I may not do honors. I have to decide soon."

Hayley tilted her head to one side. "You look tired, Joanie."

"I didn't sleep well last night. I have new neighbors. They were carrying furniture in." This was a complete lie—besides everything else, the walls at her luxury apartment dampened sound.

"Are you still thinking Phil would be into another threesome?"

"I'm not sure."

"We could negotiate it, if he wanted to do BDSM. I'm down for that." Joanie gave a noncommittal shrug. "Joanie, I'm worried about you."

Stop worrying. I need the money.

Taking Joanie's wrist in one hand, Hayley gently pushed up the sleeve of Joanie's cardigan with the other. She turned Joanie's arm so the scrapes and bruises showed clearly in the light.

"Is this consensual BDSM? Those look painful, and not in a fun way."

Joanie shrugged again. "It's basically consensual. Sometimes he pushes a little hard. I'm training him." She forced a laugh.

"I wonder if this is going to work."

Joanie drew back her arm. "Well, so do I."

"I know you want security. But if worst comes to worst,

and you have to move out, you can get a regular day job. Or do something grey market and keep your head down."

Joanie grimaced. "What I have is an awfully good deal, Hayley."

"Sure. But let me know if it stops working, okay?"

From her bed, on a Friday morning, Joanie watched out the window as the red leaves of a maple tree waved at her. She lay with her head on Phil's shoulder, trying to lose herself among the leaves. But the pain of her bruises kept her in place.

She felt his shoulder move as he stroked her hair. "This weekend I really want to see how much pain you can handle. You're so sexy when you're taking my cane."

"Mmm-hmm, Daddy."

Her eyes flickered to the clock on the bedside table.

In ten minutes, she had to get ready for class.

He caught the movement. "Sweetheart." He angled himself away from her so he could see her better. "I almost want to hurt your pretty face some way, so you have to stay here."

She couldn't tell if he was in play space or for real.

"I'm not sure I like you going out to classes. You should spend all day thinking about me, like a good sex toy."

She'd better reply to this.

"That sounds sexy, Daddy. But I do still want to go to school."

She levered herself to standing.

Sitting up quickly, he grabbed her wrist and swung her back onto the bed. Holding her down, he smacked her ass with his other hand.

Flat on her chest among rumpled sheets, she stared at him, and he stared back.

After nearly a minute, he let go.

Shaking, she grabbed clothes from the closet, threw them on, snatched up her backpack, and left.

On and off, she considered texting Cleo. But she didn't. She didn't want to have to explain her situation.

Then one afternoon, hurrying home between raindrops after a twelve-thirty class, she nearly ran into her on the street.

"Whoa! Hi, Joanie!"

"Uh—hi!"

Cleo rocked back a step, eyeing her critically, the same look Hayley had given her.

"I was going to have lunch. You want to come with? I've been meaning to text you—I've been so busy."

"Sure." Joanie fell into step with her.

They ended up at a tiny pho place. Snagging two spots at the counter, they ordered jasmine tea. The scent of hot jasmine and Cleo's sandalwood perfume surrounded Joanie like an embrace.

She wished she ever felt cared for, these days.

The pho came. They talked about classes.

"I was going to invite you to one of our community's

open houses," Cleo said. "There's an informal one tonight, if you want to come."

What did she have to look forward to tonight? Nothing. And Cleo was expressly on the list of people she could see.

"I'd love to."

"Why don't you come to my house after lunch? It's only a couple hours till we get started."

Cleo hasn't asked her what was going on in her life. Maybe she'd connected the dots. Maybe she didn't want to know.

"Okay."

Then she was in Cleo's room, in Cleo's bed, under the orange, yellow, and magenta sari glittering with gold thread. They kissed.

Her lips were so lush, like flowers or fruit. It was hard not to bite her; she wanted to eat her up.

She inched down Cleo's body. Before her orchid-like pussy, scented of musk, Joanie settled on her elbows. She licked and bit and sucked. Putting her hands under Cleo's buttocks, she propped the slender pelvis up and forward.

She slid a finger, then two, into Cleo. Slick, wet, warm, the vulva opened to her hand. She curled her fingers to touch Cleo's G-spot as she continued to lick.

"Omigod, Joanie—omigod." Cleo bucked, and Joanie used her free hand to hold her so that she could continue to mouth her flowerlike cunt. When Cleo came, it felt like a dam bursting, energy spilling and pouring.

Cleo curled up in her armpit and they lay together, their breath quieting. A current of cool air snaked its way in through the margin of the open window.

"Now let me." Cleo kissed her, kisses full of hunger but also affection, so much that Joanie's eyes filled with tears.

It was what she missed most. Even before he'd started hurting her, Phil had treated her like an object. She didn't know if he could care about people.

Cleo caught a tear on her fingertip. "Oh, sweetheart."

She sat back on her heels, gazing at Joanie from warm golden-brown eyes, the color of amber.

"I know your life is complicated. I hate to ask, because I feel as if asking is pushing you. But what exactly is going on?"

In answer, Joanie burst into tears.

In bits and pieces, Cleo got the story from her.

"I guess I'm with your friend Hayley. It's like the frog in the pot of boiling water. I worry by the time you know it's not working, something bad will have happened."

Joanie sniffled. "Hayley thinks he's a psychopath. That's ridiculous."

"I doubt your Phil is a serial killer. But he doesn't sound like he cares much about other people. Mind you, in sales that can be a gift. A friend of mine worked on the anthropology of sales."

Joanie only stared in response.

"Never mind. I wish you could come live with me."

"That'd be nice. But how would I pay the rent?"

"We'd figure something out. I have some strings I can pull."

Joanie shook her head. "I don't want to be a burden. Let me work this out. Phil hasn't done anything out of line. Mostly he just freaks me out."

Cleo gave her a look. "Except for the beatings."

"It's just BDSM." Cleo rolled her eyes. "No, Cleo, it is. If he does something over the line, I'll speak up. I'm no dummy."

"I wish I trusted you more about this." Cleo leaned and kissed her, a lingering kiss. "For now, sit back." Joanie lay down among the pillows glinting with mirrors.

Cleo's head went between her thighs. Her delicate tongue slid along Joanie's inner lips and found the best spot. "Yes, there."

Joanie buried her hand in Cleo's hair, closing her eyes.

For dinner that night, they shared lentils spiced with red pepper in Cleo's bottle-green kitchen. After dinner, Cleo pushed back her chair.

"Tonight we're having Forum, which is something we do for transparent communication in the community. You talk about your stuff and act things out, based on the facilitators' suggestions."

"All right." For Joanie, it was enough to be at Cleo's table, not at home in her empty apartment. But she was curious.

If she could find a path to a different world, something more humane, that would be amazing. It was what she hoped to address with economics. Maybe community could do it another way.

About twenty people, ranging in age from early twenties to sixties, gathered in the house's living room, full of bright-yellow sunflower paintings. Three facilitators sat on one side of the circle, a middle-aged woman in a seersucker jacket the leader. After a brief introduction, she sat forward. "We begin Forum by clapping."

The process started with two-minute shares. The surrounding circle of people formed the container, holding the speakers in close attention.

A young woman with long brown braids stood and paced the circle. "I was going to do a long share about what an asshole Randy was, and how that broke us up." Randy sat across the circle, a young curly-haired man with the look of a carpenter. A flicker of emotion crossed his face.

"But really it's not about Randy being an asshole. It's about me being sad." The young woman turned the other direction again. "I think that's all I need to say." She sat down.

Everyone clapped. "Clear the energy," the leader said, and everyone waved their hands, pushing the energy behind them.

After a few short shares, the circle opened for longer ones. Of these, the hardest was from a man in his thirties, tall and grey-faced, in an incongruous multicolored wool poncho. "My estranged father is in a coma. I have to decide whether I visit him before he dies."

The circle's container held the story. At one point, the facilitators handed him a trash barrel, if he wanted to vomit out old pain. Bent above it, he coughed and spit into the container, hanging onto it with both hands. It was as if Joanie could see the pain flowing out. The community held him, reflected things back.

"We end Forum by clapping."

Afterward, people chatted in the living room. The sunflower paintings radiated energy like lamps. Cleo drew Joanie under her arm.

"What did you think?" she asked.

"It's cool. It's—group psychodrama?"

Cleo nodded. "It helps air the emotions underneath. Otherwise we'd constantly be fighting. So, are you interested?"

"In community? Sure. Everyone is. It's a human thing."

"My herbalist friend says that everyone who comes to him these days is wounded in community. We're social animals." She peered at Joanie. "But...?"

"But I live where I live, and I do what I do."

Cleo frowned. "I don't think sex work is incompatible with community. I've done the Inanna shrines for three years now."

Joanie glanced from one side to the other. "That's kind of a grey area."

"Capitalism makes whores of us all. Or rather wage slaves. Inanna and sacred whores predate capitalism by millennia."

But Cleo was just arguing theory. It was different for Joanie. It was her life.

"We have a couple of rooms about to turn over. I wish you'd consider moving in."

"I can't. And now I really should leave."

"Can I walk you home?"

"If you like."

Cleo lent Joanie a coat to cover her cardigan. Full dark

had fallen, a hint of paler blue along the western horizon. They crossed the University District's main drag, full of students laughing and talking, the smell of weed and Indian food in the air.

"I wish you could stay at my house. I wish I could kidnap you."

"It doesn't work like that."

"It could."

They approached the stark rectangular outline of Joanie's building. A spot bulb lit the area by the front door.

"This is me."

As they stood facing each other, a figure appeared out of the shadows.

Phil.

"Hi, Phil! This is my friend Cleo."

Phil looked Cleo up and down, and smiled, chilly as the wind full of leaves. "Pleased to meet you."

"Likewise!"

Cleo had put in her whore time too.

Phil stepped around Joanie, with his key opened the door and held it for her. Joanie put on a megawatt smile and, going on tiptoes, kissed his cheek.

"Daddy," she whispered, "I'll be up in a second. Let me say goodbye."

Phil glanced from her to Cleo and back again. "Okay, baby."

The door hung on its hinge a moment, then shut. Joanie let out a sigh of relief.

Cleo stared at the closed door. "I know that man."

They exchanged a look. Cleo gazed at Joanie as if trying to drill knowledge into her.

"Obviously we can't talk now. But meet me for pho day after tomorrow at one-thirty. Same place. Can you do that?"

Joanie nodded.

"See you then."

Stepping forward, she kissed her, a kiss that was a wish and a blessing.

Joanie carried it with her as the door shut behind her.

As soon as she set her keys in the purple glass bowl on the kitchen counter, Phil spoke from the bedroom. "Clean yourself out, baby. I want to take your ass. You had sex with that black girl, didn't you?"

"I did!"

"You licked that girl's pussy, didn't you?"

"I did."

"I thought so. You like her a lot, don't you, baby?"

Coming into the bedroom doorway, Joanie nodded shyly, like a little girl with a crush.

Inside, she made herself go numb.

It wasn't good whoring. She wanted to be a good sex partner, a caring person, when she was with her clients. But she had to survive this.

"Come here, you little slut." She stepped forward. Jumping to his feet, he grabbed her by the hair and slung her onto the bed.

She fell, catching herself, foursquare on the white down comforter. He leapt on her, pinning her.

Grinding his teeth, he said into her ear, "Did I say you could have sex with that girl?"

She jerked her head up in surprise. "Yes, you did, Daddy!"

This made him pause a moment.

"I guess I did, didn't I?" She nodded hard. "Okay, you get off this time, you little slut. But never again."

"Never again?"

"You'd better never think of that black girl again. I thought I'd be okay with it, but I'm not. From now on, you're all mine. You're my piece of ass, and that's all you are. Just my hot little cunt, and my hot little ass. All for me."

"Whatever you say, Daddy. I'm all yours." She wriggled below him. He worked his hand under her, grabbing her breast, pinching her nipple hard, with his fingernails. The other hand pushed aside her skirt. Two fingers drove into her sopping cunt.

I hate this. But my body likes it. Stupid body.

He finger-fucked her a few moments, then threw her off the bed. Her head narrowly missed the side table.

"Clean yourself up."

Stumbling into the bathroom, she shut herself in, used the toilet, then turned on the shower.

She could survive this. She'd had worse.

When she returned, naked, trembling, he threw her again onto the bed. With no preamble but a condom and a handful of spit, he drove his cock into her ass.

White pain tore through her as he fucked her.

Immediately after he spent himself, he fell asleep.

The thought came unbidden, unwanted.

I won't make two years of this.

The next morning, he shook her awake, getting her out of bed naked. He was dressed for work in a polo shirt and jeans. Grabbing a straight chair from the tiny kitchen table, he put it in the bedroom and made her sit. Getting a length of his favorite black silk rope from the closet, he tied her in place.

A ray of sun fell across the floor, then disappeared. From the corner of her eye, she saw grey cloud filling the sky.

He tied her tightly, so her breasts bulged between swaths of rope. The effect seemed to fascinate him. For a few minutes, he slapped her tits, one after the other.

"Pretty," he muttered to himself. "Pretty tits."

Then he stopped and stared at her, his eyes blue marbles with nothing behind them. She gazed back, not sure what he wanted.

He slapped her across the face, knocking her head to the side.

"You don't look me in the face."

She cast her eyes down. "No, Daddy."

"You don't have any friends any more. All you have is me."

I don't agree with this.

He hit the side of her head, hard, leaving her head ringing. "Answer!"

"Yes, Daddy."

"Better."

He walked around her, watching her closely. At random, he reached out and twisted a nipple, hard, then continued circling. Suddenly he slapped her face again, almost as hard. Then he grabbed both tits and twisted, till she gasped. Stepping away, he continued walking.

Time was passing. She had class pretty soon. She hoped he hadn't marked her face.

He stopped in front of her.

"If you're good, if you toe the line, you can keep going to class. If not, you can't."

"Yes, Daddy."

He stepped forward and unzipped his fly, bringing out a hard cock. He straddled the chair, pushing his cock into her face.

"Suck me, baby. Do a good job."

Movement constrained by the ropes, she stretched forward to lick and suck.

After a few moments, he stepped back. He slapped her face again.

"Not good enough. I need your ass."

She opened her mouth to protest, and then shut it.

He untied her and threw her prone on the bed. Grabbing a condom, he lubed himself with spit and mounted her. She cried out in pain.

He hit her ass cheek, hard.

"Muffle that sound, bitch!"

She bit the pillow as he drove into her. The world was one electric fire of pain.

Finally he came, grunting, and lay down on her, shoving her face into the pillow. She managed to find a space to breathe.

After a time, he got up. "You're bleeding. Go clean yourself up. Then go to class. If you insist."

Stumbling into the bathroom, she started the shower and looked at herself in the mirror.

He hadn't bruised her face.

Joanie sat in the coffee shop, scrolling between Hayley's number and Cleo's, texting neither.

The day was misty and grey, the clouds low. A gritty wind gusted through the shop door as customers opened it.

She could barely sit. She'd found some over-the-counter numbing ointment, but it didn't work as well as she'd hoped.

She couldn't keep doing this. But what was she going to do?

She needed to clarify her boundaries, at least.

She should leave. But she needed the money.

Her mind ran in circles. She tried taking deep breaths, but it didn't work. She checked the time again.

One more class, then back home.

Maybe he wouldn't be there.

When she got back to the apartment, Phil was waiting for her in the living room, frowning.

Shit.

He jumped up. "Get your clothes off."

She dropped her backpack and peeled where she stood. Grabbing her by the hair, he dragged her into the bedroom and threw her on the bed.

"Ass in the air."

"Daddy—"

"Do what I say!"

From the closet, he chose an alder cane. "Count!"

Blood flew from her legs, flecking the sheets. Everything spun into a whiteout of pain. She couldn't count anymore. When he shoved himself into her ass, she shrieked.

Grabbing her head in one hand, he held her face to the pillow until she passed out.

Chapter 24

She woke in darkness. Finding herself alone in bed, she sat up.

The light flicked on outside the bedroom. A silhouette darkened the doorway, then moved toward her, as if out of grey smoke. She rubbed her eyes.

"I hope you like this, baby."

Phil handed her a fork, a knife, and a plate of food: steak, broccoli, and mashed potatoes, take-out from a restaurant. She was starving, and she wolfed it down.

He sat on the bed, watching her in half-darkness.

"Good baby, eating my food." When she slowed, he lifted away plate and silverware and set them on the bedside table.

He took her hands. She glanced at him a moment, then hastily down.

"Good girl," he said. Taking her chin, he tipped it so she faced upward toward him. "I've been hard on my babydoll, this last bit. I'm sorry. I'm going to turn over a new leaf and be nicer. Right now, I need you to suck my cock."

He stood, shucked his jeans, and stepped to the edge of the bed. Kneeling, she took his flaccid cock in her mouth. An image flashed across her mind, of biting it off, but she let it pass.

"Good sucking, baby. I do want to keep my little sex toy." He stroked her hair. "Lie back. I'm going to fuck you."

She lay back on the sheets, seeing how much blood had fallen. Drips and smears covered the fabric.

He mounted her missionary style, rubbing her butt against the bed. It hurt like her skin being shredded. After a few moments, he put her legs over his shoulders to go deeper, but every thrust pushed her welts against the bed. Waves of pain rose and fell.

She faked an orgasm for him. He came, grunting, and rolled off. Grey mist boiled at the edges of her vision.

"I don't want you going to class anymore, baby. School is expensive. You need just to be my sex toy."

The grey mist covered the ceiling.

"Did you hear me?"

"Yes, Daddy."

"Is that yes, Daddy, I'll quit classes tomorrow?"

She made a vague affirmative sound.

He nodded and closed his eyes. After a few moments, he began to snore, with a whistling sound.

Puabi-Ekur watched, through the grey mist that filled the room.

In her dream, Joanie watched a woman in a mud-brick temple, crumbling frankincense onto a censer.

The woman was perhaps in her thirties, long crimped brunette hair falling over a full, rounded ass. A whisper went through Joanie's mind: Puabi.

The woman was muttering to herself.

"The Lady Iltani is dead. She fell down a well."

An agony of pain and loss washed over her.

"I should have done something. I should have acted."

In the dark bedroom, as Phil snored beside her, Joanie's eyes popped open.

In the morning, Phil left as he usually did, with no goodbye. Joanie, feigning sleep, heard him shut the outer door behind him with a click.

Thank the gods he had to work sometimes.

She stood, assessing her body by feel. Her asshole was on fire, but she'd gotten used to that. The welts on her ass felt okay till she reached back and touched them.

She'd have to bandage the worst of them. Putting on jeans would be no fun.

Okay, numbing cream and bandages. Then she had a couple of things to do.

She went to the closet and reviewed her clothes.

Joanie got to the pho shop before Cleo did. Outside it was a cold day, overcast, full of gritty wind, but inside it was warm. She found a table in back, got soup, added bean sprouts and cilantro, and ate.

Warmth suffused her body, and she calmed down. Her ass still hurt to sit on, but she'd taken a double dose of ibuprofen and the pain had backed off.

She kept an eye on the door, half-afraid that Phil would enter. As if she could just manifest him out of fear.

Cleo appeared about ten minutes later, swinging her backpack down beside Joanie's feet. "Hi there!"

Joanie stood, and they hugged. Joanie's body relaxed, involuntarily. It felt like home.

Joanie started to speak, but Cleo interrupted her.

"Let me talk first. This is pretty important. I know that guy."

Joanie slurped a mouthful of soup. "Phil?"

"Yeah. He's a friend of Sasha's. I think he's her big backer. Let me tell you what I know."

Cleo had been closer to Sasha a year before, while they were still occasionally bedmates. Joanie could see it in her mind's eye: Cleo's orchid lush features contrasting with slender, pale Sasha. A fleeting jealousy passed.

"He used to come over and talk money."

"Talk money about what? The Inanna shrines?" Her brain was moving slowly. "Don't they support themselves?"

"They do, but Sasha's got other stuff going on. She's pretty secretive about it. Some kind of escort service, more straight-ahead prostitution, not goddess worship. At one point, I got the hint it had to do with her support of homeless youth."

"What do you mean?"

Cleo grimaced. "Looking back, I think she might have been pimping those girls out. I don't know for sure."

"Sasha's pimping out teenagers?"

"Maybe. We were falling apart. She was starting to see Linda and didn't have time for me. She sure wasn't going to answer any pointed questions. But it was one reason I put space between us. I'm not sure Sasha is a good person."

"Why did you keep doing the Inanna temples if you didn't trust her?"

"I like doing the temples. And I created them as much as she did, on the ritual level. If anyone was going to leave, I wanted it to be her. Maybe that was dumb." Cleo frowned. "The more I think about it, the more I think my hunch about the underage thing is right."

Joanie turned this over in her mind.

Who was she to criticize someone for pimping people out? She'd run Tammy's desk herself. But it was one thing for Sasha to help Cleo and her, adults, make extra cash under the goddess's protection. It was another thing to set up homeless youth.

If that was really happening. They didn't know for sure.

"If I had to guess, I suspect your Phil is helping bankroll things, and laundering money for her in exchange for a cut.

I saw cash pass hands at one point, when they didn't see me. A lot of it."

Joanie saw again the crooked drawer in Phil's office and the stacks of twenty dollar bills.

"I found some money he had once. A big pile of twenties. I never let on."

They stared at each other.

"It makes sense. I've wondered how exactly Phil makes so much money," Joanie said. "I mean, he's semi-high in the food chain where he works. But he's still a wage-earner. He didn't blink an eye at anything, putting new items on his budget left and right. And I wonder…"

She saw again Tammy leaning over her cheeseburger at Denny's: "If you think I'm into human trafficking, no. But there are people in this city who do something like that. Closer to you than you think. They're no friends of mine—in fact, I'm pretty sure they tipped off the cops."

"I bet he set up Tammy, too."

She remembered the night the cop had nabbed her, and the phone call from Phil that had come first. Maybe he'd been double-checking if Tammy was there for Tom the cop. When they found out no, they wanted at least to get dirt on her.

"But why set up Tammy?" Cleo asked.

"Get rid of the middleman. Make me vulnerable, so he can own me." She reached out and clutched Cleo's hand. "Cleo—he thinks he owns me. He's been getting worse. He wants me to quit school."

"Oh, sweetheart."

"I decided you were right. I'm moving out." On her chair

she'd slung her backpack and a big canvas shopping bag. From under it, she dragged a rolling suitcase. "I've got everything here, my books and computer, all I need for clothes, and all the money from the shared bank account. I got out."

Cleo nodded slowly.

"The only thing I couldn't fit was my quilt from Aunt Marie."

"Should we go back and get it?"

"No, he might come back. I think I'm done."

Joanie stared at Cleo. Cleo gulped.

"I'm glad you're out. But what now? Now Phil's our enemy. That's bad."

Joanie watched Cleo carefully, the small movements of her face. Was she going to let her down?

"You can't go directly to my house. I'm sure he recognized me the other night. We have to hide you somewhere else."

<Hey, can I call you?>

It was Joanie.

Clayton had made it through his Wednesday site-planning class by sitting in back and hiding, as students have done for centuries. His head pinged and twanged after a night drinking beer with James.

Now he stood in the Engineering building hallway. Green-grey walls held bulletin boards full of out-of-date notices, under flecked acoustic-tile ceilings. Students pushed past, eyeing him as a roadblock, nudging him with backpacks.

<Sure>

He headed outdoors to a triangular patch of grass, still emerald-green, scattered with fallen oak leaves. Sitting under the parent tree, he answered his phone as it rang.

"Clayton, I can't talk long. But I think I need your help."

He heard fear in her voice. "Sure, I'll help you."

"Meet me at the coffee shop at four o'clock—can you do that?"

"Sure thing."

When he walked in, pale sun shone onto the blonde wood of Joanie's favorite booth, a sunbreak in the grey day. Two girls sat there with Joanie: Hayley, the pretty blonde from Rahul's party—she'd been Hollie then—and a light-skinned black girl with amber eyes.

He imagined all of them, together, with him.

The tits on that Hayley—

Trying to hide his blush, he sat down by Joanie. She grabbed his thigh and squeezed.

He shook hands with the new girl. "What's up?"

"I'm Cleo. I asked Joanie to call her closest friends here. She's moved out from Phil."

No one looked happy.

Joanie cleared her throat. "It was a unilateral decision on my part. I don't think he'll like it."

Cleo leaned across the table. Clayton could see the

shadow of cleavage in the vee opening of her shirt-dress. She caught his eye and flashed a grin before she spoke.

"Phil's going to do everything he can to get Joanie back. We need to make him leave her alone. We also need a place for her to stay. And not my house—he knows we're friends, he's seen us together."

Hayley screwed up her face. "If Phil knows Sasha, he'll know I'm Joanie's friend. It can't be my house."

Clearly both Cleo and Hayley were scared of Phil knowing where they lived.

"Is this temporary, or permanent?" Clayton asked.

"Temporary," Joanie said. "In the long term, I hope to move into Cleo's intentional community. But I need to settle things with Phil first."

Clayton frowned. "It can't be a permanent solution, because eventually we'll get found out. But in the short term, you can stay in the dorm with me."

Joanie snuggled close to him, grinning. "Thanks."

"It's good, too, 'cause there's always people around," Cleo said. "Phil's not likely to do something stupid around people. But how do we get him to leave you alone, Joanie?"

Clayton pushed a shock of dark hair back from his forehead. "There's no chance he'll just accept you're gone?"

Cleo raised an eyebrow.

"I don't think so," Joanie said.

"I think I'm going to need coffee for this."

At the counter, he got a cup of drip coffee. As he sipped, Cleo and Joanie brought him up to date. "You think Phil will threaten Joanie with—what? To hurt her?"

"I don't know what he'll threaten me with," Joanie said.

"Whatever he thinks will get me back in his power. Reporting me for breaking parole might be easiest."

"He's been violent, too," Cleo said.

Joanie leaned forward. "We do BDSM. But he takes it further than I want, pretty much every time."

Cleo looked from Joanie to Clayton. "I think we need to figure out some kind of leverage against Phil. What can we use?"

Clayton shrugged. "If he's trafficking in teenagers, the obvious thing is to call the police."

The others screwed up their faces.

"I don't think we should go to the police," Joanie said. "At least not right away."

Seeing Clayton's face, Cleo folded her hands. "Clayton, there's stuff here. Some people might say, check your privilege." She said it without particular malice, looking him full in the face.

After a moment, he nodded.

"First," she said, "I want Joanie to live her life without interference. If we sic the police on Phil, he's sure to claim she's broken probation, or whatever else he can think of. And he has the money to lawyer up. Second, if we're talking about trafficking underage kids, I want them to have better lives."

Hayley nodded. "If the police get involved, who knows where those kids will end up?"

"The system is there to protect them," Clayton said.

"If they're underage, they'll end up in foster homes," Joanie said. "I've dealt with the foster system. I don't recommend it."

She turned her gaze on Clayton, and he had to look away.

"What, then, if not the authorities?" he asked.

"The threat of the authorities," Cleo said. "Not pulling the trigger. I think it's a stronger position."

"But that leaves things as they are for the underage girls," Clayton said.

"I can figure out how to get them help," Hayley said. "Talk to people in the Department of Social Work. Give them my card, let them come to me. Offer a path out."

"Possibly folks in my community would help," Cleo said.

The three of them knew the problem set, Clayton saw, and they had a plan for the girls. What else?

"It still sounds like we need evidence," he said. "How do we catch Phil and Sasha in the act?"

All eyes moved to him, amber, blue, black as ink. Joanie gave his leg a reassuring squeeze.

"One angle is Sasha's driver, Paulo," Cleo said. "I think Sasha has a house she maintains. She always gave the impression it was an informal halfway house, but now I'm thinking it's an informal brothel. He could lead us there."

"That sounds iffy," Hayley said. "And dangerous."

"I'm a big girl. I can take care of myself."

Joanie and Clayton exchanged a glance.

"Before we do anything, let's come up with a plan," Joanie said.

Over the next hour and more coffee, they worked out a rough strategy. Joanie would go home with Clayton, an idea that sent through him alternating jets of fear and joy. Cleo would go by Sasha's, see if Paulo was around, and follow him if she could.

"How will you know if he's going to the house?" Clayton asked.

"I know she makes her big bank deposit late Sunday night or early Monday morning. So he's probably going to pick up money Sunday evening. I can drop by Sunday to talk about Inanna work, then hang out till he goes. It's not a sure thing, but what else have we got?"

"It sounds risky," Hayley said.

Cleo shrugged. "I'm not stupid. I won't get caught."

Hayley rolled her eyes.

"Trust me. I did acid every other week my senior year in high school, and no one ever suspected."

The other three gazed at each other.

"It's the best we've got," Joanie said.

Once Cleo knew where the halfway house was, it would be fairly easy to stake it out. "That's where you come in, Hayley and Clayton," Cleo said.

"What?" Clayton said.

"Me?" Hayley said.

"You're the ones they know the least."

"Sasha and Paulo have both met me," Hayley said.

"Wear a wig or something. Cheap wigs are like fifteen dollars. Or wear a headscarf."

They'd take turns taking video of men coming in and out of the house. If they could swing it, if they found the right window, they'd take video of the girls having sex with the men.

"I think Hayley's right," Clayton said. "This sounds dangerous."

"What's the alternative?" Cleo asked. "I mean, Phil is not a nice guy."

"Wait him out?" Clayton asked.

Joanie sighed. "I don't think so." She looked around at her friends. "Maybe trying to fight Phil is too dangerous. I can leave town if I have to. That might be best all around."

"But you'd be breaking parole," Clayton said. He took a deep breath. "If anyone watches the house, it should be me, not Hayley."

Hayley scowled. "And why is that, Mr. White Knight?"

"I can't hold my own against Paulo, as you've described him. But I can run away from him. I'm pretty sure of that."

Joanie nodded slowly. "You are a runner."

"It's chancy, but let's give it a try," Clayton said. "I can borrow a car. I think I can get away if I have to. Which means I think we can make this work."

He'd do nearly anything if it meant he could be with Joanie.

"Okay," Cleo said. "I'm in."

Then she smirked, turning to Clayton. "If you do this, I think I can speak for all of us, you'll get a reward."

Clayton raised his eyebrows quizzically.

"You ever had a foursome with three smokin' hot professionals before? I didn't think so."

Puabi-Ekur watched the little group of humans, and their heart was heavy.

What the humans didn't see was the energy surrounding them.

For Puabi-Ekur, it showed as grey billows trailing their every movement, shot now with darker threads, blue-black as cyclone cloud.

The humans' plan took luck, and they didn't have any. Unless Puabi-Ekur did something to turn the tide.

That meant going back and reforming their alliances.

Chapter 25

I'm sorry the room is such a mess."

Done playing hide-and-seek, the sun poured deep orange light into Clayton's dorm room. The dense light couldn't hide the basket of laundry, the haphazard piles of books with dirty plates on them, the half-eaten bag of chips. Also, his room smelled.

"I don't care." Joanie seated herself in the desk chair and pushed her bags under the desk. She gazed up into his face. "I appreciate the help."

"I'll clean tomorrow," Clayton said.

"I want you. I missed you. Come up here."

They scrambled up to his loft bed. In a moment her t-shirt and bra were off, his mouth on her beautiful breasts, sucking, biting, and licking.

"Oh my god, your breasts, Joanie."

"Bite me. Hard."

He sank his teeth deep into her nipple.

"Harder. Harder. Omigod. Yes." She unbuckled his belt and pushed down his jeans with one hand, grabbing his hard cock. "I want you inside me." She frowned. "My butt is messed up. I need to be on top."

He raised his eyebrows quizzically.

"Take a look if you want." She slid off the bunk, tugged her jeans off with her panties and bent over, presenting her ass.

"Oh my god, Joanie. I didn't realize." He dropped off the bed to stand next to her, staring at her striped and bandaged ass.

His anger whipped up.

I want to kill this Phil guy.

"Mmm." She pulled her jeans inside out, inspecting them. "Looks like I didn't bleed, though. I was being real about the sex."

They scrambled up to the bunk. She dragged off his jeans and underwear, grabbed his cock, and sucked him to hardness. "Where are your condoms?" He stretched to reach one.

"Hand me that." She rolled it on and climbed on, closing her eyes. He reached up, pinching her rosy-brown nipples hard.

He'd wanted this so long.

It took a while for her to find her rhythm, but slowly she started chanting, "Yes. Yes. Yes!" He felt her muscles tightening along the length of his cock, pulling at him, begging him to come. Then came the white heat of climax, the world exploding.

She lowered himself on top of him gently. He held her

in his arms, and in the afterglow he felt their energies combined, waves subsiding into an ocean of love.

"Stay inside! You're slipping out."

"I can't help it." He felt himself subside. She shifted off to lie beside him, tossing the condom in the trash.

"Do you want food?" he asked. She shook her head.

"You sure? I could make some popcorn." The dorm had a popcorn cooker in the kitchenette, closer than the cafeteria.

"I'd eat popcorn."

When he shut the door, Joanie gave into temptation and nuzzled the pillow. It smelled like Clayton sweat.

I love him. I do.

She'd switched her phone's ring tone off. Now it buzzed her. She looked at the name on-screen.

She'd been expecting this. She needed to play for time.

She'd turned location tracking off as soon as she'd left the apartment, but she double-checked before she picked up.

"Hi, Phil."

"Hi, baby. Where're you at?"

"Out."

"When're you coming back?" Only someone attuned to the sound of his voice could have heard the menace in it.

"I'm not coming back, Phil."

A pause fell. "What do you mean, you're not coming back?"

"I've taken the things I need."

Most of them. Oh well.

"You can get rid of the rest. We're done."

Another pause. "I hope you've been seeing your probation officer regularly."

"I have been."

"Because I might have some things to tell that person. I'll have some things to say to you, too, when I find you. And I will find you."

"Really?"

It was easy to sound scared. He scared her.

Phil's tone changed. "Yes, I will." He was almost purring.

"Maybe we should talk."

"I think we should."

"Not this week. Can we talk next week?"

"Do I really have to wait?"

She needed to make him think there was a chance. But she couldn't face him now.

"Please, Phil. I'm overwhelmed. I need time to think."

A long pause fell.

How had she let it get so far?

She'd wanted the money. She'd thought she could handle it.

At last he spoke. "Okay. If you insist."

"I'll meet you downtown, at the steakhouse, next Wednesday at eight p.m.," she said.

"Goodbye, my love," Phil said. He sounded cheerful. He hung up.

That gave them a week.

Sabit, Aea, and Tessa each waited a different way.

Sabit presented as the least human of the three: a furry winged animal like a bat, but with a long, prehensile, black-skinned tail that she lashed from side to side. Tessa preferred human form but had her own red-scaled, forked tail. She was filing her nails. Aea appeared as a cloud of red smoke, from which human features—notably a pair of perfect tits—came forward when she chose. Aea billowed, a little faster and with more cohesion than any natural cloud, up and down the beach, again and again.

Tessa cleared her throat. "Stop it, Aea."

Aea blew up into Tessa's face, then subsided.

Tessa frowned, stood her full human height—six feet, ten inches—then sighed and sat down again.

This corner of the astral recalled the beginnings of the world: a lava flow, black and rusty brown, lapped gently by waves of the sea.

Sabit fluttered over and sat at Tessa's feet a moment, her black eyes gazing up mournfully.

Tessa sighed again, and raised her voice so it carried.

"Puabi-Ekur, you called us here for a reason. You know who you need to talk to. Can we get on with it?"

Puabi-Ekur stood above the rest on a promontory, looking into the mist on the nacreous ocean.

"Whom I need to talk to," they said, absentmindedly.

Tessa rolled her eyes and continued work on her nails.

Sabit flew back to her, made eye contact for a moment,

then winked out of the space. Aea blew up and down the shore a few more times, then dissipated.

Tessa put on a light coat of clear polish and blew on it to dry it, letting her breath fill with a hint of flame. Then she stood, adjusted her jodhpurs, and strode up the lava hillock to Puabi-Ekur.

Beside them, she spoke. "You've had a while to think this through. I think we've all come to the same conclusion. Hekate had a good idea."

Puabi-Ekur nodded, continuing to stare out to sea.

"I know it's hard to swallow your pride, but you say Iltani needs you."

Puabi-Ekur made no move, no sound.

"Let me know when you're ready."

Waves rhythmically rushed up the shore and retreated, a sound outside of time.

Tessa shrugged and disappeared.

In night's deep center, three a.m., something wakened Joanie from a dream of mess and confusion. Fluorescence seeped under the dorm-room door from the hallway, a grey mist.

She found herself thinking about her quilt.

Aunt Marie had tried to help her. She'd only heard she'd died last year. She'd have liked to go to the funeral.

Sorrow welled up, a sense of the brokenness of her life, overwhelming her. Beside her, Clayton was deeply asleep, dead to the world.

She could ask for comfort. But she hated to wake him.

Why did she care so much about the quilt? It was just a thing.

Was it her, or some negativity from outside?

She'd had such a hard time packing. She had to have enough clothes, her facial cream and wash, all the basics, her personal books and witch things, and her schoolbooks. And her collection of glass unicorns. She had to get everything into three bags. The quilt was huge, enough to cover a king bed. It wouldn't fit.

She'd sat a half-hour, trying one then the other, the box of glass unicorns and then the quilt. One was the fantasies that got her through her girlhood, the other her Aunt Marie. But she had other things from her aunt, photos and a letter.

The idea of going back was stupid, like someone running into a burning building for their wallet.

She started to cry.

A grey morning showed through the dorm window. Clayton had his first class at eight. Joanie gave him a soft-mouthed kiss goodbye and snuggled back under the covers.

She woke up again in a couple hours, rolling over to find a better position. Her butt hurt.

She was hiding from the day. Time for coffee.

She slid off the bunk, found a loose Indian top like one of Hayley's, and carefully pulled on some jeans. Already her backside felt a bit better.

She could ask for help. But they'd tell her she was stupid.

Maybe not. It was old stuff of hers, not asking for help. And she was embarrassed. Still she didn't want to drag them in. They were already doing so much. This was her problem and her business.

Slinging on her backpack, she went out.

The day was full of mist; she could barely see two blocks ahead. On the sidewalks, people loomed out of the fog then disappeared, like apparitions. It felt like Halloween— Samhain, as witches called it. The veils were thin, and all sorts of things were out.

The coffee shop sat nearly empty. The barista stood half-asleep, her makeup smudged. Joanie felt a bit smudged herself.

"Triple cappuccino."

For courage. Her mind was full of alarm bells ringing. Joanie ignored them and looked at her phone.

Either she went to her eleven o'clock, or she did this.

A stain of plangent sorrow rose through her.

She only wanted this one thing. He'd be at work.

Finishing the coffee, she grabbed her backpack and crossed campus. The fog made everyone seem distant. Rounding the corner, she saw the charcoal-grey box she'd lived in.

She peered up at Apartment 304. The lights were out.

She tried to feel forward, to see if it was empty, but all she felt was her own numbness, laid over dread and sorrow.

She took the stairs, the stairwell a white-painted

concrete box, and fumbling with her keys opened the apartment door.

The apartment seemed empty. She glanced around. On the white wall, the one image she'd bought, a block print of flowers, caught her eye with its color. She'd left the quilt in the bedroom closet, on the shelf above the clothes rack.

She went into the bedroom. Phil lay on the bed, fully clothed, flat on his back on the covers.

Why wasn't he snoring?

The quilt now lay on the straight chair on the far side of the bed.

His eyes opened, and he sat up. Following her eyes, he glanced at the quilt.

"I thought you might come back for that."

She turned to run.

"No, you don't."

Phil leaped on her, grabbed her wrists, threw her to the bed, and pinioned her. She fought with all her strength, but he was stronger.

"You're not leaving again."

She drifted in and out of consciousness.

He had her tied on the bed, ass upward. He'd caned her with the thickest switch till she passed out. Blood was everywhere, her blood, enough to pool on the ruined coverlet.

He woke her up and fucked her ass, first with his cock, then with the butt of a spatula. It hurt. She passed out again.

When she woke up a second time, her skin was stinging. He'd gotten out an X-Acto knife from the art supplies she'd left behind, and was slowly slicing patterns into her buttocks and back.

Seeing her eyes open, he spoke.

"You don't know whose story this is, little whore. You think this is a story where you escape with your friends. But maybe this is a story I write."

He cut her.

"I'm not going to kill you. I'm going to hurt you. Then maybe I'll take you somewhere you don't have an identity. Somewhere you're just my sex toy. As long as you live."

He cut her again.

Chapter 26

In a time outside of time, a heaven of stars rolled outward in all directions, filled with blazing suns of emerald, gold, white, and fiery red. Living jewels, each was a personality, each also part of a whole.

Among them, on an intricately woven carpet, sat a throne: gold set with lapis lazuli, carnelian, and crystal. Before it stood an incense burner, also gilded, with ever-burning coal heaped high.

Puabi-Ekur had brought frankincense, cassia, and fistfuls of sweet-burning rose petals. Sabit and Aea had made themselves into handmaidens and heaped the offerings onto the coals. Tessa, because it amused her, had become a twice-life-size black panther, carrying panniers of additional incense.

After a time, the Lady shimmered into place on her throne, wearing tiered linen with a conical crown, her huge eyes ringed in shadow. Her prominent breasts tented the sheer cloth.

All four of her supplicants threw themselves prone in obeisance.

"You may rise." The huge, ringed, dark eyes went from one incubus-succubus to the next. "Thank you all for your fealty. Sabit, Aea, Tessa, you know that Puabi-Ekur and I have a lot to talk about. Will you leave us now?"

Each bowed themselves out, disappearing among the stars.

Smoke rose from the burning incense, perfuming the nonair.

"Lady," began Puabi-Ekur, and stopped.

Silence fell.

Different currents of scent wafted by, frankincense then cassia then rose. The silence continued.

At last Puabi-Ekur spoke. "Lady, I haven't come to you for a millennium. I have been remiss. But I have done my work over time."

The Lady Inanna nodded.

"I have seduced men. I have seduced women. I have seduced folk who were both and neither and somewhere in between. I have carried semen to eggs. I have stirred the cauldron of human genetics. I have done my duty."

The Lady Inanna shifted in her seat. "You know duty isn't the currency I ask for."

The incense burned away. Puabi-Ekur emptied the final pannier of sandalwood onto the coals.

"Why did you take her, Lady?"

"I didn't take her."

"You could have saved her."

"*You* could have saved her."

Near-silence fell again, broken by sniffles.

Puabi-Ekur was crying.

Incubi-succubi cried rarely. The Lady reached out her beringed hand, palm up. Puabi-Ekur, understanding the gesture, came and rested their cheek upon it.

"Puabi-Ekur," she said gently.

Puabi-Ekur only cried harder.

The Lady Inanna, making herself larger, picked up Puabi-Ekur, settled them on her lap, and wrapped her arms around them as a mother holds a child.

Puabi-Ekur cried a long time. Each tear crystallized, fell to the carpet, turned to dust, and drifted away. Slowly they stopped, swallowing hard, materializing a bit of cloth to wipe their face.

"Can you forgive me now?" Inanna asked gently.

Puabi-Ekur nodded.

"And?"

Puabi-Ekur sighed. "I let go of the past. I offer you devotion, Lady Inanna. But let me save her now. Help me."

"I will help you. Surely you knew that! It's not me you have to persuade."

The burning suns flared behind them, emerald, red, and lapis blue.

The sense of oppression grew as the staircase spiraled downward, carved through living rock. Every few yards, lanterns were inset in the rock, the first ones ornate. The lower the staircase went, the simpler the lanterns were.

The lanterns ceased being metal and became fired clay, then chunks of rock, less and less well-hewn. Then they disappeared, and the only light was a faint red glow from below.

Puabi-Ekur was alone. They were embodied as Puabi, dark crimped hair swinging to their rounded ass. As was traditional, they'd let go their clothing and jewelry to the gatekeepers above.

Their parents had given the Lady her due millennia ago. But perhaps they'd cheated her by becoming a demon, one that didn't serve her. The fealty that Puabi-Ekur had shown was to her sister.

Lord Enki would not send someone after Puabi-Ekur to bring them back.

At the thought, a spark appeared and blossomed into a flame, which painted around itself a lantern of delicate golden mesh.

They did have a patroness.

The final gate appeared, basalt bound with silver. It opened soundlessly before Puabi-Ekur. Torches flared to either side, but no gatekeeper was in sight. The golden lantern led the way into the forecourt of the Great Below. Puabi-Ekur couldn't tell if it was a room or a cave—the walls receded into darkness.

Wasn't this place usually full of the dead?

A voice boomed from one side of the space. "I've been waiting for you."

Puabi-Ekur turned to see a huge throne, basalt inset with black chalcedony.

In it, in a seamless black robe with a deep hood, sat a bony form. Skeletal but living hands clasped the throne's arms. Skin stretched thin over a skull with deep-set eyes, red irises holding black pupils set sideways like a goat's.

"Come forward." Puabi-Ekur stepped up to the base of the throne, the floating lantern settling by their feet.

"Hail, Lady of the Great Below, Queen of the Dead." Puabi-Ekur laid themself prone in obeisance.

"You may rise. What would you have of me, Puabi-Ekur? My sister has been pleading for you." Red eyes stared at the naked succubus. A growl underlay the goddess's voice.

"My lady, I want your help so my lover can escape the djinn and take her place in the battles upcoming."

"Take her place in the battles!" Ereshkigal's laugh echoed. "Which side do you think I'm on? The side of the natural order? Would you describe Hell as a natural place?"

Puabi-Ekur scanned across the black earthen floor to the basalt gate. This place wasn't natural as the world was— it held no living being, not even an insect.

"Is death natural, Puabi-Ekur?" The goddess's eyes burned with a red flame.

"Yes, my lady."

"The war, if it is a war, is between those who deny the sacredness of the natural world, and those who affirm it. My rites celebrate the last gate, to the House of the Dead. I am on your side, Puabi-Ekur."

Great. The goddess had been messing with them. They supposed it was her prerogative.

"I'm inclined to honor your request. But what do I receive as token of your devotion?" A slight smile crooked the lipless mouth.

Puabi-Ekur stood tall, breasts presented prominently. "My talents are legendary."

Ereshkigal hiked her robe up her fleshless thighs, exposing a vulva as red as her pupils. "Prove it."

Puabi-Ekur knelt before the basalt throne. Leaning forward, they put their lips to the Lady's nether lips, stroking her thighs. Ereshkigal threw her head back against the upright back of her throne.

Puabi-Ekur applied themselves, licking and sucking. "May I put my fingers inside you, my lady?"

Ereshkigal shook her head, eyes rolled back into her skull. "Just keep going!"

Puabi-Ekur cupped the goddess's buttocks in both hands and went around and around the wet, red pussy, licking and mouthing, biting gently at the clitoris, feeling the energy rise.

She tasted like pomegranate.

Below the throne, the earth rumbled. Dust shook into the air.

Puabi-Ekur felt the energy coalesce and burst beneath her lips. Ereshkigal cried out. A gush of clear liquid spilled from between the bony thighs onto the basalt seat of the throne. A crack appeared across the dusty floor.

Ereshkigal heaved and writhed on her throne, then quieted. Slowly her red eyes opened. The crack in the floor closed.

"Again! I have a strap-on you can borrow. If you're good enough, I'll ask the Annunaki to help your lover as well."

In a time outside of time, on a bed covered with midnight-black silk, Puabi-Ekur awoke beside the goddess. Ereshkigal was sitting up beside them, red eyes staring, focused on the distance.

"It's time to help your Iltani now. If we can."

Puabi-Ekur sat up in alarm and followed the goddess's gaze.

Things weren't good. The grey mist had encircled Joanie. The djinn had played on her emotions. She'd seen it, but they'd overwhelmed her.

Puabi-Ekur turned to Ereshkigal. "You're a goddess! Can't you fix this?"

Ereshkigal shrugged. "I cry for those who come to my realm. I don't seal their fates."

Chapter 27

The morning had been misty, but by afternoon the sun was doing its best to break through, making god-rays through banks of fog. Clayton sped up, walking back to the dorm. He figured he could catch Joanie after her eleven o'clock class and go with her for lunch or coffee.

But she wasn't in the room, and there was no note or text. He sent a text but got no answer.

That didn't seem like her, not at this point. Where would she go?

She'd probably just stepped out.

Puabi-Ekur tried again.

Clayton had an odd sensation, like someone above him was shaking the air like you'd shake out a blanket. Maybe it was overprotective, but he decided to text Cleo.

<Hey, Joanie's not here. Is she with you? This is Clayton>

<No. Let me try Hayley>

Nothing happened for a minute or two, and he breathed easier. Then a text came back.

<She's not with Hayley. This isn't good. I bet I know what she did>

<What?>

<Meet me at the coffee shop in 15>

The sky that afternoon was spectacular. Sun fought with cloud; thunderheads blew up, then light tamed them into cotton candy. Even Clayton noticed the odd weather as he crossed campus.

He banged into the shop. Cleo was in the corner, her short afro framed against blonde wood. She stared at her phone, tapping furiously.

As he came up, she said without looking up, "Sit, or get coffee. Hayley should be here in a minute. My friend Tony is being a butt."

"Tony?"

"He's a martial artist. I wanted some muscle."

"What's up?!"

"Go get coffee."

Again Clayton felt turbulence in the air above him. An idea popped into his head. "Doesn't he want to be a hero?"

Cleo gave him an "oh, please" look but said, "I'll give it a try."

Clayton got drip coffee and returned. Cleo shot him half a smile.

"Your idea worked. Tony'll be here in a few."

"What's going on?"

"My guess is that Joanie went back to get her quilt. You know her quilt?" Clayton nodded. "It was the one thing from her childhood she couldn't keep. It ended up being too bulky to carry."

"Fuck."

"I know where her apartment is, and we are going there, and we are going to get in, or my name isn't Cleopatra."

"Cleopatra?"

"Don't ask."

Hayley swung in, a cloud of blonde curls and lily of the valley perfume, and they told her the situation.

"Really? Honestly?"

Cleo frowned. "We're all sentimental sometimes, Hayley."

"She could have asked for help!"

Then Tony strode up—six-foot-six and built like a basketball player, wearing a university hoodie. From his pocket protruded a flashlight, a big black Maglite. Cleo eyed it. Tony shrugged.

"If you carry a weapon, they can get you for intent. Tell me what's going on." They told him the story.

"Let's get over there and see what we can figure out," Cleo said.

Tony looked skeptical. "Just storm the place? This isn't a movie."

"I don't know what we'll do. All I know is, I'm going to call on Inanna and every spiritual guide I've got for help. We need some luck here."

The sun broke from the clouds and poured gold over Cleo's bench seat. She glanced at the sky. "It's a good omen."

"If you say so," Tony said.

"Let's go."

It was a five-minute walk. Cleo and Tony went ahead, and Clayton and Hayley followed: a small, tight group.

They were a mixed bag, but oddly balanced. Two men, two women. Two black, two white. They didn't look like they belonged together, but they were clearly all university students. They could be on some kind of class project.

The apartment building was tucked among existing trees, including a two-story maple tree in red splendor. As they turned the corner to the block where it stood, a blonde girl in yoga wear was leaving the building.

Pushing ahead, Hayley ran to the door.

"Can you hold it, please? I can never get the buzzer to work." The blonde girl smiled, and Hayley went in. The others hung back till the blonde was gone, then Hayley opened the door for them.

The building was quiet. They took the stairs.

"Apartment 304," Cleo said.

The apartment door was shut. They looked at each other. Clayton shrugged and tried it.

It opened. As quietly as possible, they entered.

The apartment was completely silent. There was a strong smell of blood: heavy, coppery, with an undertone of meat.

Hekate Soteira ruled all spirits, by definition, djinn as well as angels.

Maybe she played both sides. Maybe it was a giant cat's

cradle to her. But she'd told Puabi-Ekur to remake their alliances, and they had.

"Lady," Puabi-Ekur said to Ereshkigal, sitting among the black satin sheets, "you rule the Great Below. The Annunaki sit before you, who decide the fate of humans."

"Yes."

Puabi-Ekur found themselves dressed, standing beside the Lady as the Annunaki sat on their thrones. They sat in a semicircle, in bronze horned headdresses and tiered linen garments. At some points, they had the faces of animals, at some of humans.

"Is there anything I can give the Annunaki?" Puabi-Ekur asked.

They had no baskets of silver. What would tempt the deities?

A spark appeared in the air and blossomed into a flame, which painted around itself a lantern of delicate golden mesh. The voice of Inanna sounded, disembodied.

"The maiden Joanie presented me with beer. I shall give all her beer to the Annunaki."

Even the smallest offering enabled a connection to the gods.

From somewhere, nowhere, came a hoot of laughter.

Sumerians liked beer a lot.

With a jolt, suddenly from nowhere Clayton caught a hoot of laughter and the smell of beer.

Frat boys outside, probably. A window must be open.

He stepped through the entry, the others behind him. The smell of blood returned. To the right lay a living room with a black leather couch and a block print of flowers. To the left lay a tiny kitchen, beyond that a bedroom.

Shackled to the bed lay a body covered in blood.

Oh my God.

It's her.

She's dead.

Cleo nudged his elbow, hard. As if levitated, suddenly he was kneeling by the bed, touching her face.

She was still breathing. "Joanie."

She opened her eyes and looked at him blearily.

"Hi, Clayton." Her gaze rolled slowly to the others. "Hi, Cleo, Hayley. What are you doing here?"

Cleo gestured. "Let's get her off the bed. We can wrap her in the sheet, maybe? Call a Lyft, get her to the hospital."

"Just a second, sorry!" Hayley ran away. They heard the sound of vomiting, then running water. Then she cried, "Calling the Lyft!"

Cleo, Tony, and Clayton went to work on the knotted black silk rope holding the handcuffs. One knot after another, they took off the four cuffs.

"Maybe another layer of sheet," Cleo said. Clayton eyed her. "Or we'll never get any car to take her."

"I feel thirsty," Joanie said woozily. Clayton ran to get her a glass of water. "He's only out for a minute or two. He went to get—I forget what."

"Tony, will you watch the door?" Cleo asked. "I'll find another sheet." Tony posted himself in the entryway. Cleo was back in a moment. Clayton helped her unfold a sheet.

So much blood. It looked like he'd started taking her skin off in strips.

Clayton helped Cleo wrap her up like a mummy.

"The car will be here in five minutes," Hayley said, coming back to the bedroom. "Will you be ready?"

"Sure. Hayley, will you grab that quilt? Make sure it comes with us. Find her some clothes, too." Hayley ran across to grab the quilt, rummaged through the closet, then returned to the kitchen.

Between Cleo and Clayton, they levered Joanie to standing.

"Can you walk, sweetheart?" Clayton asked. Joanie nodded. "One step at a time."

As she hobbled out the bedroom door, they heard the building door open.

Hayley drew back toward the kitchen. Tony stretched his neck side to side and cracked his knuckles. Cleo and Clayton exchanged a glance and kept inching Joanie forward. Drops of blood showed her trail.

The door opened to a man in his mid-forties, with dishwater blond hair greying at the temples, wearing a polo shirt and jeans. He stopped on the threshold.

Joanie raised her head. "Phil."

She said it neutrally, but something in Clayton trembled.

Joanie cleared her throat.

"I'm leaving."

The man's eyes darted from one to another of the five of them. Clayton and Cleo stood to either side of Joanie, holding her up. Hayley stood behind Cleo, Tony behind Clayton, Maglite in his hands.

Phil's eyes stayed on Tony a moment. Then he turned back to Joanie.

"Okay, honey. I hope you're okay. The scene got a little intense, but I know you like that."

She stared at him. Clayton heard Cleo draw a breath, as if she were about to speak.

From below, a car horn sounded.

Hayley said, "I'll make sure the guy waits." She slipped by and ran down the stairs, clutching the quilt.

Clayton caught Cleo's eye. "Let's get out of here."

"Wait," Joanie said. She went forward, one step, two, pulling Cleo and Clayton with her. Her eyes were fixed on Phil's.

"I'm leaving. I want you to know this was not okay." Red stains had started to come through the sheets that wrapped her.

"Not okay, honey? It got a little out of hand. But you like being my sub."

"I didn't say yes to this. You and I are done." She turned to Clayton. "Let's go."

They took the elevator. Out on the street, the Lyft driver caught sight of the mummified girl and yelped. Cleo handed him a hundred dollar bill, and he shut up. They got Joanie into the back seat.

"Where's the closest emergency room?" Cleo asked.

Hayley checked her phone. "UW Emergency."

"Let's go there," Cleo told the driver.

"What are we going to say?" Hayley asked, turning from

the front seat toward the three in back. Joanie had dozed off. Clayton looked at Cleo.

"It's up to her to decide if she wants to press charges," he said.

Cleo nodded. "Right now we get her treated. She's our friend. We found her at her apartment."

"No talk of Phil, then," Clayton said.

Cleo glanced at the driver, then back at Clayton. "You know I'm not a fan, but I think we stick to the plan right now."

The car pulled up at the circular drive by the ER. It was late afternoon, suddenly a sunny day.

Tony climbed out. "I should take off."

"Thanks," Cleo said. "I owe you a beer or three."

Hayley climbed out too. "Do you need me? I can stay, but I can also make my three o'clock class. Either's fine with me."

"Don't worry about it. Text me." Hayley nodded and fled.

Clayton watched her go.

It was different from the movies. The movies didn't have smell.

In the ER, they flanked Joanie as she signed herself in with student insurance. The staff got her into a room, its major feature a metal table. Everything smelled vaguely of alcohol. They seated Joanie in one plastic chair, Cleo took the other one, and Clayton stood.

When a doctor appeared, they started, and Joanie woke up. The doctor eyed the two friends over her glasses, smiled briefly, and turned to Joanie.

"Can we get you on the table?" Joanie climbed up, with help. "We're going to have to take off the sheet. Do you want your friends to stay?" Joanie nodded.

Cleo and Clayton unwound her. The doctor examined her back.

"Some of these are probably fine as they are. Some should have stitches. What happened?"

Joanie shook her head.

"We found her at her apartment," Cleo said.

The doctor looked from one face to another. "Okay. I'll clean you up, get you a tetanus booster, sew you up as gently as I can, and get you back home with some painkillers. Okay?" Joanie nodded.

Within a couple hours, Joanie was back in Clayton's bunk. Cleo ducked out and returned with some hot pho for the three of them.

Clayton slurped it gratefully.

Now he really wished he'd cleaned his room.

Up in bed, Joanie went to sleep.

"Bye for now," Cleo said to Clayton. "I'll let Hayley know what's up."

She leaned in close, taking Clayton by both shoulders.

"Dude, she's alive."

Chapter 28

Coming from class, Clayton stood a moment, basking in sunlight on a street littered with bright red and yellow maple leaves, in front of the coffeehouse. The day had dawned unexpectedly hot.

Joanie had made it to class. She'd only missed a day. Despite everything, things felt better, as if a grey film had peeled off the world.

Maybe it was just that Joanie was back.

Inside, he saw Cleo and Hayley sitting with her in her favorite booth, in the sun. From the outside, she looked fine, though helping change her bandages was a reminder she wasn't healed.

"I did it," Cleo said. "I found where the house is."

"The house?" Clayton asked, sitting down with coffee.

"The house where Sasha's girls live."

"How?" Joanie asked.

"I followed Paulo, like I said I would. My hunch was

right. He went to a house in Renton. I was able to watch through the window—they're pretty casual. Everything was visible. He was definitely hitting up a group of teenage girls for money."

"Did you catch any video?" Hayley asked.

"I did!" Bringing out her phone, she showed it, grainy and enlarged, partly cut off by the fall of drapes, but showing a large man taking cash from young women.

"That's not all." She showed more video, of a man and a young woman pulling up to the house in a car and going in together. "It doesn't prove prostitution, but I'm guessing it would get the police a search warrant. I think it could work as a threat."

"Maybe we don't need to stake out that place any more," Joanie said. "I'd rather not, if we can avoid it. I don't want anyone hurt."

Clayton frowned. "I'd rather be sure. The more video we get, the better. I said I'd help."

He wanted to be a hero, like Tony had wanted to, though he knew that was dumb.

Joanie raised her eyebrows. "Please don't. Unless someone really thinks it's necessary."

"The main thing we need to do is frighten Phil," Cleo said. "Get him to leave you alone."

"Maybe he will now," Hayley said. "I mean, we all saw what he did to Joanie. He admitted it, too."

Joanie shook her head. "That's not going to make him leave me alone. I blocked his phone, so he borrowed someone else's." She showed them the text:

<Joanie, this is Phil. I want you back. I went a little overboard. It won't happen again. I'd like another chance.>

"Did you reply?" Cleo asked.

"No, I don't have the energy. Besides, it might encourage him. I did block the number. I should probably change my phone out, but that's one more thing to do."

"What would it take to make him go away?"

"I don't know. I think you're right, Hayley. He doesn't get that I'm a person, not a thing. You saw him trying to minimize..." Her voice trailed off.

He had tried to minimize flaying her alive.

"Based on what we've seen," Cleo said, "his weakness is overconfidence."

"Which would help if we were leading him into a trap," Clayton said. "But we're not. I think we need more video, if we can get it."

My own argument is convincing me. Shit.

"I see your logic," Joanie said.

"Yeah," said Cleo. "Without it, we saw what Phil did, but he can always say it was BDSM gone wrong. Joanie's got a prostitution charge on her record, and we already know he's willing to spend money on lawyers."

"I'll go back to the house tonight," Clayton said.

Hayley and Cleo nodded slowly.

"I hate this," Joanie said. "I want to build in some safety. How can we do that?"

"We could turn on phone tracking," Cleo said.

"You guys can," Joanie said. "I'm too paranoid about information getting to Phil."

Cleo and Hayley looked at each other.

"How if we both track Clayton, and he tracks us?" Cleo said.

Joanie wrinkled her nose. "It's better than nothing."

Blue-black thunderclouds gathered at the edge of the astral horizon. With a crack, a streak of lightning blazed across them.

Puabi-Ekur stared at it. Tessa sat near them on a boulder, her red-scaled tail flicking from one side to the other.

"I got the impression that the Annunaki changed her fate, like turning off a light. I thought it was done."

Tessa grimaced. "Do you think the djinn will give in without a fight? We've challenged the challengers. I hope you have Ereshkigal on speed-dial."

Joanie lay on Clayton's bunk going over econ notes. Clayton sat at the desk messing with a CAD package. Outside, night was falling, a long blue slide into darkness. The air felt heavy, as if one of Seattle's rare thunderstorms threatened.

Leaning over the bed's edge, Joanie eyed Clayton.

"Maybe I should fuck you for luck."

"You're supposed to hold off the night before the big game."

"This isn't a game. Come up here."

Up on the bunk, she pulled off his jeans and picked up

his cock in long cool fingers. Her touch made him twitch. She took him in her mouth.

Like heaven, liquid heaven.

In a moment, he was hard.

"Oh God," he said. "That feels amazing. But—it's up to you—are you really ready for sex?"

After a few moments, she shook her head. "Do you want a blowjob?"

He could tell from the way she moved she was in pain. "No. Just let me hold you."

She let herself down beside him and cuddled into his armpit.

In the near-dark, the only light was streetlight fallen across the desk. He could barely see her profile. He stroked the silken hair back from her forehead.

"I'm so happy you're here," he said. "At the apartment, I thought you were dead." He treasured the feel of her hair under his fingertips, her nearly silent breathing. "I love you so much."

"I love you too." A sudden wind rattled the window and angled away. "I'm going to be praying to the goddess to make sure you're okay. If you're not back by midnight, I'll call Cleo and Hayley. We'll find out where you are and come after you."

The tan-painted Renton duplex sat positioned at the end of a cul de sac abutting a ravine. Clayton parked his friend's car halfway between two houses and slid down in his seat.

He felt completely exposed. But no one was paying attention to him. He hoped the rain held off. Though rain might hide him.

The house he watched was quiet, though the front drapes were open as they'd been the past evening. No one moved inside.

As he sat there, an American-made sedan pulled up. A young girl, maybe fifteen, got out, with a man in his thirties. They headed toward the house. They seemed oblivious to him.

Clayton videoed it.

Maybe from the brush behind the house he could find an angle into one of the bedrooms. He climbed out of the car and made his way down the street. Around the corner, he doubled back and dove down into the ravine.

A lamp lit the bedroom in use. He got a clear video shot of a thirty-something man unbuttoning his shirt. The girl came up, took the man by the hand, and led him out of sight.

Twenty minutes passed, and nothing happened worth taking video of. A chilly breeze played among the trees. The mud below Clayton seeped into his jeans. It felt like time to get back in the car.

Clambering up the slope, he took the long way around. For a long time, nothing happened in front either.

Then the big, dreadlocked man, Paulo, appeared in the front window, looking out. Clayton took video.

Then the front door flew open.

Paulo came out, headed straight for Clayton's car.

Clayton scrabbled for the keys. Before he could start the

car, Paulo was opening the driver's side door. He grabbed Clayton's shirt and yanked him out.

"What the fuck do you think you're doing?!"

"What? I—nothing."

"Bullshit." Paulo pulled a pistol out of his back pocket. "What's your name?"

"Clayton."

"Clayton, you're going to give me your phone." Clayton handed it over. "Now you're going to take me for a ride."

Paulo held the gun on Clayton the whole time, positioning it in his lap below the level of the car windows. Clayton eyed it as he drove.

He had to get out of this before midnight. He didn't want the girls coming after him.

At Paulo's direction, Clayton stopped at a house not far from the University District. Keeping his eyes and gun on Clayton, Paulo took out his phone.

"I'm sitting outside with a kid who was taking video of the Renton house. I'm going to take him to the basement and ask him some questions. That all right with you?"

Straining his ears, Clayton heard a female voice say yes.

"Get out of the car."

At the back of the house, they went down a flight of concrete steps and through a door into the basement, Paulo with the muzzle of his gun in the small of Clayton's back. Paulo marched him into a small room painted mint-green. It had a single overhead light fixture, one boarded-over window, a folding table, and two matching chairs. Its floor was unpainted concrete.

Paulo pushed Clayton down into a chair and leaned against the wall, facing him.

"Now, what the fuck were you doing?"

"Nothing."

Paulo carefully set the gun down on the table, then lunged forward and punched Clayton in the stomach.

"Ungh!"

"I'm going to ask you again. What were you doing at that house?"

"Nothing!" Paulo punched Clayton once more. He doubled over.

That one had hurt. But he'd rather Paulo hurt him than anyone hurt Joanie.

"What were you doing?"

"Nothing." Another punch.

It was pissing Clayton off. He wanted to rush Paulo, but he knew better.

"You're a tough guy, huh? Okay." Paulo got up and left the room, shutting the door behind him. A lock clicked.

Clayton jumped up and tried the door anyway, but it was dead-bolted.

He grabbed the chair, stood on it, and inspected the window. It was nailed tight. His anger was cooling, and the fear rose, like grey mist. It curled around his heart.

They were alone. Paulo could really hurt Clayton.

What had he meant by "You're a tough guy"?

Behind him, the door scraped open. Paulo grabbed the chair out from under him. He fell to the ground.

Paulo picked Clayton up by the shirt collar and put his face in Clayton's. "What the fuck were you doing?!"

Clayton stared, immobilized, too scared to speak.

"How about this, tough guy?" Paulo shoved a black rectangular object into Clayton's arm. Two prongs touched.

A huge electrical pain broke over Clayton, with a smell of burning. The pain kicked him back to anger.

"Ow! Fuck you, asshole!"

Then it stopped. Clayton looked at his arm and saw two tiny burn marks.

A stun gun?

"Fuck you!" He pulled out of Paulo's grasp. "I'm not going to tell you anything!"

Paulo stepped up close. "I'm can do this all night. Or something else—I'm creative." Grabbing Clayton, he stunned him again.

Clayton felt woozy. "Fuck you," he slurred.

"I need you to tell me what you were doing, asshole."

"I wasn't—I wasn't—"

"Fucking tell me." The pain hit again.

Then everything went jumbled, and Clayton was falling. Paulo moved to grab him, but he slid past. His head hit the table.

Puabi-Ekur poured themselves from one corner of the ceiling to another.

They wished Clayton were more psychic.

They'd gotten him knocked out so he couldn't give everything away. But that wouldn't last.

Tessa was right. The djinn were fighting back. Who was doing this?

Puabi-Ekur stepped back, and back again, to see a morass of grey threads going all directions.

Too complicated. They needed to ask for help.

They hated it when Tessa was right twice in a row.

Chapter 29

By ten o'clock, doing homework in the dorm, Joanie knew something was wrong. But she wanted to keep her agreement with Clayton.

A minute after midnight, she called Cleo.

"Clayton's in trouble. I just know it."

Cleo sounded resigned. "I bet you're right. I should've gone."

"We decided by consensus the other way."

"I'm showing him at an address near the University District." A couple more clicks, and Cleo gasped. "It's Sasha's house!"

A pause fell on the line.

"Well, we knew it already," Joanie said.

"I was thinking the underage girls might be Paulo's side gig, but not if he's brought Clayton to Sasha." Cleo took a deep breath and let it out slowly. "I think I can guess where they're holding him, anyway. If we're lucky, we can get him out of there." Cleo explained her idea to Joanie.

"That will take luck. And a crowbar."

"I've got a crowbar. I'll call Hayley."

"Not Hayley. I want to go."

Cleo made an uncomfortable sound. "Joanie—you're still injured, your back—"

"I love Hayley, but if anything serious happens, you know what she'll do."

"She'll throw up." Cleo sighed. "Okay, I'll come get you."

By three a.m., Sasha's house had fallen dark.

Blue-black clouds hung overhead, clotted thick. A block from Sasha's house, Cleo's phone alarm went off. She sat up, momentarily confused—she'd gone to sleep in her car.

Seeing Paulo's car finally gone, she shook Joanie awake.

"Time to do it."

From the glove compartment, Joanie grabbed the flashlight. From the trunk, Cleo took a crowbar and several feet of rope. Luckily no dogs on the street were awake—no barking to alert anyone. They crossed the yard. Behind the house, they found the boarded-up basement window they wanted.

Cleo paused, her crowbar at the edge of the first board. Even she had a few compunctions.

"Do it," Joanie said. "It's our best chance."

Cleo pried the first board up and off. It made a couple of squeaking sounds, not loud. Flat on her stomach in grass and mud, Joanie shone her flashlight into the basement room.

"Bingo," she said.

"Is he okay?"

"He looks like he's asleep."

Cleo pulled the other boards off, as quietly as she could. At any sound on the street, she stopped, till the sound passed. Then the two of them clambered through the window and jumped down into the basement room. It was chilly and smelled of mildew.

"Oh my gods," Joanie said.

She'd caught sight of Clayton's head, a big gash on the side. No one had bothered to clean it up. Blood pooled on the floor.

Joanie handed Cleo the flashlight and knelt beside him. After a moment, she looked up at Cleo.

"He's breathing, but he's completely out."

They stared at each other.

"We have to get him out of here," Cleo said. "Get him in the car, take him to the emergency room. Say he got in a fight, which he did."

It'd be their second ER visit in a week. "I don't want to move him till I see how bad his head is. Hold the flashlight."

Cleo did. Joanie examined his scalp gingerly, shifting his head as gently as she could. Clayton remained unconscious.

"I can't really tell. I think it's mostly surface stuff, a big lump and bruising. I don't think his skull is broken." She looked up again at Cleo. "I don't know. If we move him, we might mess him up."

"If he stays, they might kill him. I think we should get him to the ER."

With the help of the table and the rope, the two of them maneuvered Clayton's limp body up and out the window. The trickiest part was carrying him to the car.

"I'll go open the back door. Then we'll just do it."

"What happens if someone sees us carrying him?" Joanie asked.

"Unlikely, at three a.m. But if they do, he's our friend, he got in a fight, we're taking him to the ER. You can do the talking."

Joanie nodded. She was the white girl. It was a white neighborhood.

Luckily Clayton wasn't a big guy, and they were strong. But it took three tries to get him across the lawn and into the car.

At their second pause in the grass, Joanie rubbed the back of her wrist across her forehead. "If we get through all this, Clayton is going on a diet."

The clouds above churned and twisted. Thunder sounded, far away.

"Do you think it's going to rain?" Joanie asked.

"In a few minutes."

Just as they managed to drag him all the way into the car —Joanie pushing, Cleo pulling—a light flicked on in the house. The front door banged open.

Sasha stood in the doorway, legs wide, arms together, a gun trained on them.

"Stop!"

Time paused. Puabi-Ekur hovered in darkness.

So many grey lines pointed here, to this nexus.

Ereshkigal, Annunaki—I vow you so much beer.

Hundreds of battles coalesced on the astral and exploded. Ereshkigal keened. The Annunaki spoke.

Puabi-Ekur fell into Clayton's bruised body and rebounded.

"Sasha! You going to shoot me now?" Cleo yelled.

Joanie shut the door on Clayton and ran to the driver's side. Cleo could keep talking. She could drive.

Sasha wavered and stood down.

"Is that you, Cleo? I thought someone was breaking into my house."

"Weird," Cleo said. "Well, gotta go."

"Who's that with you?"

"A couple friends." Cleo unlatched the passenger door. "See ya!"

She dove into the car and threw Joanie the keys.

Start, you fucker!

Joanie revved the engine and zoomed down the street.

The rain fell down, suddenly, with a rip of lightning.

"She saw me. I don't know if she saw you," Cleo said. "Watch that corner!"

The car skidded. "Slow down! She's not chasing us."

Joanie slowed it and turned a corner onto a main drag.

The rain poured down in curtains. Now that the storm had broken, it felt calming.

"If she and Phil are business partners, she already knows you're in deep," Joanie said. "I'm glad she's not cold-blooded enough to kill you."

"Huh. If I know her, she was worried about prison. And I bet she's not that good a shot."

They drove up to the ER, stopping at the entrance circle.

"How are we going to get him in there?" Joanie asked.

"Grab that wheelchair, why don't you?"

They wheeled him in. They were in luck. The emergency department was nearly empty, and the intake nurse got Clayton to a room right away. Joanie didn't recognize any of the staff from earlier.

"The doctor will be with you in a few minutes," the nurse said, closing the exam-room door behind them.

After a minute or two slumped in a chair, Clayton twitched, and then suddenly he cried out, "Hey!"

He sat up, looking around him.

"Joanie! Cleo! What's going on? Where are we?"

Joanie jumped up and hugged him.

"We're in the emergency room. We got you out of Sasha's basement."

"My head hurts like fuck."

"I'm not surprised," Joanie said. "You should see yourself."

"You're going to have the mother of all headaches for a while," Cleo said. "And I totally beat you at stake-outs, Mr. White Knight."

The doctor called it a concussion and sent Clayton home with a bandage wrapped around his head. Clayton got a prescription for a week of ibuprofen and no hard thinking, which in the morning he took to his professors.

That afternoon, the war council met at the coffee shop.

"We still don't have enough to video take to the police," Clayton said, accordion-pleating a straw wrapper. All they had was what Cleo had shot. His phone was gone for good. One morning errand had been reporting it missing and getting it blocked. He'd have to retrieve his friend's car later.

Cleo rolled her eyes, and Hayley made a sad-trombone sound.

"We got as much footage as we're going to get," Joanie said. "The whole point is having it as a threat. Phil's never going to see it."

They looked at each other.

"I guess I call Phil next," Joanie said. She sighed, looking out the window to the sunny afternoon, students walking by talking and laughing.

None of them was trying to get rid of a psychopath.

"He's not going to climb through the phone and attack you," Cleo said gently.

"I wish I felt certain this would work," Hayley said.

"Who the fuck knows what will work," Cleo said. "We have to keep trying."

A glum silence fell. In the pause, the barista called out a coffee order.

"What do we need to make this happen?" Clayton asked.

"A bottle of red wine and my cell phone," Joanie said.

"I'll buy you a bottle of wine, honey," Cleo said. "You can call from my house."

Joanie shot a glance at Clayton, whose face was carefully blank.

She sighed to herself. At some point, they needed to have the "Joanie is polyamorous" conversation.

Right now, she was going to Cleo's. She needed some girl time.

In the fall afternoon, sunlight poured yellow through the leaves. In Cleo's scent, sandalwood perfume overlaid musk. They'd fallen to walking hand in hand; something in it gave Joanie a turn of the heart. How intoxicating it was to see Cleo smile.

A drift of yellow-brown leaves led up the steps of Cleo's house. They stopped on the sidewalk in front. Joanie drew her in and kissed her, stepping up on tiptoes to reach Cleo's orchid-like mouth.

"You're so beautiful," Joanie breathed. "You're luminous."

"Look who's talking, sexy girl. Come inside, let me get you that wine."

Inside, in the bottle-green kitchen, it was cooler. Cleo grabbed a bottle of syrah off the counter, three-quarters full. They ascended to Cleo's room.

The tented sari above Cleo's bed moved in the breeze, casting a reflection of pink and yellow down onto the mirrored pillows. Cleo pulled her tight t-shirt over her head, and Joanie jumped on her, hot to put her mouth on her, licking, sucking, and biting her prominent nipples. Cleo moaned and fell back. Joanie ripped off Cleo's unzipped jeans and pressed her hand to Cleo's pussy, wet and hot.

She slid down between Cleo's thighs and licked. The musk and taste made her so hot that she snaked a hand down to her own pussy.

"Put your fingers in me," Cleo moaned, and Joanie obeyed: two then three fingers in the warm, wet cave of Cleo, soft tissue encircled by bone.

"Can you take more?"

"Yes, omigod, yes—"

Slowly, Joanie inserted a fourth finger, fucking Cleo with her hand.

"More?" Vigorous nodding. Gently, slowly, patiently, Joanie compressed her fingers and pushed her hand bit by bit into Cleo's cunt. A little tight around the knuckles, but there was more than enough juice pumping from Cleo to make things slippery.

Joanie's hand passed the narrow spot. She passed the test.

This is holy. Hail Inanna.

She felt a ripple in the air of the room. The goddess statue on the dresser smiled.

She made a fist, holding it within Cleo's cunt, focusing once more on licking Cleo's clit. Cleo moved rhythmically, bucking and twisting. Knowing she was close, Joanie held her down with her free hand.

Cleo shouted, nearly bouncing off the bed. Her cunt

contracted around Joanie's hand in waves. Joanie closed her eyes and let go into the ecstasy that poured through and filled the room.

Then, slowly and gently, she slid her hand out, wet and wrinkled now. She pillowed her head on Cleo's thigh. They lay still, breathing heavily.

After a time, Cleo's breathing calmed. "Omigod, girl, you are the best sex person in the universe." Joanie mumbled her thanks. "I mean it. You're the best sex ever."

Joanie turned and looked up along Cleo's body, the scoop of belly, the hills of breasts. Cleo caught her eye.

"You're a keeper, Joanie."

A wave of sorrow passed. Joanie found tears in her eyes.

"Oh, honey. Come up here." Joanie moved up, and Cleo took her in her arms.

"What's wrong?"

"I don't know."

"I love you, girl. You know that, right?" Joanie nodded.

"I love you too."

But saying it made Joanie cry.

Chapter 30

Not only did Cleo feed Joanie a couple of glasses of syrah, she also heated some homemade tikka masala and shared it, ensconced in the cozy, shiny space of her room.

"I owe you an orgasm," Cleo said.

"Don't worry about it." Setting down her plate, Joanie kissed Cleo's forehead. "It means at least as much that you took care of me."

"It's nothing."

They finished eating. "I'd better make this call."

"Okay. I'll be downstairs."

Joanie heard Cleo's footsteps retreat. She pulled out her phone and stared at it blankly a moment. Then she tapped in Phil's digits.

Phil picked up on the second ring.

"Hi, Joanie. I knew you'd call. Ready to see me?"

"No, Phil."

His tone changed. "Why'd you call?"

"We got video of the house in Renton. If we take it to the police, you and Sasha will both end up in prison."

A pause fell. Joanie looked across for reassurance at the goddess on the dresser. Inanna sat half in shadow, and her face was grave.

Phil laughed. "I don't believe you. We got that boy's phone, your friend who thought he was so smart. There was nothing on it at all."

They'd made the connection. Her number must have been in the phone.

"That's not what I'm talking about. We were hoping to get more video, but we don't really need it. I think we have enough already to get a warrant and get you both arrested."

"Do you now." Phil's voice was hard. "You're messing with the big time here, baby. Are you sure that's what you want? Come back now, and maybe I'll forget this."

She sighed. "Phil, I'm not coming back to you. Think about it, talk to Sasha, figure out what you want to do. I'll call back in—" a week seemed too long— "three days."

"You do that." Phil hung up.

Joanie set the phone on the bed, glass face down.

Outside, twilight had fallen. The sunny day had given way to a night lidded with cloud. In the distance, she heard thunder.

She found she was trembling.

She could call Officer Tom and tell him about this. But that wasn't what she wanted to do. It'd be a mess. Their way was better for the girls in Renton, too.

She hugged herself a second, staring into space.

She needed to get back to the dorm.

Puabi-Ekur stepped back and back.

A universe, seven universes, whatever it took for perspective.

They saw the astral connections now. The djinn were Sasha and Phil, though likely neither of them knew it.

Puabi-Ekur felt a tug, and turning in its direction, let themselves be pulled. Stars passed in the void. A wash of galaxies flew by.

They arrived at a throne encircled by red flames. To either side stood torches. Puabi-Ekur made obeisance.

"Hail and greetings, Lady Hekate."

"Greetings. You are curious about the djinn that challenge your Iltani?"

Puabi-Ekur nodded. "Do they know who they are?"

A half-smile. "They know as Iltani knows, as a dream, nothing certain."

"My lady, may I ask who this Phil was in an earlier life? I have a particular life in mind."

"Show me, Puabi-Ekur."

What scene should they choose? There were too many.

Late in life, after Puabi had ended her performance career and instead taught young dancers, she sat in the audience for a show by three of her students. Another girl just come to womanhood played the harp for them.

Torches encircled the mud-brick courtyard under the darkening sky. The girls stamped their way in, making their coin-hung girdles jingle. The dance started slow, then grew faster, the girls wheeling about each other, shaking their hips, braiding their arms together and letting go. The drummer was good, an old hand, but the young harpist was better, her notes plangent and perfectly timed.

Afterward, the aficionados stepped up to compliment the dancers. Puabi saw that one man lingered by the harpist. From across the courtyard she studied him, a noble judging by his dress, his turban studded with lapis lazuli and gold.

Oh, no. No, no, no, no.

She strode up to the pair, her own girdle jingling, and swept around to stand behind the girl protectively.

The years had not been kind to Kirkaru. His body looked as if lard had been poured over it; even his nose was bulbous. Only the narrow, sharp black eyes remained as before.

His smile didn't reach those eyes. "My dear Lady Puabi! As always, your students gave a brilliant performance."

She gave him a look, then turned to the harpist. "What is your name, dear?"

"Kitara."

"Kitara, I would warn you—this man stole my lover, a harpist, long ago. Literally stole her like a bag of meal, against her will. He is not a kind person. He is not a good person. Do not encourage him." The girl's eyes went wide.

Puabi turned back to Kirkaru. "You know I sit on the temple council myself, now, Lord Kirkaru? Stay away from the girls."

He frowned. "You mistake me. I—"

"There is no mistake, Lord Kirkaru. Stay away from the girls."

At least she could save the young ones now.

"Is Kirkaru Phil, my lady?"

"Yes, Puabi-Ekur. You have done as I asked, and remade your alliances."

Puabi-Ekur nodded.

"That was wise."

Then throne, flames, and lady were gone. Puabi-Ekur found themselves hovering over Clayton's bunk.

In the dorm room, Clayton's desk fan barely moved the hot and sticky air. Joanie lay on the bunk half-asleep, econ text open beside her.

Climbing up beside her, Clayton kissed his way down her body, inch by inch. He kissed her eyelids, fluttering like butterflies, and lingered on her lips, invading and claiming her mouth. Slipping off her t-shirt and bra, he mouthed and kissed and bit her lovely breasts, their prominent nipples, their shadowy undersides. He kissed down over her lean belly, her hip bones, and her pubic mound with its narrow dark strip. He lingered on her vulva, tongue slicking her labia, finding her clit. She was moaning.

He sat back, grinning. "Do you want something?"

"Keep doing what you're doing!"

"Are you sure?"

"I'm sure!"

He returned to licking her clitoris, touching the bud itself rarely, mostly just circling it, teasing her.

"I want you inside me!"

"No, I'm going to make you come first."

He settled before her vulva, her hips propped on a pillow, licking, nuzzling. Her hand caught in his hair, clutching. She writhed and moaned.

Her body tensed. Her breath paused. She groaned.

Then she cried out, throwing her head back.

He kept licking through her orgasm, holding her pussy to his face. When she stopped moving, he gave her vulva a last kiss and sat back, waiting, watching. After a few moments, she blinked and caught his gaze.

"Come up here." He moved up next to her. "You're getting really good." Her hand went to his crotch, rubbing his hard-on through his jeans. "I want you inside me now."

He peeled off his jeans, put on a condom, and mounted her gently, moving so her body stayed in one place. He let go to the tight wet slide of her pussy.

If there was heaven, this was it.

He let himself climb the ramp and jump, that white-hot moment of oblivion. A moment afterward, she cried out herself. He felt the contractions of her cunt around him.

She came again too.

Always it was a thing of marvel to him.

He lifted himself off and clasped her in his arms. He kissed her gently, across her face, her hair and ears at random, then snuggled against her.

He'd half dozed off when he heard her voice. "You know, there's a couple things I want to talk about. Like whether we should fluid-bond."

"Fluid-bond?"

"Stop using the condoms. I'm up-to-date on my tests, and I'm STI-free. I assume you are, too, though you should get tested. But there's something else we should discuss."

"Mmm?" He could listen to Joanie forever, but he was three-quarters asleep.

"You know I'm seeing Cleo, right?"

He froze in place.

Joanie sat up, gazing down into his face. "Sweetheart. You did know, right? Or should I have said?"

"I knew. I guess I didn't want to think about it."

She nodded. "I'm polyamorous, Clayton. I always have been, and I'm pretty sure I always will be. You should think about how that works for you."

He stared up into her ink-black eyes. "I don't feel poly, myself. Sure, I'm attracted to other girls. But the only one I want to be with is you."

She brushed back the shock of hair from his forehead. "You're not required to do anything. You just need to realize, I'm going to keep seeing other people."

I guess I always knew that.

"I don't know if I'll ever want an ordinary life. I don't

know if I want children. I'll probably stay in the sex industry if I can."

He stared up at her.

None of this was news.

He sat up, took her hand, kissed her knuckles, and looked into her eyes.

"I don't know about the future," he said. "I might change my mind. But at least for now, I'm okay with this. I just want to be with you when I can. I love you."

She leaned across and kissed his mouth. "I love you too."

That was plenty for now.

The next day, the weather was unsettled, big cumulonimbus piling up only to fall away. The war council gathered at the coffee shop midafternoon, sunlight falling in wide bars across their table, then hiding.

"I have a story for you," Cleo said.

In the middle of the night, a sound outside her window had awakened her. "My subconscious kicked in, which was lucky. I was up and out of my room in ten seconds."

She'd run to the kitchen, which was empty. Hearing movement upstairs, she woke a roommate.

Together they crept back to Cleo's room to see the window open, muddy footprints on the bed, and out the window, a man running down the street.

Cleo looked across at Joanie. "I'm almost certain it was

Phil. Same build, same hair. He must've climbed the drainpipe."

"How does he know where you live?" Hayley asked.

"I'm sure Sasha told him."

Hayley shook her head, blonde curls going all directions. "What was he after?"

"I think he was trying to scare me."

"This is not okay," Joanie said. "He can't go around frightening my friends." She propped her head in her hands. "I should just leave town."

"And break parole? No, I'll sleep down the hall with Katarina. I'm not going to let him win."

"Maybe we should booby-trap the window," Clayton said.

Cleo shook her head. "Booby-traps backfire. Firebird House will keep a watch out. But we all should be careful."

The next day, the war council convened in the afternoon at the coffee shop. The talk was chit-chat, above a heavy feeling of waiting. Outside, leaves fell and piled in the street.

The following morning, Joanie and Clayton woke up slowly.

She ruffled her fingers through his shock of brown hair, climbed on top of his back as he lay, face buried in the pillow. She rubbed his strong, warm, muscled shoulders rhythmically, rocking with the motion of it. Then he caught her hips with both hands and twisted around to face upward, so his hard-on pressed her pussy, only a thin layer of sheet between them. She leaned and kissed his mouth, deeply, sucking his tongue. He reached up and mauled her pretty tits, pinching the nipples till she moaned.

Then she wriggled and set his hands aside. "We should finish our conversation." She lay down beside him on the bunk. "I think we should go for it. Fluid-bond, think of each other as partners. For now. Keeping in mind I'm still really into Cleo."

They'd talked about this, in bits and pieces, for several hours the previous night. He'd gotten tested recently; he had no STIs. Neither did she, through a combination of luck and rigorous care. They could dispense with condoms. Partners translated, in his terms, into boyfriend and girlfriend, which is what he'd wanted all along, but with her seeing other people. He could live with that.

He scratched his head. "You sound pretty ambivalent about being partners, though."

"That's not about you. You're awesome. You're solid and smart and kind. And you've never been weird about what I do. I've just thought of myself as damaged goods for so long."

"Sweetheart! You're the most beautiful girl I've ever seen, inside and out. You're kind, you're hard-working, you're a good person. You're courageous. You've gone through more than anyone I know, and you're amazing. "

"Oh, honey."

He wrapped her in his arms, reverently, as he might a goddess, her straight dark hair falling across him like strands of silk. Cupping her breasts in his hands, he kissed her mouth deeply, and then lightly all over her face dropped butterfly kisses.

"I worship you."

He felt in her a deep movement, emotion like the sea. Sitting up, she pulled aside the sheet, fondled him a few moments, then mounted him. He thrust into her. She rocked on top of him, moving like the sea against the shore. He held her hips, but she drove.

"I love you," she whispered. "I love you so much."

The sensation climbed. He closed his eyes. It was like being magma, liquid fire, his veins and his body on fire, his heart open, her energy all around him. She was crying, warm drops like rain. He touched her face.

She shook her head gently and kept rocking, nudging them both higher. The volcanic energy rose. They drove toward a white-hot center circled in red, the end and the beginning.

They came one just after the other, the energy reverberating between them. She fell on top of him, sobbing, and then he was crying too, not in sorrow, just excess of emotion.

He felt deep in the goddess's ocean. It was like being reborn.

She lay down on top of him, and he held her, a thin layer of sweat between them, till her breathing evened out. She grabbed a tissue and slid off him, wiping herself.

They lay there maybe half an hour, energy pinging and dancing, slowly subsiding.

"It's never been like that before," she said. "I guess it's how I feel about you." She grinned. "And you're the god of cock."

He laughed. "I have so little to compare it to. But that was—I'm not religious, but it was like seeing God."

"Goddess."

They went to sleep.

Later in the morning, Clayton went out to get them both something better than dorm coffee. She slipped into the long t-shirt that served her as nightgown, went to pee, returned, and lay half-asleep.

There was a knock on the door, quick, rat-a-tat-tat. A blond head poked in.

James.

She'd been expecting this.

She sat up, instinctively looking for a weapon. The only thing handy was her econ text, but it would do in a pinch, at least as a shield. It stood a foot tall and was thick as a brick.

Standing in the doorway, he eyed her, and she eyed him.

"Hi, Joanie."

He knew her name now.

"Hi, James."

He came further into the room, shutting the door and sitting down in Clayton's desk chair.

"I know you've been staying here," he said.

"Are you going to tell the RA about me and get me kicked out?"

"That wasn't my first idea." He lounged comfortably, swiveling the chair back and forth. "A guy came around yesterday, asking about Clayton. Someone must've told him he lived here."

"A guy?"

"Middle-aged guy. I talked to him a bit. He said he knew you. I knew what he meant." He smiled, showing his teeth.

"James—"

"He gave me five hundred bucks to let him know when you were around. I have his number in my phone." Pulling it out of his pocket, James dangled his phone, smirking. "But honestly, I'd rather fuck you than call him."

She stared at him.

You bastard.

Sliding off the bed, she stepped up to him and stroked his hair and shoulder.

"You're fun to fuck, James, it's true." Though she'd rather have a dildo.

She straddled his lap and began to rock, pressing her pussy against the front of his jeans. She felt him get hard.

Putting her arms around his neck, she leaned in, rocking, squeezing the muscles of his shoulders. His body loosened, and he smiled into her face. She slid her palms down his arms, slowly, to clasp his hands.

Grabbing the phone, she threw it hard against the wall.

It bounced off, ricocheting under the desk.

"You bitch!" He stood, and she fell backward.

Go for the door or the phone? The phone.

She dove under the desk, scrabbling, and got it.

He grabbed her, dragged her out, and holding her by the arm, backhanded her face.

"You whore. Selling yourself to that asshole for money,

but you won't have me. You—" he swung at her again, but she dropped, falling on her back.

Ow, ow, ow.

The momentum pulled him on top of her. Seizing her wrists, he pinioned her arms above her head, the phone still clutched in her hand. He applied pressure, trying to get her to drop it, but she held on.

"I'll get the fucking phone," he growled. Taking both wrists in one hand, he shoved the fingers of the other hand into her cunt.

"Nice and wet for me. I'll fuck you and then call your sugar daddy, get five hundred more." He unzipped his jeans one-handed.

The door opened. Clayton stood in the doorway, holding two steaming coffees.

"Take the phone!" she cried.

Too late. James grabbed it himself. He rolled off Joanie.

Joanie caught Clayton's eye. He gave a tiny nod.

James got to his feet. "I can explain—"

"No, James," Clayton said. "You can't explain."

James looked from Clayton to Joanie and back. "Oh yeah?" He took a step toward Clayton. "Your whore girl-friend here—"

Clayton threw a punch at James, the coffee cup still in his hand. On impact, the lid popped off, covering James's face and chest with scalding coffee.

James yelled and dropped the phone, falling against the desk. Leaping up, Joanie grabbed it and rushed to Clayton. She took the other cup, peeled off the top, and shoved the phone in.

"You bitch! That's a six-hundred-dollar phone!" James yelled.

"You were trying to rape her!" Clayton yelled back. He turned to Joanie. "What's going on?"

"He's been talking to Phil. He was going to tell him where I was." She set cup and phone down and wiped her hands on her t-shirt.

James got up. "Fucking burned all over my body. Give me that fucking phone."

Clayton stood aside. "Take it."

James picked up cup and phone, glaring at Joanie. "Bitch, I'll take you to small claims court."

"You were fucking trying to rape her, James."

James sneered. "You can't rape a whore."

"Fuck off. I never want to see you again."

Clayton and James stared at each other a moment. James shrugged and left.

As Puabi-Ekur watched, a big grey strand broke with a snap.

A hundred other, smaller tendrils parted after it. Cut loose, an entire timeline floated away.

I think that might be it.

Was this Hekate Soteira's doing? The Annunaki's?

Maybe they'd never know.

Chapter 31

"Okay, you get points for the coffee trick," Cleo said.

The day had turned to sun, as if for now the legions of grey had been beaten back. Joanie sat in the corner, sipping a cappuccino. Hayley munched a biscotto.

"It wasn't a trick," Clayton said. "It was a reaction."

He'd let his anger take over. He didn't want to be someone driven by anger.

"Still, it worked."

"I can't keep staying in the dorm," Joanie said. "I'm sure James has told the RA already."

"Tonight you're going to call Phil, right?" Hayley asked. "What's our plan if he doesn't back off?"

"Officer Tom, I guess," Joanie said. "Though I feel like it'd mean a worse outcome for the girls in Renton."

She and Cleo exchanged a gloomy look.

That night, Joanie went home with Cleo, bringing her things. "For the phone call, I might as well continue as I started."

Cleo eyed her. "I'm thinking no sex first. I'll leave you in peace."

Under the tented sari, light bouncing off orange and magenta, Joanie sat cross-legged on Cleo's coverlet, staring at the picture on the face of her phone, a circle of trees.

She had to get it over with.

She tapped in Phil's number.

The phone rang once, twice, three times.

Then it was answered, by a woman's voice.

"We're sorry. You've reached a number that is disconnected or is no longer in service."

She tried again, with the same result, then set down her phone, staring at it.

Maybe Phil had cut and run.

Had he gotten caught?

They could find out. For now, this was good news.

She went downstairs. Cleo sat in the living room, reading on her tablet under a sunflower painting. "Phil's number is disconnected."

They stared at each other a moment.

"I'll try calling Sasha." Cleo retrieved her phone and called.

Joanie watched her face.

After a moment, her eyes went sideways, and she set the phone down.

"It went right to voicemail. I'll give it a few minutes. My guess is she's blocked me." Joanie's eyes went wide. "I found out how that works after phone wars with an ex. Maybe they've blown town. I can find out if I ask around. Carefully." She grinned. "I don't want to ask Paulo, for example."

Joanie came over and snuggled next to her on the couch. "Anyway, I don't have to deal with Phil tonight."

Cleo put her arms around Joanie, resting her chin on Joanie's head.

"It's too early to tell," Cleo said, "but I hope he's gone. If he is, I want to know what happened with the girls in Renton."

"Mmm-hmm. If we can help them, I'd like to."

"I have a few ideas who to ask about Phil and Sasha. I'll text Hannah in the morning."

"Hannah?"

"She's an ex of Sasha's. She used to help run the temples, and she's still in the community. If anyone knows the gossip, she will."

The next morning, a story appeared on the city newspaper site. Clayton found it, bored after class, checking news in the dorm common room. He forwarded it to everyone.

In the sunny back booth of the coffee shop that afternoon, he read it aloud to the war councilors who hadn't seen it.

"Two men and one woman have been charged with promoting underage prostitution following an investigation that resulted in the shutdown of a brothel in Renton, according to police and prosecutors.

"Phillip Collier, age 45, has been taken into custody..."

When he was finished, they looked around at one another.

"Two men and one woman," Joanie said. "But they only name Phil."

"Maybe Paulo? And Sasha?" Cleo said.

Just as they spoke, her phone pinged with a message. "It's Hannah!"

"Ooh, what does she say?" Hayley asked.

"I should come see her, and she'll tell me what she knows. She doesn't want to put it in text or email, I guess." Cleo and Joanie made plans to go to Hannah's that evening.

In the periwinkle twilight, the west almost green above coral, Cleo and Joanie parked and walked. Hannah's small white bungalow, one and a half stories, had a trellis to one side of the door, still full of yellow roses tipped with pink. Her teenage son was clearing out for the evening as Cleo and Joanie came up, Cleo carrying a bag with white wine, crackers, and some brie. He glanced at them curiously but went by.

"I remember him when he was twelve," Cleo said. "He doesn't remember me."

"Or he's just running off to do his own stuff," Joanie said.

At home, she'd do that, if her parents' friends had stopped by.

That had been a long time ago. She never had to see any of them again.

Cleo rang the doorbell. "Come in," said a voice from inside, and they did, following the voice to the living room.

The wall was covered with a large Celtic-knot hanging.

Below it was a nondescript, cushiony couch, covered in throws. All around the rest of the room, on almost every surface, stood statuary and candles.

This woman had to be a pagan. Those were altars.

Holding court from the couch sat a big woman wearing a purple sarong, head shaved but for a tuft of cobalt-blue bangs. It had been a hot day, for Seattle. A fan was on across the room.

"Come in, sit down. Want some iced tea? I'd ask you to get it out of the fridge, if you don't mind. My fibromyalgia is acting up today."

"I brought some wine," Cleo said. She pulled the bottle out of the bag. "You're a pinot grigio girl, right?"

"Yep, that's right!" Hannah said, with a Southern twang.

Cleo and Joanie got wineglasses, and Cleo poured. Facing the couch were two overstuffed chairs. Joanie took one, Cleo the other, and Cleo introduced Joanie.

"So, tell all, girl!" Cleo said, matching Hannah's accent.

Hannah grinned.

"I've had to piece it together," she said, "but you know anyone who Sasha crosses comes to me with the dirt. I think I got most of it. Maybe you can fill in the rest."

She rested her glass of wine, beaded with condensation, against her forehead. "Just can't take the heat anymore! Anyway, what was it, a week ago? Y'all's boy toy came and got got, and then *you,* young miss," she cocked an eyebrow at Joanie, "called and threatened that Phil guy. Phil went to Sasha, and Sasha freaked out. You know she's always been all about plausible deniability."

"Mmm-hmm," said Cleo, meaningfully.

"Apparently she went to the police. And sang like a canary. I'm guessing she's trying to get some deal and pin her underage stuff on Phil, though of course she did most of it. Did you know about her Renton establishment before all this?"

Cleo shook her head.

"How did you find out?" Hannah asked.

"She always talked about it as if it was a halfway house, but then Joanie's friend left town—well, you tell this part." Cleo looked across at Joanie.

She felt like Hannah would understand. She'd helped run the Inanna shrines.

"I was working at an escort service," Joanie said. "Sasha ran my friend who owned it out of town by telling the police my friend was doing human trafficking. In the process, I got busted."

"Oh, that's a shame," Hannah said, shaking her head. "Hateful what they do to our profession."

Bingo.

"Afterward, Phil covered my bail. I didn't have a lot of options, so I let him be my sugar daddy. He thought he owned me."

"Oh, no! He's as bad as they come."

"I guess I thought I could handle it. But I had to get out. Cleo helped me." She met Cleo's eyes, amber velvet.

I love her so much.

"Then Phil started threatening me, and we figured the best way to keep him off was to get something against him. So Cleo followed Paulo and got some video. Then Clayton tried to get more, got jumped, and we rescued him. So I called Phil and told him we had enough video to take him down. Maybe we did, maybe we didn't, but it was time to bluff."

Hannah nodded. "He must have run to Sasha."

"He came to my house to try to intimidate me," Cleo said. "Maybe he hoped to keep Sasha from talking. Where is she now?"

"They're all in jail. And you know they all deserve it."

"What happened to the girls in Renton?" Joanie asked.

Hannah shrugged. "I'm curious myself. I'm guessing the youngest ones went to social services. The older ones are probably out on their own."

"I wish I could help them," Joanie said wistfully. "The system sure isn't going to."

The kids would go back to their abusive parents, or equally abusive foster parents. The older girls were going to need to find another place to live, at least.

"If I were more mobile, I'd go check the house out," Hannah said. "Maybe go ask some girls on the street near there."

Joanie glanced at Cleo, who inclined her head.

"If you go over there, let me know what you find out," Hannah said. "I'd love to help if I can."

When they pulled up to the tan duplex the next evening, it was silent and dark, the drapes drawn. The house felt lifeless.

"It looks empty to me," Joanie said.

"To me too, but let's wait a bit and make sure."

Half an hour passed, with no sound or light showing. "I think Hannah's right," Cleo said. "We should go to the closest track."

"Pacific Highway South?" Cleo nodded.

That Saturday early evening, with the flash of car lights passing, there was movement and life even in strip-mall desolation. Near a convenience store, at the edge of the aura of fluorescent light, they saw a couple of teen girls, a blonde and a girl with hair dyed pink. The girls wore t-shirts and jeans with high heels, nothing that would be outlandish in a high-school hallway. Maybe they were more heavily made up than most high schoolers.

"Let's talk to them." Joanie nodded.

They parked and walked up. In the darkness, passing cars' headlights flashed. Grit crunched under the leather soles of Joanie's boots.

When they came up to the girls, Joanie knew. A wave of sorrow crossed her heart.

They were so young.

"Hey," said Cleo, "can we take you to Starbucks? We're wondering about some girls who used to work around here. They worked for Paulo."

"You know Paulo?" the taller girl said, the blonde. "Where's he at?"

"Honestly, I'm not sure. But I think he's in jail."

Joanie cleared her throat. "We're trying to find his girls. We want to help you out."

The blonde girl frowned, biting the corner of her pink-lipsticked lip. "Why?"

"Because I was you," Joanie blurted. "I worked the street a while as a kid. But I got out. Now I'm in college. I still work in the sex industry, but I'm in control."

The girls stared.

"Come have coffee," Cleo said. "I'll pay you for your time. Thirty bucks, each."

Pink-haired Lexi didn't need a lot of money to get back to her parents—Cleo and her community collected two hundred dollars. Even Joanie, looking forward to some low-paid office or restaurant job for the next months, put in twenty five. Lexi had stormed out of her parents' house after a fight, but her house was still a home for her, if imperfect. Her parents wanted her back.

Alyssa, more wary, agreed to meet Joanie a second time, at the Starbucks where they'd talked earlier. Joanie borrowed Cleo's car and drove south. Highway branched to highway, under an overcast of thin cloud broken by sun. The low, brown building lay among trees just gone yellow, losing their leaves.

Coming in from the sunlight, the place seemed dark. Then Joanie saw the girl's blonde hair shining across the room.

Closer up, Alyssa seemed barely awake, propped against the wall studying her phone.

Nodding out, Joanie guessed. Heroin.

"You want a Frappucino? Vanilla?" Alyssa mumbled yes, so Joanie went and got it, and a cappuccino for herself. She set the drink in front of the girl, who latched onto it, sucking the straw.

She'd been lucky. She'd never gotten addicted to anything. She drank for a while. Then she realized what it had done to her family.

As Joanie stared at her, the girl barely glanced up, just poked at her phone.

"Do you want to talk, Alyssa?" Rousing herself a little, the girl looked at Joanie. "You're on something, I can tell. I'm guessing heroin. Are you smoking it?"

If she'd been shooting it, she wouldn't be in that tank top.

"Yes. I'm sorry." Alyssa shook her head. "Maybe this wasn't the greatest idea." Leaning down, she fumbled on the floor, grabbing at her candy-pink purse.

If she left, Joanie would never see her again.

"Don't go. I don't want you to be on heroin, but I also don't care if you're stoned. I just want you to get out of this life, if you want to. I sell my body, but I do it on my own terms."

Alyssa stared a moment, then set her purse down again. She put her face in her hands.

"It doesn't have to be like this," Joanie said. "What do you want to do, where do you want to go?"

"I used to want to be a dancer," the girl mumbled through her fingers. "Now I don't know."

It was like Joanie saw her drowning.

Joanie closed her eyes a moment.

Inanna, help me.

uabi-Ekur found themselves in a Starbucks off Pacific Highway South, above two young women, one golden-haired, one brunette, only a few years apart in age. The brunette was her Iltani.

Puabi-Ekur remembered wanting to save the young ones.

Drawing together their power, Puabi-Ekur pushed aside the grey smoke surrounding the younger girl. This drug was like the fog of the djinn. They grounded out the smoky cloud and drew out the personality of the girl herself.

There now.

Alyssa blinked her eyes and sat up straight.

"Wow," she said. "For some reason, I don't know, it passed off." She turned toward Joanie, a puzzled frown on her face. "I don't even know why I smoked today. Marcus offered it to me, and I got high. Anyway, I feel like talking now."

Thank you, goddess.

Alyssa's story wasn't unlike Joanie's. A neglectful family, a stepfather who abused her; when she ran away at fourteen, she ended up on the streets almost immediately.

"Paulo was a step up," she said. "He didn't hurt me, or not a lot; he mostly just got us high. He took our money, but we got stuff back." She shook her head. "Marcus is an asshole, but I have to pay rent."

"Rent?"

Alyssa twisted her face. "Whatever I make." She sighed. "You can get out of this? How do you get out?"

Joanie had to get Alyssa out right now. If she left her, she'd never see her again.

"Come with me, now."

"And leave all my stuff?"

A couple hundred dollars' worth of cheap clothes. But Joanie understood.

"Can you pick it up?"

"Maybe? I think so. If Marcus isn't there. He thinks I'm out making money."

Alyssa's directions took them to a low-slung small house, set in a weedy yard. Joanie guessed it'd originally been built for an aircraft worker's family.

"Hurry, okay? I don't want to meet Marcus. If he's there, we should just go without your stuff."

Waiting was an ordeal. The day was hot. The sun beat down on the little Beetle, which had no air conditioning.

If he showed up and fucked with her, she'd leave.

Put on your own oxygen mask first.

But the girl came out quickly, lugging a trash bag of clothes. She opened the car door, but even shoving with both hands had trouble wedging the bag past the front seat into the back.

As Joanie leaned to help, an older-model red-orange Camaro pulled up behind them. Alyssa shrieked.

A short, squat, goateed man, maybe half again Alyssa's age, leaped out of the Camaro, staring. He power-walked toward Joanie's car.

"What the fuck you think you're doing, Alyssa! Don't you know you owe me three hundred dollars!"

The bag popped into the car. Alyssa dove into the passenger seat, slamming the door behind her.

"Don't listen to him! He makes things up. Let's go!"

Marcus strode alongside the car, reaching for the handle of Alyssa's door. Joanie gunned the engine, swerving away from the sidewalk, and shot down the side street.

Alyssa looked through the back window, giggling.

"Fuck you, Marcus! Oh, shit! He's got his gun out!"

A shot rang past.

Another clanged into the side of the car.

Shit!

"Now he's climbing back in his car!"

She only had half a block on him.

Skidding, Joanie turned the corner. She floored it, swerving, spun around a corner, then another.

"He's pointing his gun at us!" Alyssa cried.

"Get down!"

Alyssa ducked. The shot went wide.

She had to get on the highway. He wasn't going to pull this shit there.

She found a straightaway, floored it, made a sharp turn. Another turn, and she saw the highway. The ramp was empty. In a moment, they were on it. Alyssa's phone rang.

"Block him."

"You'd better believe it," Alyssa chortled. "He's gone!"

Joanie swerved into the carpool lane and drove like a madwoman. She didn't care if she got pulled over. She had to get Alyssa away.

"Do you still see him?"

"Yes!"

She floored the gas pedal and changed lanes, nearly hitting a semi.

"Shit, Joanie!"

Inanna, save us.

She dodged cars, skipped lanes, wedged herself into tiny margins. "How about now?"

"Not anymore—wait, yes! He's way far behind."

Everything was a blur with a center of laser focus. This lane, that lane, that space, squeezing in, speeding. "Now?"

"I don't see him now." Alyssa scanned the highway. "I think he's gone."

Joanie settled into the carpool lane, going a good fifteen over the speed limit.

By getting out the gun, Marcus had lost the time it would have taken to catch them.

Joanie had Alyssa call Cleo. "Hold the phone for me.

Cleo, do you think Hannah meant it, when she said she'd like to help?"

"I think so."

"Because I have Alyssa with me. You think she'd put her up for a while? Maybe we can pool our money and get her on her feet."

Or at least away from her pimp.

In a few minutes, Cleo called back. "Hannah wants to meet her."

Then they were in Hannah's living room, in front of the whirring fan. Hannah held court from her throw-covered couch, under the Celtic hanging.

She quizzed Alyssa. Thin as a blade of grass, hair shining, the girl answered in low tones.

"I think this could work," Hannah said at last. "I've been wanting to rent the side room. Now, I don't care if you smoke weed, but I don't want any heroin in this house. If you steal from me, you're out immediately." Alyssa nodded. "And I need you to get a job, double-quick."

Hannah turned to Cleo. "You say you can cover rent for a couple months, between you and your community?"

"If it's as low as you say," Cleo said.

"It's a deal."

Hannah's gaze returned to Alyssa. "We're taking a chance on you, young lady." She looked meaningfully at Joanie. "Some of us have been where you're at, so we know what it's like."

She hefted herself to her feet. "I'll show you the room."

That evening, Joanie found herself alone in Cleo's room. The statue of Inanna was watching her.

It had been forever since she'd meditated with the Lady. And she owed her. She'd helped her again and again, her friends as well.

She lit Cleo's candle, grounded and centered, shielded herself, and let herself fall into trance.

But it wasn't the goddess who appeared. "Who are you?"

Joanie got the rough outlines of a female form, a face with brown eyes, and the hint of a sweet nature.

"I've been watching you for some time," said Puabi-Ekur. "I knew you in another life, long ago. I've been trying to help you."

"Well, thanks," said Joanie. "Do you want something from me?"

"No. I just want to help."

Joanie looked at the spirit quizzically. She almost said, "What's in it for you?"

But she knew. She'd wanted to help Alyssa not because it did anything for her, but because she wanted to protect her. Alyssa was just a kid.

Maybe it was true sometimes that someone wanted to help her, just to help her.

"We've known each other many lives," said Puabi-Ekur.

Joanie found herself in a temple, red mud-brick. Ahead of her stood an altar that held a copper dish where incense burned. Past that lay the open door to the shrine, where a white-gypsum statue of Inanna faced her, with huge lapis-blue eyes. Inanna smiled and held forth her beautiful breasts to Joanie, in both hands.

The Queen of Heaven, the Sacred Whore, giver of love and nurturance.

Oh, Lady.

The scent of frankincense wafted to her, and an old sorrow.

"In that life, you were Iltani, and we were lovers. I was Puabi then."

Joanie caught a glimpse of a woman, a dancer's coin girdle around her wide hips, long crimped brunette hair falling down her back.

"What was I like then?"

"Dark eyes, dark hair, like now. You were a harpist."

As if dealt from a pack of cards, a half-dozen scenes fell into view. In a dusty courtyard, women danced in a line. A desert sky at the end of sunset bled from coral-red to cobalt blue. One oil-fed lamp lit a tiny, close room. A set of robed men and women faced her across a table, frowning. The mouth of a well opened onto darkness.

Fear clutched her stomach.

"You died in that well," Puabi-Ekur whispered. "But now you're alive, and you have friends."

"Who else do I know from that life?"

"You know."

It came to her with a wrench.

Phil.

"I will protect you from him, and your friends too."

Joanie bowed her head. "Thank you."

Blowing out the candle, she went to sleep.

$$\sim$$

She woke to a body curling itself around hers. "Cleo?"

"Mmm-hmm. You want some dinner? I made stir-fry."

"No, I'm fine. Just hold me."

Cleo laughed. "It's a tall order, sexy girl, but okay."

It was Joanie who, after some time, rolled to face Cleo and kissed her.

Sensation washed over her: the lush lips, the scent of sandalwood, arms around her, clever hands, clever teeth nibbling her neck.

"Do you want…?" Cleo whispered.

"I just want you. Whatever that looks like."

Cleo kissed Joanie's palms, her neck, her breasts, and moved down to her pussy. Cleo licked her till she cried out, then got out the glass dildo and played with it, teasing her then filling her.

"Yes!" She came, a huge release. She found herself crying. "Oh, my love."

Cleo held her till the reverberations of orgasm died away. They went to sleep.

At the turn of October, Joanie got a room in Cleo's community house. Clayton started coming to Forum there when he could. Joanie took the first job she found, as a barista— she'd done it before, briefly, during one of her attempts at a straight-world life.

They followed the story of the trafficking ring in the news, periodically asking Hannah for gossip. Sasha got off light, a suspended sentence, and dropped out of sight.

Alyssa seemed to be working out as a renter, and Joanie talked her management into taking her as a barista in training.

Mid-October, in Clayton's dorm room, Joanie stood looking over Clayton's shoulder at Halloween costumes on the computer. "Sexy ear of corn? Sexy lobster? Really?!"

He pulled her into his lap. "You would totally be a sexy ear of corn."

"The trouble with both those costumes is that you boil these things and eat them. Would you boil me and eat me?"

"Well, I'd eat you." He was beginning to kiss her when her phone rang.

"Wait a sec." Finding it in her purse, she frowned at the number. She didn't recognize it.

Maybe a customer from before?

"Hello?"

"Hi, baby."

A buzz like an electric shock went through her.

"Hi, Phil."

She could block him immediately. But maybe it was better to hear what he had to say. Maybe he wasn't even in town.

"Did you miss me, baby?"

"Sometimes." She missed the money.

She felt a knocking at her psychic bubble.

She had help.

"Draw him out," Puabi-Ekur whispered.

"What's going on with you, Phil?"

"You may have seen, I made bail. I got fired, but there's a lot of new startups."

Startups that didn't do background checks.

"I'm working down in Palo Alto, but I'm in Seattle on a business trip. You want to have a drink, maybe dinner?"

Puabi-Ekur appeared before her, bulked up like a muscle-builder.

"You know, Phil, I'd love to. But I have a new boyfriend. He's pretty jealous. And he's a martial artist. I wouldn't want you to get hurt."

Clayton, who'd been listening, grabbed the phone.

In his deepest register, he said, "I don't want you talking to her again. Ever. Or I'll kick your fucking ass."

Then he hung up.

"Oookay," said Joanie. "I guess it's worth a try. Next step is a restraining order."

But that week, that month, Phil didn't call back.

"My gods, woman—you're working your pretty ass off," Cleo said, as Joanie stumbled in, having worked all day as a barista, still with an hour of econ to study. "This weekend, let's go talk to Hannah. I want to start the Inanna shrines again. I think between you and me and her, we can make it work."

Joanie slumped down in a kitchen chair. "Right now that just sounds like one more thing to do. But you're right."

She did believe it was her path.

The alder leaves were falling, yellow-brown, wet piles now the rains had started. The following Saturday morning, sun sparkled off dripping leaves and puddles as they walked over to Hannah's for coffee.

"I've been thinking about starting the shrines again myself," she said. "Come see the ritual room."

They climbed down the steps to her finished basement, a big room with alcoves, a couple of couches, and another big Celtic hanging, a tree of life with branches woven together.

"We could drape the ceilings, get a few pillows," Cleo said. "We could take the circle down and put it back up each time, not to mess with the coven energy too much."

"That would work. My coven actually works with Inanna fairly often." Hannah gestured to the altar, where a statue of Inanna sat draped with bead necklaces. "As a matter of fact, what are y'all doing for Samhain? We're going to do a ritual to Ereshkigal. You ever work with her?"

In her mind, Joanie heard a psychic gasp.

Puabi-Ekur had.

"I'd love to come to your Samhain ritual, if I'm invited," Joanie said.

"Of course!" Hannah beamed. "The Ereshkigal we work with is syncretized with Hekate, like in the ancient Greek curse tablets. Goddess of the witches—good for Samhain."

Laughter floated in—not the Annunaki's, goddess voices.

They were conspiring against Puabi-Ekur. For their own good, perhaps. But it was still a conspiracy.

An old petulance made Puabi-Ekur want to run away,

but they felt a draw to the voices and let themselves drift there.

They heard the torches flicker before they saw the flames.

The goddess, enthroned, wore a cloak with a deep hood that shadowed her face. Puabi-Ekur prostrated themselves, lying a long time face-down. Slowly they recognized their own exhaustion.

They'd won, at least for now. Iltani was free.

But they felt how much of a stretch it had been.

"Puabi-Ekur," Hekate said. "you've done as I asked. You've remade your alliances. You've re-engaged."

They knew where this was going.

"A spirit like you, who can walk both dark and light paths—you can be of use to me. Would you enter my service?"

They wondered what happened if they said no.

"If you refuse, there will be no reprisals. But you know how this dance goes. You can drift, if you like, till life leaves the planet. Or you can act. Would you dance with me?"

Puabi-Ekur lifted their gaze to see the goddess. Her face was hidden, and yet from her flowed the calm of the center of the universe.

How could they not?

"Yes, my lady."

A swirl of the cloak enfolded Puabi-Ekur for a moment before the goddess disappeared.

∾

Samhain night, in darkness lit by candles, they all stood there with the coven: Joanie, Cleo, Clayton, Hayley, even Alyssa, who looked small and lost. Hayley put an arm around her.

"Before all else," Hannah said, "we honor earth and sky, without which we would not be."

Drawing a circle around the space with her ritual knife, she continued, "We cut this circle from time and space, that this may be a ritual place." Her high priest cut the second circle, and she the third.

The ritual space rose around Joanie like a homecoming. Coveners called the elements, and Hannah called Ereshkigal.

"Lady of the Great Below, Goddess of Witches, Ruler of the Dead, come to us now as a strong protectress, to we witches who stand at the edge of darkness. Come to us now."

The dark queen came in, like a wind at night. At the edges of Joanie's perception, she overheard a conversation.

"Hi, honey," the goddess said to Puabi-Ekur. "What are you doing after the ritual?"

About the Author

Mary Trepanier writes fantasy, horror, and erotica. You can find her short stories in the *Blood in the Rain* anthologies of vampire erotica, among others. *The Queen of Heaven's Daughter,* first book of *Tales of the End Times*, is her first novel. *The Deer Stalker*, the second book in the series is also available.

Tumblr : https://marytrepanier.tumblr.com/

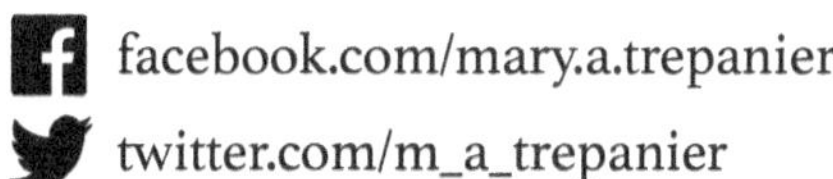

facebook.com/mary.a.trepanier
twitter.com/m_a_trepanier